BOOK TWO
THE DRAGON'S RETURN

BOOK TWO
THE DRAGON'S RETURN

WRITTEN BY
STAN LEE AND STUART MOORE

ART BY
ANDIE TONG

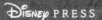 PRESS

Los Angeles • New York

Printed in the United States of America

First Hardcover Edition, January 2016
First Paperback Edition, January 2017

1 3 5 7 9 10 8 6 4 2

Library of Congress Control Number: 2015936647

FAC-020093-16344
ISBN 978-1-4847-5255-5

Visit disneybooks.com and disneyzodiac.com

SUSTAINABLE FORESTRY INITIATIVE   Certified Sourcing
www.sfiprogram.org
SFI-00993

THIS LABEL APPLIES TO TEXT STOCK

We know what you're thinking!

"How could anything be more exciting or filled with more surprises than Volume One?"

We know how grateful you are, how much you'd like to thank us for bringing you this great second volume of Steven's adventures. But that can come later. First, turn the page and join our fantastic cast of characters as the thrills, surprises, and dangers keep ever growing.

Excelsior!

— Stan

This one's for everyone who's worked so hard to make THE ZODIAC LEGACY a reality—especially Andie, Brittany, Nachie, and of course Stan the Man!

— Stuart

To Zoe and Joshua, my happy shiny lights.
To Nicole, Shaun, and Megan, for always loving what I do.
To Steph, for always believing. I could not have done this without you.
And to the people reading this, thank you for making this happen!

— Andie

PROLOGUE

THE AUSTRALIAN OUTBACK was a life-

less place, a wilderness of red sand and withered trees.
Satellite cameras, staring down from orbit, picked up only
the occasional flash of movement, a kangaroo or wallaby
darting across the cracked earth.

In the midst of this desolation sat a strange, high-tech
complex of buildings. The satellites couldn't see it, and it
wasn't listed on any map—but it was there. From far above,
it resembled a clutch of smooth white eggs half-buried in
the sand, spread out in a wheel formation around the central dome.

In the very center of that dome—the largest one—a man named Malosi stood waiting. He was in his mid-twenties, with a wide face, and a nervous look in his eyes. He wore a crisp, well-pressed uniform with the insignia of the Vanguard Company on its breast.

Why? he wondered. *Why have I been summoned? Why me?*

In his hands, Malosi held a strange object. It was about the size of a softball and almost perfectly spherical except for a few dents. Its surface was bronze, tarnished and discolored in spots.

Malosi looked around. He was alone in a giant featureless chamber. The ceiling rose up to a central point; the floor was uneven, rising up and down, as if it had once been landscaped. But the only thing covering it was a thin layer of gray sand.

Malosi shifted from one foot to another. He brushed lint off of his uniform. He shifted the bronze sphere from one hand to the other.

The sphere, he realized. *It's warm.*

He looked up, startled, as a door in the far wall whirred open. He reached for his energy rifle, then realized he didn't have it on him. No weapons were allowed in the main dome.

A large, muscular figure strode into the room, action ready in boots and his own unique uniform. Malosi drew in a sharp breath. The man was Maxwell, founder and leader of Vanguard.

"Sir," Malosi said, snapping to attention.

Maxwell regarded him for a long moment with cold eyes. "It's just Maxwell," he said.

Malosi nodded quickly. "Maxwell."

Maxwell stepped forward, crossing the sandy expanse between them. His stare remained focused on his visitor. "Something wrong, Malosi?" he asked.

Maxwell had kept a very low profile for the previous year, spending most of his time there in his inner sanctum and in a secret lab. He'd left the running of Vanguard to his lieutenants, and he hadn't pursued any new military contracts. That left Vanguard's field agents—including Malosi—wondering what Maxwell's plans were.

But Malosi couldn't say that out loud.

"No, sir," he said. "Maxwell, I mean."

Maxwell stopped before Malosi. "You've been with us for four years. Is that right?"

"Yes."

"And a year ago, you were up for . . . let's call it a promotion."

Malosi felt a stab of anger. He tried to control it, but he knew Maxwell had seen his mouth tighten.

"Sometimes," Malosi said carefully, "things don't work out."

"And sometimes they do. It just takes a little longer." Maxwell gestured at the bronze sphere. "I see you have the item I requested."

"The Operator gave it to me personally." Malosi hesitated. "I have to ask, Maxwell . . ."

"Yes?"

"Anyone could have brought this to you." Malosi forced himself to look Maxwell in the eyes. "Why did you request me?"

A slight, amused smile crept onto Maxwell's lips. "Are you bored, Malosi? Tired of guarding bushes and cacti? Wondering if I've lost my fire, my thirst for greatness, along with the Dragon power?"

Malosi took a step back. "I—I didn't mean—"

"At ease." Abruptly, Maxwell turned and started toward the edge of the room. "Walk with me."

Malosi grimaced. He shot a glance at the bronze sphere in his hand, then followed. Maxwell led him past an area where the floor of the room rose up like a hill.

"Have you been here before, Malosi?"

"Once," Malosi said, still cautious. "It looked very different."

"This used to be my garden." An edge crept into Maxwell's voice. "A place of peace and contemplation, an oasis of streams, bridges, and waterfalls. But the Zodiac power ruined all that."

"The Zodiac power," Malosi repeated.

"Now this place must serve a new purpose. As must we all." Maxwell whirled around, addressing Malosi directly. "But you know all about Project Zodiac, don't you? You were fully briefed."

"Last year," Malosi agreed. "I was to be . . ." He trailed off, unable to speak the word. Malosi had spent the past year trying not to think about the power that had been promised to him and then snatched away.

"The Tiger," Maxwell said. "You were chosen to be my Tiger."

Malosi looked down, not wanting Maxwell to see the anger in his face.

"And since that time," Maxwell continued, "you've observed our Zodiac agents in the field. Snake, Monkey, Rat . . . you know what they can do. You've seen, firsthand, the power that should have been yours."

"I've been treated well by Vanguard," Malosi said stiffly.

"That's gratifying. But irrelevant."

Maxwell seated himself on a slight rise. He stared straight ahead, for so long that Malosi began to think he'd forgotten his visitor's presence.

Finally, Maxwell said: "I've made mistakes, Malosi."

Malosi cleared his throat. "That's, uh, that's human."

"Human." Maxwell smiled. "Yes. *I* am human, but the Dragon power is not. It's the greatest of the Zodiacs— orders of magnitude more potent than any of the others. It's very . . . seductive."

Malosi sat down next to his leader. "I'm, uh, sure you can handle it. Sir."

A flicker of doubt crossed Maxwell's face. The weight of the past year's actions visibly weighed on him. His eyes, his face, his whole body looked tired.

"I've strayed from my path," Maxwell continued. "When I held the Dragon in my hand, I lost perspective. I said and did things that I regret. And as a result, the power was lost to me."

"That . . ." Malosi paused, thinking of the Tiger power. "That's not an easy thing to live with."

Malosi looked away, lost in his own dark thoughts. He wondered how he could miss something so much when he'd never had it at all.

Then he felt Maxwell's eyes on him. When he looked up, Maxwell was staring at him with a frightening intensity.

"There is rage within you," Maxwell hissed. "The rage of the forgotten, the lost. But rage at whom?"

Malosi said nothing.

"At your father? Who walked out on you?"

Malosi shook his head. "No."

"No," Maxwell agreed. "We have ways of finding ourselves . . . new fathers."

Maxwell didn't look away. Malosi felt exposed, as if all his secrets were being revealed, one by one, under Maxwell's piercing gaze.

Then Maxwell reached into his pocket and pulled out a tattered photo. It showed a lean, athletic boy of about fourteen, with a shock of dark hair and a cocky expression on his face. The raging form of the Tiger rose up above him, roaring into the wind.

"*Steven Lee*," Maxwell continued.

"Steven Lee," Malosi repeated.

He took the photo in his hand. It looked as if it had

been crumpled up, thrown away, and then massaged flat again.

"This boy stole what is rightfully yours," Maxwell said.

"But . . ."

"But what?"

"No. My chance—it passed me by." Malosi straightened his uniform. "Like I said, sometimes things don't work out."

"Malosi." Maxwell's voice turned dark, hard. "I am about to gain my second chance. The Zodiac powers will be mine—ours. All of them, this time."

"All of them." Malosi's eyes went wide. "Including the Tiger?"

"Oh, yes."

Malosi nodded slowly. He felt hope burning inside him, a fire he thought had been extinguished long before.

"Sir," he said, "what can I do?"

"You can start by giving me that."

Maxwell gestured at the bronze artifact in Malosi's hands. Malosi looked down in surprise. He'd almost forgotten about it.

"What is it?" he asked.

"It's called a *jiānyù*."

Malosi held out the sphere—the *jiānyù*—but only partway. Something, some instinct, made him stop. He felt that he was about to cross a line, to fall into a pit he could never escape.

"Give it to me," Maxwell repeated, "and I promise you, the second chance begins now. For both of us."

Malosi studied the sphere. It seemed to grow even warmer, almost hot to the touch.

Then Malosi looked back down at the photo. He'd seen videos of Steven Lee in action, leaping and striking gracefully, the fierce Zodiac avatar blazing above his young figure. *That should be mine,* Malosi thought. *It's supposed to be mine.*

It will be mine.

He handed the sphere to Maxwell.

Maxwell held the *jiānyù* up to the light, gazing intensely at it. Malosi had the strange impression that Maxwell was seeing *through* the sphere, far beyond it. To the cosmos above, to the ley lines beneath the earth. To the ancient forces that had birthed the power of the Zodiac.

"The rise of the Tiger," Maxwell whispered, "shall herald the Dragon's return."

Then he shook his head and turned to Malosi. He placed a fatherly arm around Malosi's shoulders and stared, fiercely, into the younger man's eyes.

"Are you with me?" he asked.

Malosi nodded. "I am."

Maxwell smiled, an unusually warm smile for him. Malosi felt a sudden unfamiliar surge of pride.

"Then I have already won," Maxwell said.

PART ONE

THE STORM

CHAPTER ONE

STEVEN LEE was twenty meters in the air, descending slowly by parachute, when the truth of his situation struck him like a hammer to the head.

I just jumped out of a plane, he thought.

Steven had done a lot of bizarre things over the previous year. He'd traveled to Hong Kong, Greenland, and strange caverns underneath China; he'd battled armed soldiers and superpowered agents all over the world. Along the way, he'd acquired the incredible power of the Tiger.

But I've never jumped out of a plane before!

He reached down with trembling fingers and double-checked the buckle across his waist. Below, his destination lay spread out across a clearing in the desert: a multinational school consisting of several low buildings. A rounded water tower rose from the roof of one building.

Steven peered down. He couldn't see Kim, his teammate, from that height. But he knew she was already on the ground.

A fierce wind rose up, blowing sand into Steven's face. He coughed and turned to look behind him. In the distance, a raging sandstorm was rolling its way across the desert sand. It would be at the school in minutes.

And then, he thought, *it'll reach Dubai. A city of two million people.*

A sharp crack caught Steven's attention, rising above the roar of the wind. He looked down just in time to see the water tower break loose from its mountings on the roof of the school. In an instant, he forgot about skydiving into a new country and about looking for his teammates. His total focus moved to the events in front of him, and the tower falling toward the school.

Steven reached across his chest and unsnapped two safety buckles. As the chute flew free, fluttering up into the air, he twisted his body and dove toward the ground.

The energy-shape of the Tiger flared all around him. Wind roared past, sweeping back his hair and spitting

moisture into his eyes. The storm was growing stronger.

The water tower rolled along the roof, moving toward the edge. The school was a square, wide building, only two stories high. On the ground below, a teacher in a hijab was hustling a group of kids out of the building onto the playground.

The water tower was about to fall right on top of them.

Steven arched in midair, kicking out to strike the water tower on its side. It clanged loudly and rolled back into the middle of the roof. But as he bounced up and away, he saw it start to roll toward the edge again.

Inside him, the Tiger roared in frustration.

Steven reached out and grabbed a flagpole protruding from the side of the building, then used it to swing his body around. He was barely thinking; the Tiger operated mostly on instinct.

Swinging to the ground from the flagpole, he saw the last few children straggling out of the schoolhouse. Steven grabbed the three remaining kids in both arms and tossed them onto the playground, aiming toward a grassy area. They landed in a heap, winded but unhurt.

Steven touched down, stumbled, and looked up to see the huge bulk of the detached water tower plummeting straight toward him.

A blur of motion caught his eye. He turned to see Kim running his way. As she leaped up into the air, an energy-construct in the shape of a bounding rabbit blazed into existence around her. Steven felt her arms close around him, heard a soft *poof*—

—and then they tumbled to the ground together. When Steven looked up, dazed, the first thing he saw was the water tower crash to the pavement, exploding in a fury of water and plastic.

The second thing he noticed, as a few drops of water splashed his face, was that he was at least eight meters away from the school. The water tower had missed him.

Kim tried to climb to her feet but stumbled. Steven reached out to help her.

"Thanks," she said. "Teleporting with a passenger . . . it still takes a lot out of me."

Steven shook his head. He'd seen Kim use her power a hundred times, but he still wasn't used to it.

"Thank *you*," he replied. "You saved my butt."

She smiled that shy smile of hers. As always, it made Steven smile back.

The teacher approached, holding a girl's hand. The last of the children followed, staring at the shattered remains of the water tower. They all looked between five and seven years old.

"Thank you," the teacher said. "You arrived just in time." Then she paused, frowning. "You look very young. Are you from the government?"

"Sort of," Kim said. "They called us for help."

Steven looked around. They were in the middle of the

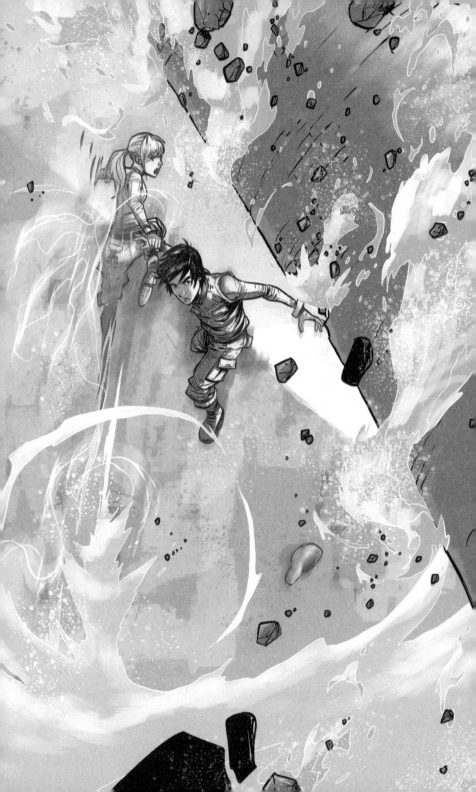

playground, near a basketball hoop with no net. On the far side of the yard, an old bus stood by a grove of brightly colored trees. Some of the kids were starting to climb aboard.

"We're here to help you evacuate," Steven said. "What's your plan?"

The teacher looked at him for a moment, unsure. A huge wind blew up, almost knocking them off their feet. Kim reached out to help the woman, who kept a tight grip on the little girl's hand.

Steven looked up. The sky was dark, almost black, a roiling mass of rain and sand. It looked like a blanket of smoke, reaching all the way down to the horizon. Steven squinted and tried to make out the Zodiac stealth plane, which he knew was hovering overhead. But it was lost in the thick cloud cover.

The woman gestured toward the bus. Steven nodded, and he and Kim followed her.

"The school buildings are old," the teacher explained. "They're not safe during a storm, so we're supposed to take the kids to that old factory. It's got a shelter in the basement."

She pointed. Over the trees, past a long line of open fields, Steven could see the factory building in the distance. It was at least a kilometer away.

As they approached the bus, a young boy stuck his head out the window. "Miss Maya!" the boy shouted. "The driver can't get the bus to start!"

Kim turned to Steven. "Don't suppose you know how to fix a bus?" she asked.

He shook his head.

Sweat broke out on Steven's brow. The air was incredibly thick now, full of moisture. The wind was a constant barrage.

The boy climbed out of the bus. The teacher moved to help him, and five more kids followed, stepping down to the ground. Then another five.

Steven turned to Kim and looked her grimly in the eye.

"Fourteen kids, plus Miss Maya and the driver," he said. "We'll never make it on foot. The storm's too close."

Kim knew instantly what he was thinking. Her eyes grew wide with worry.

"Can we ask the others for help?" she said.

Steven shook his head. "Liam's busy helping people at a half-collapsed construction site on the edge of the city. Roxanne is dealing with a traffic obstruction that's blocking evacuation efforts. And Duane has to keep monitoring from the plane."

"What about Jasmine?"

Steven shrugged helplessly. Jasmine was the Dragon, the most powerful Zodiac of all; at first she'd shared that power with Maxwell. When the Zodiacs defeated him at

Dragon's Gate, Jasmine absorbed all the power. That had seemed like a good thing—but since that time, Jasmine had become very withdrawn and quiet. Steven barely knew how to talk to her anymore.

Kim grimaced. She turned to look across the fields, at the factory in the distance.

"Can you make it that far?" Steven asked.

"I'll have to," she replied. "But I can only carry one at a time."

The teacher looked at them, baffled. "What are you talking about?"

Steven cocked his head at her. "Who's your most adventurous student?"

Miss Maya turned to face the children. They stood together, eyes wide, waiting for instructions. Another gust of wind blew up, and they shrank away from the swirling sand.

"Aadab?" the teacher called.

A small girl stepped out of the group. She had dark hair and big eyes, and she looked completely unafraid.

Kim held out a hand. "C'mere, cutie."

She pulled the little girl close. Then she turned toward the open fields, staring at the factory building beyond. She tensed, clutched the girl tightly, and leaped into the air.

Rabbit energy flared around Kim. Then, together with little Aadab, she disappeared with a soft *poof.*

Miss Maya gasped. So did the whole class—except one

boy, taller than the others, who stepped forward.

"Zodiac," the boy said, cocking his head to stare at Steven. "You guys are from Zodiac!"

Steven frowned. "How do you know about that?"

"My dad works for the emirate."

Steven nodded. The Zodiacs were cautious about letting the public know of their existence, but recently Jasmine had started spreading the word discreetly among the world's government officials. That was how the Dubai authorities had known to ask the team for help.

Kim's been gone awhile, Steven realized. He touched a button on the small receiver clipped to his ear. "Kim? Rabbit? Are you okay?"

"Yeah," her voice crackled in his ear. "The girl's safe. I just needed to rest for a second. . . ."

With a faint *poof*, she reappeared in front of him.

"But now I'm ready to go again," she finished.

The students and their teacher stared at the girl who'd disappeared and reappeared out of nowhere.

Then the children all pressed forward, reaching toward Kim.

"Me next!"

"No, me!"

"Meeeee!"

Smiling wearily, Kim reached out for another child. As they vanished, the wind whipped up again. Rain began to sprinkle down.

Miss Maya gestured for the group to move up against the bus. "Everybody stay calm," she said. "We'll be safe here for a few minutes."

Then she turned to Steven with an odd, stunned look on her face. "Zodiac?"

"Zodiac," he replied.

Kim *poofed* back for another child and carried her to safety, as well. Then another. The sky was turning very dark. Steven, the teacher, the driver, and the remaining children lifted their shirts up to their mouths to keep out the rising dust.

After the fifth child, Kim didn't come back right away. "Kim?" Steven asked over the radio.

"I'm . . . this is really hard." Her voice was crackly, exhausted. "I don't know if I can keep it up."

Steven flinched from the rising wind. "I'm sorry," he said, "but you have to."

"Talk to me," Kim said in his ear. "Distract me with something."

"Like what?"

"Anything."

Steven's mind went blank. He couldn't think of anything to say—except the one thing that had been bothering him for the entire mission.

"I'm worried about Jasmine," he said.

"Me too," Kim said. "What do you think happened to Carlos, anyway?"

Steven grimaced. Carlos was the scientific genius who, along with Jasmine, had founded the Zodiac organization. Three months before, in the middle of a mission, he'd suddenly disappeared.

For Jasmine, it was like half her heart had been torn out. She'd searched, put out feelers, called in every favor she had in the world. Nothing. It was as if Carlos had vanished off the planet.

"I don't know," Steven said.

Kim reappeared in front of him, breathing hard. She caught a face full of dust and coughed.

"I'm okay," she said. "Who's next?"

Kim took another child in her arms and turned to Steven. Her eyes were sunken with exhaustion.

"Keep talking," she said. "Does Jasmine really think Maxwell took him? Took Carlos, I mean?"

Poof.

"Uh," Steven began, touching his earpiece again. "I don't know. Maxwell—he doesn't have the Dragon power anymore. Jasmine's got it all now."

"But Maxwell still has his private army. Vanguard." She paused. "Is he gonna come looking for the rest of us?"

"He's been lying pretty low," Steven said. "But at least a couple of Zodiac operatives are still working for him. Carlos used to be able to track those guys' every move, but . . ." He trailed off, feeling helpless.

Kim *poofed* back in, grabbed another child, and vanished again.

Steven couldn't shake the dread he felt about Jasmine. He was worried about Roxanne, too—the Zodiac's Rooster. She was expecting a visit from her mother shortly after this mission. Steven had a terrible hunch that Roxanne might be planning to quit the team.

A shiver ran through his body.

"Steven?"

He looked up. Kim stood before him, lashed by the wind. She was breathing hard, leaning forward to rest her hands on her upper thighs.

"Nobody left but the teacher," Kim said. "And us."

"Wait!" Miss Maya yelled. She looked around, frantic. "We're missing someone. Where's Jana?"

Steven swore softly under his breath. He clenched his fists and willed the Zodiac power to rise up all around him. The Tiger's main attributes were strength, speed, and agility. But it was also finely attuned to danger, and its senses were superhumanly sharp.

Steven turned from side to side, searching the area. The energy-Tiger mirrored his movements, its deep green eyes seeing farther than Steven's own could. At last he noticed a small figure, cowering against a brightly colored flame tree down at the end of the playground.

A huge wind whipped up—the biggest gust yet—and rocked the bus. Steven, Kim, and Miss Maya backed away from the bus into the open field.

"I see her," Steven said, turning to Kim. "You take Miss Maya to safety. I'll get Jana."

Kim nodded and moved to take the teacher's hand. Miss Maya hesitated.

"Jana will be okay," Kim said. "Steven's the best."

The teacher nodded grimly. Together they leaped into the air and vanished.

Steven was already in motion, loping tigerlike toward the grove of trees. Rain spattered against him as he ran. Behind him, the bus toppled and crashed to the ground.

The Tiger howled into the wind.

A cloud of wet dust flew into his eyes, blinding him momentarily. He waved it away, peering through the thickening rain. For a moment, he couldn't see little Jana anymore.

Then he caught sight of her again, cowering behind a tree. Its leaves were a vivid shade of red, so bright that they almost looked artificial.

The girl was only five or six meters away. But as he took a step toward her, she retreated, scurrying behind the next tree.

"Jana!" Steven yelled. "I'm here to help you!"

"Go away!" she screamed. "You're a *tiger*!"

With great effort, he willed the Tiger energy to subside. He could feel it fighting him. It wanted to be free, to protect him from the elements.

But there was a downside to the Zodiac power. Steven knew that the sight of a raging ghostly tiger was terrifying to the little girl.

"I'm just a kid," Steven called. "Like you!"

She stared at him, her eyes still wide with fear. He realized that she was the girl he had seen holding Miss Maya's hand when he first arrived.

"Come out, okay? Miss Maya is worried about you."

She shook her head.

Steven clenched his fists, frustrated. He could leap out and grab the girl, but he didn't want to scare her any further. And he wasn't sure if even the Tiger could outrun a terrified seven-year-old.

There was a soft *poof* beside him.

"Jana," Kim called out, stepping forward. "Will you listen to me?"

Jana stood perfectly still, staring.

"I know this is scary," Kim continued. "I used to be scared, too. When this boy here"—she pointed a thumb at Steven—"when he first came to sign me up for his group, I ran away from him—how many times?"

"Three times," Steven said. "Four, maybe."

"Four times," Kim said, taking another step toward Jana. "But then I realized he was only trying to help me. Just like we're trying to help you."

A hint of doubt crossed Jana's face.

"You don't have to be afraid." Kim smiled. "I had to learn that. I had to learn to trust people."

She held out both hands. Jana took a hesitant step, then ran forward into Kim's arms.

Steven smiled. "Nice speech."

Kim smiled back at him over the head of the little girl who clung to her. "BRB," she said, and vanished.

Kim's grown a lot, too, Steven thought. *Just like Roxanne. Do they need us anymore? Do they need* me?

A moment later Kim reappeared. She took a step toward him and stumbled.

"They're all safe?" he asked.

She nodded, then spat out a mouthful of dust and coughed violently.

"I can't," she gasped, collapsing into his arms. "I can't do it again."

He nodded, wrapping an arm around her shoulders. "Come on."

Staggering against the rising wind, he led her over to the trees. The wind raged all around them, whipping and lashing them with tiny grains of sand. Steven shrugged off his jacket and draped it over Kim's shoulders, holding the sleeve up to her mouth.

"Breathe through this," he said.

She nodded and gasped in a breath.

Steven pulled her up against the trunk of a tree. Kim slumped against it and coughed again. Then she looked up sharply, through the dust and spattering rain, at the tree. He followed her gaze.

"Those are the brightest leaves I've ever seen," Steven said. "Never thought I'd see that in a desert."

She smiled weakly.

A huge gust of wind slammed into them. Steven reached for Kim, bracing her up against the tree.

"The heart of the storm," he whispered. "It's passing over us now. We'll just have to wait it out."

She buried her head in his shoulder.

The storm grew even stronger, rising and whirling all around. Steven pulled her close, raising his shirt to his mouth so he could breathe.

Kim pulled his jacket tighter around her shoulders. Her presence was warm and comforting beside him. She was only trembling a little.

As they stood together, the pelting rain and sand began to rip into the brightly colored trees. Fiery red leaves tore loose and whipped all around, vivid dots of color that flashed bright and then vanished into the thick cloud of dust.

"They're beautiful," Steven said, peering up over the collar of his shirt.

Kim said something into his shoulder, but it was muffled and lost in the roaring wind.

"What?" he asked.

"I said it's just nice being here with you."

An enormous gust of wind rose up, almost blowing them off their feet. Steven closed his eyes, concentrated, and willed his power to come forth. The Tiger wasn't invulnerable, and it couldn't stop the storm. But its energy might be able to protect them, just a little bit.

The Tiger felt Kim's heartbeat even more clearly and

vividly than Steven did. It roared into the wind, raging against the violence of nature. It reached out a spectral claw and swiped at the bright blood-colored leaves.

Gradually, the storm passed. The wind died down. The dust and sand subsided, leaving only a steady pelting of rain.

"You okay?" Steven asked.

"A little wet." She smiled, exhausted. "And there's sand in my hair."

He looked up. The sky was still blanketed by a gray cloud, but it was clearing fast. He could see a blurry glow starting to shine through the haze and sand.

"Look," he said.

Kim followed his gaze. As the clouds parted, they could just barely make out the tiny circling figure of the Zodiac plane. And next to it—hovering in place high in the air—was the source of the glowing light. It was too small to make out, but it was clearly a human figure. They both knew who it was.

"Jasmine," Kim said.

Steven nodded. Jasmine was the key to this whole mission—but could they rely on her? The storm was moving on, but that black cloud looked as huge as ever. And it was still on course for the center of Dubai.

"I think I can jump again," Kim said.

"Can you carry me?"

She looked at him, pretending to be doubtful. "You're bigger than a schoolkid. But smaller than a teacher."

Steven laughed.

He looked up again. Jasmine's glow was brighter, and she seemed to be drifting toward the storm front. But she wasn't taking any direct action yet.

Jasmine was the most powerful of the Zodiacs—the only one who could take on the forces of nature. The only one who might be able to actually stop the storm.

Maybe, Steven thought.

Before Steven could speak again, his earpiece crackled. Kim touched her ear at the same time he did, and together they heard Roxanne's strained voice.

"Liam? Steven? Jasmine? *Kkkkk*-ybody? I need backup."

Kim looked up at Steven. As she reached out a hand, the Rabbit energy flared up around her small form.

"Let's go," she said.

CHAPTER TWO

ROXANNE RAN AND JUMPED through
the wide Dubai street. Cars honked and swerved. She
dodged sideways to avoid an SUV, yelled "Sorry!" and
moved on.

Up ahead, a concrete barrier separated her from Sheikh
Zayed Road, the main highway through the center of town.
Stupid Zodiac plane, Roxanne thought. *Why couldn't they have
dropped me closer to the highway?*

She knew the answer, of course. There was no place to land a plane there, in the middle of Dubai's skyscrapers and narrow streets. The city looked very different up close than it had in Duane's briefing. It was a real place, vivid and colorful, full of actual people living their lives.

Of course, Roxanne could have parachuted down instead. But she wasn't ready to do something *that* crazy. Not yet.

When she reached the highway, a barrage of shouting and honking hit her from the other side. She hoisted herself up, vaulted onto the top of the barrier . . .

. . . and stopped, staring in surprise.

A large two-segmented truck had overturned and lay sprawled across the entire southbound half of the highway, blocking all four lanes. The trailer had cracked open, spilling small blue and white objects onto the highway. They formed a spreading pile in front of the honking cars.

As Roxanne dropped down onto the road, she realized what the objects were.

"No way," she whispered. "Muffins?"

She walked up to the truck. Its cab was still upright, but smoke was pouring out of the engine. The back segment had been twisted around and lay sprawled on its side.

Roxanne picked up a muffin and sniffed it. Blueberry.

A crowd of people ran up to her. They gestured and pointed angrily at the truck, then back at their own stalled cars. They were dressed in a wide variety of clothing, from western formal to traditional Arab garb; they yelled and chattered in different languages.

"Hold up!" she cried. "I can't understand you all. *Calmez-vous!*"

The people moved closer, pressing her up against the truck. Smiling nervously, she held up the muffin. A hungry-looking man grabbed it out of her hand.

"I'm here to help!" Roxanne cried.

"*You'rrrrre* here to help?"

She looked up, stunned.

The crowd parted, all staring nervously at the newcomer. He was covered with yellow fur, and his bared teeth gleamed. Even hunched over, he was half again as tall as a man.

"Dog?" Roxanne said in disbelief.

Dog was a Zodiac but not one of Jasmine's team. He worked for Maxwell, the military leader who'd engineered the Convergence, the event that unleashed the Zodiac powers onto the world. Of all the Zodiacs, Dog experienced the most drastic physical change when he used his power, growing thick, savage fur all over his body. He was a loose cannon, a weak link on Maxwell's team. But he was also a soldier.

He let out a low, menacing growl.

"Easy," Roxanne said, holding up both hands. "Easy, boy. . . ."

Then a terrible thought struck her. They hadn't heard much from Maxwell since his defeat at Dragon's Gate,

where Jasmine and Carlos had extracted the Dragon power from his body. But Maxwell was still out there somewhere. . . .

"Is Maxwell behind this?" Roxanne asked. "Is he trying to steal Dubai's strategic supply of . . . uh, muffins?"

Dog lunged forward. "I don't have to answer you," he growled. "Why don't you just get back in that *plane you stole from us* and fly away. *Now.*"

Roxanne flinched away from his bad breath. Now she could see: Dog looked a lot rougher than the last time they'd met. Part of his left ear was missing, and a long scar ran down that side of his face.

Is he missing an eye, too?

She gritted her teeth and clenched her fists. The majestic form of the Zodiac's Rooster rose up to surround her, shrieking with power.

"Hey!" came a deep female voice. "There's no need for that."

Roxanne whirled around. On top of the truck, a large muscular woman stood with her arms crossed, glaring down.

"Horse," Roxanne hissed.

"Hey, Rooster girl."

Horse tensed her muscular legs and leaped off the truck. As she tumbled down to the pavement, landing hands first, the galloping figure of a stallion appeared briefly around her.

Instinctively, Roxanne shrank back. The crowd backed up a few steps, watching warily.

Horse smiled. "What's the matter, girl? Remembering how I whooped you, tied you up, and dragged you through the snow?"

Roxanne clenched her fists. "More like how I whooped you back, later on," she said. But her voice was trembling.

"With a *lot* of help from your friends." Horse made a big show of looking left, then right. "I don't see 'em anywhere."

Roxanne took a step back and touched her earpiece. "Liam? Steven? Jasmine? Anybody?" She grimaced, keeping her eyes on Horse. "I need backup."

"How's the *music* going, little Rooster?" Horse taunted, taking another step toward her. "Mommy still supporting her spoiled little girl?"

The jab struck home, in ways Horse couldn't have intended. Roxanne's mother had been terrified at the first sight of her daughter's Zodiac powers and kicked her out of the house—right after a disastrous manifestation of Roxanne's powers had ended her musical career. That had been a terrible time for Roxanne. In a single day, she'd lost both her music and the person who'd always loved and supported her.

Horse didn't know any of that. She didn't know that Roxanne's mother had just gotten back in contact, either. Or that Roxanne was considering leaving the team.

Don't think about that now, Roxanne chided herself. *Focus on the two Zodiac-powered goons that are about to attack you!*

"Listen," Roxanne said. "You can tell Maxwell I'm not here to fight anybody. I just want to clean up this mess on the highway so people can get to shelter before the storm hits. That's all."

"We don't work for Maxwell anymore," Dog growled. "He crossed a line."

Roxanne raised an eyebrow, startled. "Must have been some line."

"Besides," Horse said, "cleaning this up is *our* job. A rich guy hired us to make sure he and his family got out of the city—and now he's trapped back there, someplace." She waved a hand at the long line of cars.

"A rich guy. Great." Roxanne took a tentative step forward. "What exactly *happened* here?"

Horse and Dog seemed uncomfortable. They stood silently, not looking at each other. Dog spat on the highway.

Finally, a heavyset man in a business suit stepped out of the crowd. "He did it!" the man said, pointing at Dog. "He was chasing the truck and the driver panicked. That's when it tipped over!"

Roxanne turned to Dog again. "*Chasing* the truck?" she asked.

Dog turned slowly toward her, glaring at her with his one eye. Then he let out a growl that chilled her bones.

"*It's my nature,*" he said.

"It's been a rough few months," Horse added, clenching

her hand into a fist. "Not much work out there for Zodiacs. I'm looking forward to cutting loose a little." She laughed, a very unpleasant laugh. "This is like old times."

Dog smiled. "Let's kick her tail feathers."

Roxanne glanced up. The storm cloud was very close now. The rain was increasing in force, and the air was thick with sand. Roxanne twisted her sweatshirt around to breathe through its hood.

When the rain subsided, she lowered her hood and turned to face Horse.

"It's not like old times . . . *Josie*," she said, taking a moment to remember Horse's real name. "Back then, I'd only had my powers for a little while. Now I know how to use 'em. Now I'm . . ."

She paused, unsure. *I'm what?* she thought. *Stuck in a rut? Fighting for no reason? Far from everything I love?*

Suddenly, Roxanne missed her old life.

Horse smiled. "Let's see *what* you are."

Horse took off, leaping into the air. A fierce steed flashed to life above her, snorting with power. Two fists and two energy-hooves reached out for Roxanne, who shrank back—

—just as something struck her on the back of the neck. Pain exploded through her skull as she rolled to the hard pavement. She whirled around and looked up to see Horse and Dog, both glaring down at her.

Dog's furry brow was hard, cruel. "I owed you that one," he said. "From last year."

Roxanne shook her head, dazed. Wet sand blasted her in the face, blinding her. *Liam,* she thought. *Steven! Where are you guys?*

Dog kicked her in the stomach. Then he balled an enormous hand into a wet-furred fist.

"This one's gonna be just for fun," he said.

CHAPTER THREE

NOBODY'S GONNA SAVE ME, Roxanne

thought. *But I can do this myself.*

I'm a Zodiac.

She opened her mouth and let out a deafening Rooster-cry. Dog shrank back, grabbing at his ears. Horse cried out, flailed, and fell backward. She twisted in midair, barely managing to land on all fours.

The civilians stepped out of range, watching anxiously. Several of them ran back to their cars, slamming the doors behind them.

Roxanne braced herself against a stalled car and cried out even louder.

The energy-Horse recovered before Josie did. It turned and fixed black eyes on Roxanne, wailing an eerie, inhuman cry.

Roxanne stared back, briefly mesmerized by the display of Zodiac power. Rain sliced through the Horse, pelting its dazed host as she lay on the pavement.

Then something very strange happened. A beam of light flashed down out of the sky, bathing Dog in a yellow glow. He whirled around to look up. "Huh?"

When Dog turned back, he seemed different. It took Roxanne a minute to realize why: His fur was shorter. She blinked, rubbed sand out of her eyes, and looked again.

Dog's fur was almost gone. Skin showed through the thin hair on his arms and face. His scar was redder, clearly visible against the pale flesh of his cheek. He looked almost human.

Roxanne scrabbled to her feet just as the yellow light flashed again. This time, she saw where it was coming from.

Duane was floating down out of the thick storm cloud, a bright-colored parachute trailing from his back. He held a small metal device shaped like a flashlight, studded with electronic switches and triggers. He was aiming it

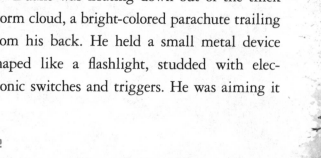

straight at Dog, immersing the rogue Zodiac in its yellow light.

I've seen that gadget before, Roxanne realized. *It's a smaller version of the power drainer Carlos used once!*

Carlos had set the device aside after that, after Maxwell had learned how to nullify its effects. But Horse and Dog weren't working for Maxwell anymore. Duane must have been listening to her comms, Roxanne realized, and taken a chance that these "freelance" Zodiacs wouldn't be protected from the power drainer's effects.

Roxanne looked around. The rain was pelting them harder now. Horse still lay dazed on the ground, rubbing her head. Most of the bystanders had climbed back inside their cars, seeking shelter from the storm.

Dog rose slowly to his feet. He seemed unsteady, as if he weren't used to walking around in human form anymore. Roxanne wondered: *Does he use his power all the time? That must be exhausting.*

Duane was five meters up now, still descending slowly. "Thanks!" Roxanne called to him. He turned, smiled shyly, and waved down at her.

A murderous growl filled the air.

Roxanne whirled around. Dog was crouched down on all fours. His face was pointed at the sky, his eyes fixed on Duane. The yellow light still shone down on him.

But Dog was hairy again.

"Duane!" Roxanne cried. "Look out!"

Dog leaped off the ground. He grabbed hold of

Duane's foot, catching him by surprise, and swung him through the air. Duane lost his grip on the power drainer; it flew away, clattered to the pavement, and rolled under a car.

Dog grunted, reached up to unsnap Duane's parachute, and flung Duane sideways. Duane soared through the air and smashed hard into the truck. He cried out in pain.

Roxanne rushed to catch Duane as he tumbled to the pavement. He grunted as he landed in her arms.

"Sorry," he said. "Thought I could build the drainer from Carlos's notes. But its effects . . . just short-term." He gasped for breath. "I can find any information, follow any engineering instructions. But the principles . . . so complex . . ."

"Don't try to talk," Roxanne said.

She set him down on the ground, using the side of the truck to shelter him from the storm. But he grabbed at her collar. He seemed desperate to tell her something, to justify himself. Duane, she knew, had always felt insecure about his lack of fighting ability; no matter how often Roxanne and the others reassured him, he felt like a lesser member of the team.

"I tried," he said, his voice weaker now. "But I failed . . . again . . ."

"It's okay—"

Two sets of arms wrenched her away from Duane. Horse's thick fist smashed into Roxanne's face, and Dog's

huge foot slammed into her stomach. That foot was covered with fur again, as if Dog's powers had never been gone.

Roxanne doubled over. Before she could recover, Horse chopped an elbow into the back of her neck. Roxanne slumped to the ground in a haze of pain.

"The great Zodiac team," Dog sneered. "What makes you better 'n us?"

"Shut up," Horse told him. Then she turned to point down at Roxanne. "And you—just lie there like a good wet hen while I see if I can salvage the job my *partner* screwed up—"

"See, that? That's the answer to your question right there."

Roxanne turned sharply in surprise—just as Liam sailed through the air. He'd pulled his knees up to his chest, forming an almost perfect sphere as he plowed into the surprised Horse.

"*UHHHHH!*" Horse cried. She toppled sideways, off balance, and cracked her head against the side of a car.

"What makes us better?" Liam said. "We don't blame mistakes on our teammates."

He bounced onto the side of the truck with a loud rattling noise. Then he unfolded his body in midair and landed in a perfect crouch on the ground. The energy-construct of the Ram raged and snorted above him.

Roxanne struggled to rise, marveling at Liam's

resilience. That impact with the truck would have killed a normal person—but there wasn't a scratch on Liam. There never was.

"About time you showed up," Roxanne said.

"Sorry." Liam gave her a crooked smile. "I had to dig some kids out of a pile of rubble, bash down a wall before it could fall on some people, and knock a rogue satellite out of the sky with my head."

"See, I almost believed you until the last one."

Liam started to reply, but his words were lost in a sudden rush of wind. The rain began to beat down harder, becoming a sheet of water mixed with sand. Roxanne could hardly see the buildings past the road.

People began to panic, blinking their headlights and revving their engines. A few people rolled down their windows slightly to yell for help.

Then Horse tackled Roxanne. Liam grabbed Horse, who jabbed him in the stomach. Liam leaped on top of Horse, and Dog jumped at Liam, dragging all four of them down to the pavement in a heap.

Cars honked. Rain pelted everything. Sand and dust filled the air.

With a grunt, Roxanne threw Horse off her back. Then she turned, startled by a soft *poof.*

Great, she thought. *What now?*

Steven stood in the rain with his arm around Kim. He looked around at the scene, rubbing sand from his eyes.

Kim ducked down and stumbled a little in the rain. She looked exhausted.

All at once, the fighting seemed to stop. Liam pushed Dog off; Dog made a show of unruffling his fur. Horse turned away, shaking her head.

Duane staggered to his feet, rubbing his head.

Steven's brow furrowed and the fierce, majestic Tiger rose up around him. He stared at Roxanne in disbelief.

"I'm glad you're all having fun," Steven said. "But has anybody noticed there's a *giant freaking storm about to wreck this city?*"

Roxanne opened her mouth to bark back at him. She wanted to say: *I'm doing the best I can. You weren't here, and neither was Jasmine!*

But she didn't say that. She raised a hand to brush wet sand off her face. Then, slowly, she nodded.

"What do we do now?" she asked.

CHAPTER FOUR

STEVEN CAST HIS EYES across the scene. The truck was still blocking all four lanes of the highway. Hundreds of cars were backed up, the line stretching back as far as he could see.

The storm grew stronger every second, coating everything in a blanket of wet sand.

And what had the team been doing while Steven and Kim were off rescuing children? Wasting their time fighting with Horse and Dog. Now Steven had to fix things—fast.

He sighed. *This should be Jasmine's job,* he thought. *Not mine.*

But it *was* his job. Ever since Carlos's disappearance, Jasmine had retreated further and further inside herself. All her energies were directed, almost obsessively, toward finding Carlos. Sometimes she holed up in remote corners of their headquarters for days, staring at computers, not speaking to anybody.

So Steven had stepped into the role of leader, directing the team in the field. At first he'd felt awkward. He hadn't asked for that responsibility, and as one of the youngest members of the team, he worried that the others would refuse to take his orders.

Well, he thought, *it's time to see if I can cut it.*

"Roxanne," he said, "is that man hurt?"

Roxanne followed his gaze. A man lay dazed, rubbing his head, by the side of the road.

"He must have gotten knocked down in the confusion," she said. "He might have a concussion."

"Okay. Kim." Steven turned to take the small girl by both shoulders. "You remember the clinic we passed on the last jump, a mile back that way?"

Kim grimaced.

"I know you're exhausted, but—just take him there. Then sit down for a while." He smiled at her. "We'll take care of this mess."

Kim nodded, moving toward the man. "I'll be back. As soon as I can."

"You've done more than your share."

Kim took the startled man by the hand. As the Rabbit-halo rose up around her, she flashed Steven a grateful smile. Then she leaped away, and the two figures vanished with a *poof.*

Steven turned to address the others. "Duane," he began—then flinched as a blast of sand hit his face. He coughed and waved it away.

"Duane," he repeated. "You and Roxanne get these people to safety. There's a police checkpoint half a kilometer past the truck—just take them there a few at a time."

"People?" Duane repeated. "I'm n-not so good with people."

"Just follow my lead," Roxanne said. Then, smiling, she walked up to a car and rapped on the window. A little girl stared out at her skeptically.

Reluctantly, Duane followed. "It's p-perfectly safe," he explained to the girl's mother.

"Now," Steven said, turning to Liam. "We've gotta move the truck."

"I can bash into it if ye want," Liam said. "Be fun. But I don't think I can move it."

"No. We're going to need Josie and Nicky for that."

Horse and Dog were standing over by the truck, arguing in low tones. At the sound of their real names, they turned to look sharply at Steven.

"We ain't helping you," Dog said.

Steven moved toward them, allowing the Tiger to flare up around him. Dog flinched, but Horse stood her ground, watching him carefully. Steven turned very deliberately to look at her.

"You two are the strongest Zodiacs here," he said. "The three of us should be able to handle a few crates of muffins."

Horse stared at him. Then she laughed.

"All right, kid," she said. "I guess that's why we're here."

"I'm here for the cash," Dog grumbled.

But soon the three of them stood at the back end of the truck, Horse and Dog each gripping a corner and Steven taking the middle. Dog growled at the mass of cars shining their headlights through the gloom.

Roxanne and Duane eased their way around the truck, holding up a blanket to cover a family of tourists. The group disappeared quickly in the storm.

"We don't have to move the truck far," Steven said, banging a fist against it. "Just enough to open up a lane. Two if we can manage it."

Dog brushed wet fur out of his eyes. "Rain's gettin' thick."

"So let's do this already," Horse said.

Steven strained his muscles, feeling the Tiger flare up inside him. To his left, Horse stood with her feet planted against the pavement, her snorting Zodiac avatar whipping back and forth in the wind. On his other side, Dog growled, scrabbling and clawing as he leaned his shoulder into the truck.

"Hey-up," Liam called. "Incoming!"

Steven ducked just in time. Liam soared through the air, balling himself into a projectile again. He struck the side of the truck, shaking the entire vehicle, and bounced harmlessly away.

Steven shook his head and studied the truck. Liam had made a thick dent in the side. But the truck hadn't moved an inch.

Dog turned to Steven, threw back his hairy head, and laughed. "Looks like you're as big a loser as we are, kid."

Steven shook his head. "We're not done yet."

Keeping his grip on the truck, Steven squeezed his eyes shut and banished all outside stimuli from his mind. Dog's complaints. Liam's suggestions. The cars revving and honking and shining their headlights.

And most of all the storm, the sand and dust and rain whipping and whirling around him.

Steven shut out all distractions, one by one, until he was conscious of only one thing—one force, radiating and vibrating through the air like invisible cords.

Zodiac energy.

He reached out and took hold of the first cord, which belonged to Liam. Liam knew what Steven was doing; they'd practiced this power-sharing technique in training sessions. The Ram's power washed over and through Steven, strengthening both of them.

Then Steven reached out and made contact with Dog.

"Hey!" Dog said, almost breaking Steven's concentration. "What're you doin'?"

"Yeah—oh!" That was Horse's voice. "I know. I know what this is. This is how they beat us last time."

When Steven opened his eyes, she was staring at him.

"The Tiger," Horse continued. "It can *link* the Zodiac powers. Bring them together."

"Yeah," Steven replied. "And when it does . . ."

He pressed his shoulder against the truck. Horse saw what he was doing and strained her muscles. Dog grunted, frowned, and pushed, even harder than before.

With a heavy scraping noise, the truck began to move.

"Liam?" Steven called.

Glowing like a comet, Liam sailed through the air again. When he struck the truck this time, it lurched and wobbled, its outer wall scraping against the pavement.

Steven frowned. The truck had barely moved a few inches—not far enough to clear the traffic lane.

Then Roxanne was at Steven's shoulder. "Let me in on this jam," she said.

He smiled.

Roxanne stepped back and let out a massive, wide-angled sonic cry. The whole back half of the truck began to vibrate like an enormous tuning fork. Steven could feel the vibrations in his fingers, lifting the truck slightly off the pavement.

The more we work together, he thought, *the stronger we are.*

Five minutes later, the back half of the truck lay at a right angle to its front half, freeing up two lanes. The cars honked and roared past, frantic to escape the wild, pelting storm.

Dog leaped up onto the truck, yelling down at the cars, "You're *welcome*, losers!"

Steven let go of the truck. His arms were sore, his fingers bleeding. But the job wasn't finished yet.

"Thank you," he said to Horse.

Slowly, she turned away from the truck to face him. Steven tried to read her expression. Horse had fought against them in the past, had taken Roxanne hostage and helped Maxwell in his dangerous plans. But Steven had always thought there was something decent about her. He'd even wondered if, out of all Maxwell's agents, Horse might join his team someday.

She lunged forward and kicked him in the face.

Steven fell back, stunned. He struck a puddle on the ground, and water splashed into his nose. He coughed, whirled, and looked up.

Horse looked furious.

"You *humiliated* us," she said. "You think we need you to come in and clean up our mess?"

"It—" He coughed up water. "It kind of looked like it."

She kicked him again, in the stomach.

Then Dog was next to her, looking down and laughing.

"Big scary Tiger," Dog said.

"Shut up," Horse snapped, turning to her partner. "I'm not too happy with you, either."

Steven scrambled to his feet. By that time, Liam, Duane, and Roxanne had gathered behind him. Liam stepped forward, smiling a dangerous smile. He balled up his fist and stared straight at Dog.

"Care to see how tough *I* am, mate?"

Dog growled.

Horse cast her eyes from Dog over to the Zodiac team. She seemed disgusted with all of them, as if the entire world had disappointed her.

"Come on," she said.

She grabbed hold of Dog's hand and leaped toward the two lanes of cars rushing down the reopened highway. They sailed through the air together, arcing over the truck to land on the roof of a moving car.

The car lurched as its driver struggled to keep control. But by that time, Horse and Dog had separated, each of them surfing on top of a different car. As Steven watched, they leaped from car to car, hopping down the highway until they were lost in the storm.

Steven gathered his team together. They retreated against the truck, watching through the thick sandstorm as the cars streamed by.

"Did we—" Duane paused, coughing. "Did we do it?"

"We cleared the road," Steven replied. "But it's too late.

The storm's about to reach full force, and there's gonna be massive damage." He gestured at the cars. "A lot of these people will be caught out in it."

Roxanne flinched from a high gust of wind. "*I'm* not crazy about being caught out in it."

"Is there anything else we can do?" Liam asked.

"No," Steven said. "There's only one hope now."

He looked up, shielding his eyes from the fury of the storm. The cloud was directly overhead, a thick mass of water and sand. It blocked out the sun, blanketing the whole area in a gray-black shroud.

Then, as they watched, a light shone down. The cloud began to part.

"Jasmine," Steven said.

CHAPTER FIVE

JASMINE HOVERED in the sky. She spread her arms, glowing brightly, and the storm receded from her touch.

Then she surged with power. The Dragon whipped its spectral head through the air, scattering the storm cloud with a sweep of its tail. It hissed, breathing fire; then it coiled up again, winding itself tight around its human host.

On the ground, Steven felt a nudge. He looked over to see Liam frowning at him.

"Should we help her, aye?" Liam asked.

Steven gestured up at the sky. "I think this is her show now."

Jasmine blazed white-hot, stronger than before. Then she reached out her arms and clenched her fists. The cloud, the enormous gray-black mass, seemed to reverse course, pouring *into* her arms and legs, her mouth and eyes. She tensed, taking in all its elemental fury.

Steven closed his eyes and concentrated. Once again, he reached out with his consciousness—and touched Jasmine's mind.

It's her show, he thought. *But maybe I can see if she's okay.*

Steven's power, the Tiger, reached out for its big sister. The Dragon's touch was like electricity, like the empty void of space, like freezing and being boiled alive at once. Its power was so great, so inconceivable that the sensations it evoked were beyond human description.

Steven gritted his teeth and pushed forward. He could feel the Dragon, its ancient strength, the dozens of people who'd hosted it before. He felt the enormous power of the storm, too—kilometers wide, fiercer than any human creation. The Dragon drew it in, slowly, and killed it dead, smothered it.

He could feel the storm; he could feel the Dragon. But he couldn't feel Jasmine. For a moment he feared that she would be absorbed by the power and lose her humanity— that she would *become* the Dragon.

And then he was there, in Jasmine's mind. She gave

him a condescending smile, as if he were still a little kid. Like when they'd first met.

Leave me alone, Lee, she said. *I'm working!*

Then she tossed him out of her head.

Steven stumbled to the ground. The others ran to help him: Liam and Duane and Roxanne. Even Kim, who'd *poofed* back in during Jasmine's light show.

Seeing them, Steven felt another shiver of fear run through him. He'd grown very close to all his teammates over the previous year. Jasmine had taught him to use his power; Liam was like the big brother he'd never had. Roxanne was the coolest person he'd ever met, and Duane had showed him how to solve complicated problems, step by step.

And Steven was starting to really like Kim, in a way he couldn't quite explain yet.

The Zodiac felt like his family—more than his *real* family ever had, except for his grandfather. But deep down, some instinct was telling Steven that everything was about to go wrong.

Could it be the Tiger—his own power—warning him of some unknown danger?

"Hey," Kim said. "Look."

Steven looked up. The rain had stopped; the storm cloud was almost gone. The dust was

clearing, and for the first time since the Zodiacs' arrival, the sun shone down on the spires of Dubai.

Jasmine hovered, wobbling a little. The Dragon hissed one last time and then faded from view. Jasmine's glow softened and she started moving through the air toward the hovering plane.

"She did it," Steven said. "She beat the storm."

He slumped to the pavement, relieved. One by one the others joined him. Kim held up a muffin, soggy and covered with grit, and made a face.

Steven laughed.

They'd won. But despite everything, he was disturbed by what he'd seen in Jasmine's mind. She'd taken every step to reassure him, to let him know she was in control. But there'd been a point, early on, when she'd almost lost control of the Dragon power.

Could that happen again? And if so, what would it mean?

Roxanne shook her head, scattering sand from her thick hair. "Anybody else need a shower? Like, very badly?"

Steven nodded, stood up, and dusted himself off.

"Let's go home," he said.

PART TWO

OX IN THE FOLD

CHAPTER SIX

BY THE TIME THE ZODIAC plane reached
Greenland, everyone was exhausted. Liam sat sprawled out in the pilot's seat, issuing the occasional lazy voice command to the plane's autopilot. Kim slumped next to him in the copilot's chair, dozing.

Steven sat at the table behind the cockpit, changing the bandages on his fingers. Next to him, Duane and Roxanne were playing a lopsided trivia game on tablet computers.

"Black Flag, the band," Roxanne said. "Name the founder and main songwriter."

Duane looked uncomfortable. "Ummm . . ."

"Greg Ginn. One point for me." She looked up and gave him a challenging smile. "Your turn."

Duane tapped his tablet. "Atomic weight of lithium," he said.

Roxanne grimaced. "Uhhh . . ."

"I'll accept an approximation."

"Uhhh . . ."

Steven smiled. He got up and crossed over to Jasmine. She sat on the floor against the bulkhead, working furiously on a laptop computer.

"Hey," Steven said. "That must have really worn you out, back there."

For a moment, her eyes tracked across the computer screen. Then she seemed to notice him for the first time.

"Not at all," she said. "Using the Dragon power—it actually energizes me now. I've been using some of those meditation techniques I showed you, to control the power. Spirit guides, yoga—it's complicated."

The computerized voice of the autopilot filled the room. *"Approaching Zodiac headquarters."*

"Establish hover mode," Liam said.

Steven walked over to the cockpit. Liam's screens showed the snow-covered mesa of Zodiac headquarters. It was three stories high, filled with living quarters, military hardware, and scientific equipment—but it didn't look like much from the outside. It wasn't supposed to.

"Be nice to get home," Steven said.

"Aye," Liam replied. "Home." But something in his tone seemed off.

Steven frowned. He couldn't shake that sense of dread he'd had back in Dubai. The feeling that everything was about to go wrong.

Liam gestured at Kim. "Should we wake her?"

Steven watched her for a moment. She was snoring softly; she looked more peaceful than he'd ever seen her. He hated to disturb that.

"Ahhh," Liam continued. "She'd kill me if I didn't."

He elbowed Kim softly. She made a sleepy noise, and then her eyes shot open. She looked around for a moment, disoriented. Then she noticed the video image of Zodiac headquarters.

She yawned, stretched her arms, and turned to smile at Steven. "See you on the ground," she said.

With a *poof*, she vanished.

Liam smiled, shaking his head. "She loves to do that."

"I guess I would, too, if I were her," Steven said.

The plane lurched slightly, then settled into a perfectly still position above the mesa. "Hover mode established," the autopilot said. "Doors opening."

Down below, a large hatchway slowly slid open in the roof of the concealed building. On the screen, Steven could see the scattered machinery of the hangar bay inside.

"Begin descent," Liam said. "Ye bloody circuit board."

"Last command not recognized," the autopilot replied. But the plane was already descending.

"You let the autopilot do everything," Steven said, smiling at Liam. "Do you even know how to fly this plane?"

"Sure." Liam smiled lazily. "But why raise a finger when ye don't have to?"

"Guys?" Kim's voice came over the radio, startling them. "You better get down here."

Liam and Steven exchanged alarmed glances. Duane and Roxanne moved to join them, watching as the building loomed closer.

Steven thumbed on the radio. "On our way," he said.

The plane was a tight fit. Its wingspan was only a few centimeters narrower than the hatchway, but the autopilot steered the plane expertly, maneuvering it sideways to enter the building safely. In less than a minute, they were on the ground.

Roxanne and Duane rushed to the jump door, preparing to disembark. "Hold it," Steven called, stopping them.

He turned to Jasmine. "You and me first," he said.

Jasmine snapped her computer closed. "Why?"

"Something in Kim's voice."

Steven led the way out of the plane, looking around. A slight Tiger glow surrounded him. His senses were heightened, on high alert.

Above, the hatch slid silently closed, shutting out the frigid northern air. Steven shivered—and then he looked toward the main door.

Kim stood with several members of the Zodiac staff, including Mags, the group's tough mechanic. Except for Kim, they were all armed. Most of the people who worked there had no enhanced powers, but they were experts in various fields of medicine and science. Right then they were serving guard duty, and their energy guns were all pointed at a single large, muscular figure.

Liam pushed his way past Steven and Jasmine, staring. "Ox?" he asked.

Ox was another one of Maxwell's former operatives. He stood with the Zodiac staff, bound and manacled. His wrists were chained in front of his stomach; thick straps held his arms tight against his body. A short chain held his ankles together.

Cautiously, Steven led the team over to join Kim and the others. Kim looked wide awake now; she was casting furtive glances at Ox.

"What's he doing here?" Steven asked.

"He just arrived," Mags said.

One year before, Jasmine's team had thwarted Maxwell's plans to steal the Zodiac power for himself. Since that time, very little had been heard from Maxwell's remaining Zodiac-powered agents. Monkey had been sighted a couple of times, carrying out minor errands for his boss. Snake and Rat, the Black Ops agents, were keeping a very low profile. Horse and Dog seemed to be operating freelance.

And then there was Ox. Rumor said he'd left Maxwell's

company, but nobody had seen the muscleman for several months.

Steven studied the rogue Zodiac. Ox seemed grim but calm. When he spoke, his voice was deep and imposing.

"I came here alone," Ox said. "And I agreed to being tied up so I could talk to you." He held up a small flash drive, waving it slightly in his bound hand. "I also brought some intel you might find interesting. On Maxwell."

At the sound of Maxwell's name, Jasmine's eyes widened. She marched up to Ox and snatched the drive out of his hand.

"I'll take this," she said.

"What about him?" Steven asked, pointing at Ox.

"You handle it."

And then, without looking back, Jasmine shouldered past Mags and Ox. As Steven watched, astonished, she left the hangar bay and disappeared into the building.

Duane frowned. "I like flash drives, too."

Ox rustled his chains. The guards waved their guns at him.

Steven exhaled sharply. He turned to look at Ox, who towered over him.

"Okay," Steven said, "so you're here. Why?"

Ox looked at him, very serious. "You want the long or short answer?"

"Short."

"I want to join up."

Mags and the guards stared at Ox. Steven and Kim exchanged astonished looks. Roxanne let out a high whistle.

Liam stepped forward. "Mate," he said to Ox. "I think we're gonna need the long answer."

"I'm a soldier," Ox said, "but I don't like Maxwell's tactics. He's gone too far."

"We're with you," Steven said.

"So far," Roxanne added warily.

"I was taught that any mission where you have to fire your gun is a failure," Ox continued. "Maxwell doesn't agree. He's always going to be a 'shoot-first' type."

Steven frowned, narrowing his eyes. "So you're saying you don't *want* to work with Maxwell anymore? Because that's a little different from what we heard."

"I know what you heard," Ox said, returning Steven's gaze. "He thinks—Maxwell thinks I ran out on him."

"Did you?"

"No. But it's true that he believes it." Ox looked away, as if remembering something unpleasant. "When we fought your team, at Dragon's Gate, somebody—or something—I hate to admit it, but they coldcocked me. Hit me from behind, knocked me right out. I woke up in a side passage, hours later, after the fight was over. Everybody was gone."

"And Maxwell thought you'd turned against him." Steven paused, thinking. "Who would do that to you?"

Ox shrugged. "I figured it was one of you."

"It wasn't," Kim said quietly.

"Wish it was," Roxanne said.

Steven cast his eyes across his team. Kim still looked exhausted; she'd been running on adrenaline, he realized. Duane seemed really uncomfortable, and Roxanne was nervous. Only Liam was calm, staring intently at Ox's chained form.

"Okay," Steven said, turning back to Ox. "First of all, that's a pretty ridiculous story. Couldn't you come up with something better? Like, maybe you and Maxwell had a big kickboxing fight on top of a volcano, with ninja stars?"

"And lightsabers," Kim added. "Always throw in some lightsabers."

"It's not a story," Ox replied. "It's the truth."

"Second," Steven continued, "it doesn't sound like you're here because you don't *want* to work with Maxwell anymore. It sounds like you're here because he kicked your butt to the curb."

"That's—"

"And third . . ." Steven paused and realized his hands were trembling. "Third, you used to hit me. A lot."

"Like I said," Ox replied slowly, "I'm a soldier. I follow orders."

"Until you don't," Kim said.

"Until those orders become unethical." Ox turned to Steven, a pained look on his face. "But if it helps, I'm sorry."

For a long moment, Steven stared into Ox's eyes. He tried to gauge the man's sincerity, to judge whether Ox meant what he said. But all Steven could remember was that very large man kicking him, punching him, and knocking him down—all at Maxwell's command.

"Listen, I'm a simple guy," Ox continued. "Liam, you know me. Have I ever lied to you?"

"No, ye haven't," Liam said. "Even when we were tryin' to bash each other's skulls in."

Duane stepped forward, a suspicious look on his face. "I—I think Mister Ox might be afraid of Maxwell coming after him."

"Is that right, Ox-y?" Roxanne asked. "You just come here so we could protect your sorry butt?"

"My name is Malik," Ox replied, a new edge creeping into his voice. "And yeah, Maxwell is dangerous. He'll throw anybody under the bus if it'll advance his agenda. I'd be stupid *not* to be afraid of him.

"But he's right about one thing: the Zodiac powers are *also* dangerous. I need help with mine—I need a group to work with. And since Maxwell's out, that leaves you guys."

"What a moving appeal!" Roxanne rolled her eyes. "I'm all choked up."

"But forget all that," Ox said. "I'm here now, and I came to you in good faith. Would you rather have me out on the streets, selling my powers to the highest bidder? Or *here*, where you can watch me?"

Selling his powers, Steven thought. *Like Horse and Dog.* That hadn't worked out very well for anyone.

Keeping one eye on Ox, he gestured for the team to form a huddle. Mags made a show of rattling Ox's chain, just to remind him he was a prisoner.

"What do you all think?" Steven asked.

"I don't trust him," Duane said.

"Me neither," Roxanne said. "Where we can watch him? More like where *he* can learn all our secrets."

"I don't know," Kim said, casting a quick glance back. "I think he might be telling the truth."

"And we *are* supposed to help people with Zodiac powers," Steven said. He paused, frowning. "Liam, you know him better than anybody. What do you think?"

"I might be able to find out."

Before Steven could respond, Liam broke away from the group and yelled out, "Ox, mate! You say ye want to join us?"

Ox nodded.

"Training room," Liam said. "Twenty minutes."

Ox seemed confused, caught off balance. "I—okay. I guess so."

"We'll sort this out, mate. Just you and me."

Roxanne leaned toward Steven. "Is this a good idea?" she whispered.

Steven shrugged.

"Okay, sure," Ox said. "Your turf, Liam. Your rules."

"Yeah," Kim said. "We'll all be there to—"

"Oh, no," Mags interrupted.

Her voice was like iron. Everyone turned to face her.

"The last six weeks," she said, "you kids have missed thirteen days of school. You might be *Zodiacs*, but you still need an education."

Duane raised a hand. "But—"

"No buts. Makeup session starts immediately."

"It's okay," Steven said, turning to his team. "You guys go with Mags. I'll back up Liam—"

"Ahem," Mags said. "You too, Tiger."

"What? And did you actually just say 'ahem'?"

"You might have been chosen by an ancient mystical power, but you're still only fifteen. With Carlos missing and Jasmine distracted, somebody's got to keep you in line." Mags leaned down and gave Steven a harsh, accusatory look. "Have you read the book I assigned you?"

"Well . . ." Steven began.

"I have," Kim said brightly. "Well, half of it. Part of half, anyway."

"But—but—" Steven sputtered. He looked around at the hangar bay, the high-tech machinery, the plane still covered with mud and sand. "We just saved Dubai."

"And I'm sure they're very grateful." Mags gestured toward the door. "Now let's go. No matter what happens, our new friend's not going to hurt Liam."

Duane started after her, followed by Kim and Roxanne. Steven hung back, leaning in for a quick word with Liam.

"Be careful," Steven said, eyeing Ox. "I don't trust him."

"I will, mate." Liam clapped Steven on the back and gave him a wide, charming grin. "Now you go learn something, aye?"

Steven nodded and moved toward the door.

As he edged past Ox's bound form, he thought, *We're supposed to help other Zodiacs. But we've got to protect ourselves, too.*

What happens when we have to choose?

CHAPTER SEVEN

STEVEN WATCHED the computer screen, shaking his head. In a small security-cam window he could see Liam and Ox sitting in the middle of the vast gymnasium-like training room. Ox was free of his chains, and Liam had set up a small folding table. The two men sat across from each other, hunched forward . . . playing chess.

"Chess," Steven muttered. "Really?"

"Mister *LEE*!"

Mags's voice made him jump. He grabbed for the screen and hastily closed the security-cam window.

On the other side of the small classroom, Roxanne snickered. She sat at another desk, reading listlessly on a screen. When Steven glared at her, she put in her earbuds and turned away.

Duane sat off to the side, staring at a holo-display. Numbers floated in the air before him.

"Sorry, Mags," Steven said.

"It's Doctor Oberdorf, now."

"Sorry, Docto—you're a doctor?"

"Yes. Of comparative literature." She smiled proudly. "Just got my degree."

"But . . . but you spend most of your time fixing cars and planes."

"I *like* fixing cars and planes." She bent down to glare at him. "Something wrong with that?"

He shook his head.

"What about the reading?" she asked. "Have you even looked at *One Hundred Years of Solitude?*"

"More like one thousand pages of solitude." He picked up the hardcover book and hefted it in the air. "I can't carry a big book like this on a mission."

"That's why we gave you the e-book version, too!"

"Did I mention we saved Dubai?"

The door creaked open and Kim walked in. Immediately, Steven knew something was wrong. She trudged across the room, staring straight ahead, her phone dangling loosely from her fingers.

"Good of you to *join* us," Mags said sarcastically, gesturing for Kim to take a seat. "If you're finished tweetering for the day."

Kim sat next to Steven in a daze. He flashed her a worried look, but she didn't even notice.

"Okay," Mags said, "we'll delay talking about *One Hundred Years*. How about *Slaughterhouse-Five*? That's a nice *short* book. Did either of you read it?"

Steven looked at Kim. Usually she could be counted on to have done the reading, but she just sat staring at her phone's blank screen.

"I read some of it," Steven said. "The part about the city being destroyed. It reminded me of . . . of Maxwell."

Mags nodded. "That's one reason I assigned it to you."

"It's still hard to believe. I mean, Maxwell is a tool and all, but that he could kill so many people . . . the entire city of Lystria."

"That's worth discussing." Mags cleared her throat. "But right now, can we talk about the book?"

"Yeah," Steven said. "The book. There was something else about it."

He paused. He had a strange feeling, one he couldn't put into words. It felt as if something were gnawing at him from the inside.

"The soldiers," he continued. "They're friends . . . I mean, they *act* like friends, but they're not really friends. They're just people who got thrown together." He looked

up at Mags. "How do you know which it is? Are people your friends just because they're *like* you, because you share some experience? Or are they really just . . . strangers?"

She looked at him for a moment. "I don't know how to answer that," she said. "Kim, do you have any thoughts?"

Kim started to say something. She looked at Steven, and he saw some strange new pain behind her eyes.

"Excuse me," she mumbled.

She stood up and ran out of the room.

Duane and Roxanne turned to watch her go. "Is she okay?" Roxanne asked, pulling out her earbuds.

Steven stood up. "I'll find out."

"*No,*" Mags said, pushing him back down into his chair. "I'll check on her. When I get back, you be ready to tell me about the first chapter of *One Hundred Years of Solitude.*"

Steven groaned.

As Mags headed for the door, Duane turned to her with a half smile. "You won't find her," he said. "Kim, I mean. She can escape from anyone."

"Just work on your multivariable calculus," Mags told him.

Steven picked up his book and opened it. He read the enthusiastic blurbs on page one. He read the title, the author's name, and the titles of other books the author had written. He read the little type with the copyright notice and the Library of Congress information.

By that time Mags was long gone. Feeling a little

guilty, Steven turned back to his computer and opened the security-cam window again.

At first, all he saw was the overturned folding table. Chess pieces lay scattered on the floor. He widened the view and saw Liam and Ox, both on their feet, circling each other like boxers.

"Uh-oh," Steven said. "You see this, Roxanne?"

No answer.

"Roxanne?" Steven called.

He turned to look. Roxanne had her eyes closed, and her head was bobbing up and down to the music in her earbuds.

Steven laid down *One Hundred Years of Solitude*—not at all reluctantly—and got up. He walked up behind Roxanne and yanked one earbud out of her ear.

"Hey!" she said.

"Sorry. Didn't mean to scare you."

"I'm not scared." Roxanne glanced at the door. "Herr Oberdorf?"

"She's still out looking for Kim."

Steven reached forward, ignoring Roxanne's protests, and opened a new window on her screen. He cycled through the security feeds until he came to the camera mounted in the training room.

Liam and Ox were rolling around on the floor like wrestlers, grappling and punching. The energy-forms of the Ram and Ox flashed up around them, flaring bright whenever either of them struck a blow. Ox jabbed his fist into Liam's stomach twice, in rapid succession. Liam just laughed.

Roxanne turned to Steven. "Yeah?"

He stared at her. "Does this seem normal to you?"

"For them it does." She gestured at the screen. "You've seen those two mix it up before. I wouldn't jump in unless somebody's guts are hanging out."

He nodded, fidgeting.

Roxanne raised an eyebrow. "Something else, kid?"

Steven frowned; he didn't know quite how to bring it up. "Is your mother still coming?"

Roxanne nodded. "She'll be here in a few hours."

"So you two are talking again."

She shrugged. "Guess we'll find out."

"That's good. I suppose."

"Look, man. I know what you're thinking." She turned to face him directly. "I haven't made any decisions yet."

Steven waited. He had a feeling she wasn't finished.

"Nothing lasts forever," she added.

"I'm just worried," he said.

"About Jasmine," Duane said.

Steven turned, startled, to see that he'd scooted his chair up to join them.

"Yeah," Roxanne said. "Me too."

"Ahem!"

The three of them went stiff all at once. Mags was back.

"There it is again," Steven said. "The dreaded 'ahem.'"

Mags strode over to the group. Duane scurried back to his desk; Roxanne turned to face her computer. Steven suddenly thought of the storm in Dubai, rushing in and driving people out of the city.

"D-did you find her?" Duane asked.

"Find the fourteen-year-old teleporter who's been running away from people all her life? No, I did not. But I'm sure she'll turn up." Mags glared at Steven. "You—back to your book. Roxanne, you've got a French history quiz coming up."

"I hate history," Roxanne grumbled. "I'm too old for this anyway."

"You missed a lot of high school while you were touring with that band of yours, *mamsell*," Mags replied. "Time to catch up."

Roxanne shot her a look and mimed a big guitar stroke in the air. Then, reluctantly, she turned back to her work.

"This computer is too slow," Duane said. "It keeps shorting out. See?"

He ran both hands along the holo-display, sending the columns of numbers spinning wildly in the air. The Zodiac Pig appeared briefly above his head, and the holo-display flashed bright. Then it winked off.

"It's not too slow," Mags said. "It's your power—it disrupts the machinery. Stop using it." She sounded like she wanted to hit something.

Duane balled up his fists in frustration. "But if I don't

use my power, I can't take in the data fast enough—"

"Doctor Mags?"

Steven turned and gestured to her. He pointed to the window on his monitor, the one that showed the training room.

"Steven," Mags said, "for the last time, *turn that thing . . .*"

Her voice faded as she saw the image on the display. Steven panned the view across the floor of the training room, past the overturned table and scattered chess pieces. There was no sign of Ox—and no sign of Liam, either.

"We better get down there," Steven said.

Mags nodded. Roxanne rose to her feet, and Duane clicked off his display. They moved together toward the door—

—and almost ran into Liam.

His hair was mussed, his jeans dirty. There was a small rip in his jacket. But he smiled warmly at his teammates. "Learn everything already?" he asked.

"Are you okay?" Steven asked.

"Course I am," Liam said. "You know nothing can hurt me."

"Where's Ox?"

"I set him up with living quarters," Liam replied. "Don't worry, I had a guard posted on 'im."

Mags frowned. "What do you think?"

"About Ox?" Liam shrugged and plopped himself down in Steven's chair. "He's still a hell of a fighter. Good strategist, too. I think we can use him."

"Yeah," Steven said, "but can we *trust* him?"

Liam thought for a moment. "I *think* he's trustworthy," he said. "But we won't know for sure until he's fighting by our side."

Steven frowned. For a moment, they were all silent, thinking.

"Here's an idea," Liam said. "Maybe we should have a little, I dunno, party or something. Then you can all get t' know old Ox." He paused. "Decide for yourself if he's membership material or not."

"Yes!" Roxanne exclaimed. "A party. That way I won't have to talk to my mother one-on-one."

Liam held up the torn collar of his jacket. "I might need some new gear, though."

"Great. Wonderful. You guys go plan a party."

Everyone turned at the sharp tone in Steven's voice.

"Meanwhile," he continued, "I'll go tell Jasmine that Kim has run off, Roxanne's thinking about leaving, and one of our enemies has just joined the team. I'm sure she'll be thrilled."

Steven turned and marched out the door.

Liam swiveled in his chair, watching Steven go. Then he caught sight of the book lying open on the desk.

"*One Hundred Years,*" Liam said, holding up the big volume. "This'd drive anybody out the door."

Mags threw up her hands. "Class dismissed," she said.

CHAPTER EIGHT

JASMINE WASN'T in the war room. She wasn't in her quarters. She wasn't even in the third-floor labs, where most of the complex's scientific equipment was stored.

Steven knew where to find her. Carlos had a second laboratory called the Vault, deep underground. The Vault was a secret to most people, even within the complex; Steven had never been down there before. But he had to talk to Jasmine. So he climbed down a long ladder, going deeper into Zodiac headquarters than he'd ever been before.

Behind a heavy steel door, the Vault was huge and dusty. Thick cables lined the stone walls, feeding power to computers, incubators, large freezers, and other assorted machinery. In one corner, an old freestanding sink stood next to an arrangement of shelves and Bunsen burners.

And in the center of the room, at the end of the thickest cable of all, a huge metal sphere floated a meter or so off the ground. It measured about five meters in diameter, and its surface was shiny and opaque.

Steven walked up to the sphere and knocked on it. "Jasmine?"

Then he noticed the door. It was small, like a hatchway—just big enough to crawl through. He reached for it, wrenched it open—

—and found himself falling, tumbling into the center of the sphere. His stomach lurched, and he flailed in midair.

Down! he thought. *Which way is down?*

"Zero gravity field," Jasmine said. "Takes some getting used to."

Steven tumbled through the air and grabbed on to a built-in handhold inside the sphere. He shook his head and looked around.

Jasmine floated in midair, her legs crossed, in the exact center of the sphere. The walls were lined with screens, more than a hundred of them, stretching 360 degrees around the inside of the chamber. Some of the screens

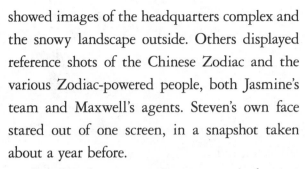

showed images of the headquarters complex and the snowy landscape outside. Others displayed reference shots of the Chinese Zodiac and the various Zodiac-powered people, both Jasmine's team and Maxwell's agents. Steven's own face stared out of one screen, in a snapshot taken about a year before.

But Jasmine was staring at a particular row of screens. One of them showed a long aerial shot of a series of giant white balls, laid out across a barren desert landscape. It took Steven a moment to recognize it as Maxwell's Australian headquarters. He'd never been there, but he'd seen the satellite photos.

Steven cast his eyes across the other screens. They showed various angles of Maxwell's sanctum—a close-up on a single white sphere, a half-hidden access road leading to the property—and a short video clip of Maxwell himself, glaring and dark, from before the time of the Zodiac Convergence. Even without powers, Maxwell was a formidable presence.

Jasmine hadn't turned around. Cautiously, feeling his way, Steven drifted closer to her.

"I thought zero gravity was impossible," he said.

"He cracked it," she said.

She pointed at one of the screens, which

showed an image of Carlos. Jasmine and Carlos had founded the Zodiac team together; he was a very serious man who usually wore a studious frown. But in that photo, he was smiling broadly. His eyes sparkled at the camera, as if he wanted to share some wonderful secret.

"It's how I think of him," Jasmine said, as if reading Steven's mind.

"Still no word?" Steven asked.

She shook her head.

Steven stared at the photo. It winked off and reappeared elsewhere on the wall, next to the big surveillance shot of Maxwell's headquarters.

"It only works within a five- or six-meter radius," Jasmine continued. "The zero G, I mean. And it requires an incredible amount of power. We're a long way from having a gravity-defying plane."

"For some reason, that's a relief," he replied.

The image of Carlos vanished again, only to reappear in yet another spot—still within Jasmine's field of vision. *She's using it,* Steven realized. *Carlos's photo . . . it's anchoring her, focusing her attention.*

"He called this the Infosphere," Jasmine said. Then she shook her head, as if angry with herself. "I mean *calls.* He calls it that."

Steven frowned. Jasmine seemed even more distant, more obsessed than she had on the Dubai mission.

"Liam, uh, he thinks Ox is for real," he said. "We're letting him stay. For now, anyway."

She didn't reply.

Steven pointed at one of the close-up shots of Maxwell's complex. "Is that from the flash drive Ox brought?"

"Yeah," she said.

"Is it . . . does it seem accurate?"

"As far as I can tell." She made a gesture in the air, and the image zoomed in to show the outline of a small door on the side of the otherwise featureless white building. "There's a few interesting details here. The main air defense seems to be these guard towers flanking the access road."

He nodded, watching her.

"But the intel is out of date," she continued. "All these shots are more than a year old."

"Ox was separated from Vanguard right after Dragon's Gate," Steven said. "He probably hasn't been in touch with Maxwell since then." He thought for a moment. "At least I *hope* he hasn't."

"There's not much new here." Jasmine swept her hand across the screens. "But we're committed."

Steven blinked. "Committed to what now?"

"Maxwell." She gestured, and the video clip of Maxwell expanded to fill six screens. "He's still at large, and we know exactly where he is. I've been drawing up plans for an assault on his headquarters."

"Jasmine, I'm not sure that's a good idea." Steven fidgeted in midair and started drifting to one side. "For one thing, I think Roxanne is about to quit."

"Then convince her not to."

"I'm not sure if I can."

She turned toward him for the first time, giving him a harsh look. "You wanted to be the leader."

"I didn't, actually," he said. "Also, we can't find Kim right now."

"Can't find . . . what? What do you mean?"

"I'm just saying, I'm not sure a full-scale attack is the best idea right now."

"It's our only option," she said, staring at the screens again. "Maxwell must be stopped."

"I know he's bad news. But he hasn't made a move for months. Vanguard hasn't even taken on any new military contracts—"

"We've got to get Carlos back!"

Steven stared at her for a moment. Jasmine was wide-eyed, acting obsessed. *How long has it been since she slept?* he wondered.

"He's there?" Steven pointed at the long shot of the Vanguard headquarters. "Maxwell has him?"

"Yeah."

"You've, what—tracked him?" Steven frowned. "Has he been in contact? What did he—"

"I just know."

Keeping her legs crossed, she tipped sideways, turning away from Steven. The images followed her around the sphere, sliding from one screen to the next, mirroring her movements.

"Carlos betrayed Maxwell," Jasmine continued, "when he and I sabotaged the Convergence. Then, later—when Maxwell and I were linked by the Dragon power—I saw things in his mind. The hatred he holds for Carlos . . ." She paused, shivering. "Maxwell is capable of anything."

"Jasmine. Look at me."

He swam through the air, coming to rest right in front of her. She frowned and tried to look around him at the screens on the wall. But he reached out and took her shoulders in his hands.

A small flare of Dragon energy rose up from her. A warning.

"Remember how all this started?" Steven asked. "When I stumbled into that creepy Convergence chamber under the museum and we both got zapped by the Zodiac power?"

"Of course," she said.

"I'm grateful to you, for taking me in. And I have never questioned your orders."

"Sure you have. Hundreds of times."

"I mean—"

"Thousands, probably." She looked at him, puzzled. "Has there been a day when you *haven't* questioned me?"

"*My point is*, this team—it's a very delicate thing." He gestured at a group portrait. "Roxanne and Duane, they're mostly here to learn about their powers. Liam doesn't really need us. And I don't know what's going on with Kim."

She was staring at him—and something in her expression made him feel cold. *She's only looked at me like that once before,* he thought, but he couldn't remember when.

Then it hit him. *On the cargo ship, right after the Convergence. When she first explained what the Zodiac powers were, what had happened to us.*

"What?" he asked, a quaver creeping into his voice.

"I always thought it was odd," she whispered.

"Huh?"

"The way you happened to stumble into the Convergence chamber"—her eyes narrowed—"just in time to get charged up with Zodiac power."

"I . . . what?" He released her shoulders and floated back toward the wall. "What are you saying?"

"I don't know." She shook her head, as if banishing a bad dream. "It's just a weird coincidence, is all."

"Yeah. Yes, it is. A coincidence!"

She turned away. As her hands danced in the air, menus scrolled down the wall screens. When she stopped, a series of silhouettes filled a row of screens, running all the way around the sphere. A rooster, a rat, a monkey. A tiger. A dragon.

When Jasmine spoke, she seemed almost in a trance.

"There are legends about the Zodiac power," she said. "Stories about its former wielders. The records are hazy, incomplete. But a lot of them didn't end up very well."

"Jasmine," he began.

"Sometimes I sit down here and I think, maybe the team is a bad idea."

She reached out and touched the dragon silhouette. The image zoomed in to show a gaping mouth with sharp fangs.

"Maybe the Zodiac power is meant to be wielded alone."

This isn't really a conversation, he realized. *She's not listening to me at all.*

She's not listening to anybody.

Jasmine waved her hand again, and the white spheres of the Vanguard complex reappeared on the screen before her.

"I'm going to do this," she said. "If I have to, I'll do it alone."

Before he could answer, a blinding flare of power rose up from her. The ghostly Dragon appeared, filled with ancient rage and passion. Its long neck whipped around the Infosphere, spitting fire at the screens. Steven tried to duck down, then realized that "down" didn't really mean anything in there.

When he looked up, the Dragon had coiled itself tightly around Jasmine. Its face hovered near hers, like a mother protecting its child.

And its image was now on every screen—dozens of them—whipping and flashing its fangs at the world.

"The Dragon," Jasmine rasped, "is more powerful than all of them. All of you."

Then she turned toward Steven. On all the screens, above and below and on every side, the dragon silhouette turned to fix its dark eyes on him, as well.

"If you're hiding something, I'll deal with it," she promised. "I'll deal with *you*."

The gaze of the Dragon seemed to bore into him, to penetrate every inch of his being. He knew she was right. The Dragon was the strongest Zodiac sign; he'd seen it in action against its enemies. It could move tons of rock, quell fierce storms, stop a madman from killing its friends.

But he'd never felt its power directed at *him* before. He felt helpless, paralyzed—like a tiny flame-red leaf in a sandstorm.

He scrambled for the door and got out of there.

CHAPTER NINE

BY EVENING, the third-floor labs had been cleared out. All the chemicals and equipment had been stowed away, replaced by tablecloths, napkins, and a few half-wilted flower arrangements. A big banner read WELCOME MRS. ROOSTER.

Duane edged up to Steven, frowning at the banner. "I thought it might be funny," he said.

Steven poured himself a cup of red punch. "Not too good with the funny, Duane."

Duane's expression turned even sadder.

"I'm sorry," Steven said. He forced himself to smile. "It's fine."

He looked around the room. Mags stood with a group of the civilians, drinking punch and laughing. Over by the coffee machine, Liam and Ox were talking and waving their fists at each other. It looked like an argument, but Steven knew they were just having a conversation.

Near the door to Carlos's lab, Roxanne leaned against a sink, a pained smile on her face. Her mother gestured all around, alternately smiling and pointing a sharp-nailed finger at her daughter. Mrs. LaFleur, Steven remembered, was an animated, larger-than-life woman. She was also the only person on Earth who could make Roxanne go quiet.

Jasmine wasn't there. Neither was Kim. Despite the noise and the laughter, Steven felt oddly alone.

"They put me in charge of party planning," Duane continued. "Which is odd, because I'm not comfortable at parties. Also, there's no place out here to get supplies on short notice."

"Duane," Steven said, "chill."

"The streamers, for instance," Duane continued. "I had to make them out of shredded intelligence reports."

Steven fingered the thin strips of paper hanging from the wall. He could just make out the word CONFIDENTIAL running down the side of one piece.

He closed his eyes. Duane was clearly feeling insecure, in need of reassurance. But Steven's thoughts kept drifting back to something Jasmine had said: *Maxwell is capable of anything.*

Maybe I blew off her concerns too quickly, he thought. *If Maxwell is holding Carlos prisoner, he could be doing anything to him. . . .*

"I'm getting better at controlling my power," Duane said. "Did you notice I haven't shorted out the training room systems for more than a week?"

"Um. No. I mean, I hadn't noticed."

"Nobody does." Duane looked sad again. "But I bet everybody notices when I get thrown into a truck in the middle of a highway."

"Duane, I'm sorry," Steven said. "I've just been really busy lately."

"Hey, kids," Mags said, walking over to join them. Two men followed her. One was Dafari, a brilliant computer programmer from Africa. The other, a short man in a jacket and bow tie, wasn't familiar to Steven.

"This is Billy," Mags said, putting her arm around the bow-tie man. "He just joined us."

"Hey," Steven said. "Where are you from?"

"I just graduated from Oxford," Billy said, shaking Steven's hand.

"Billy's smart as a whip," Mags said. "He's my new assistant."

Billy frowned. "I was promised the title 'quartermaster.'"

"Yeah, yeah. Get me a coffee, Billy?"

Billy gave her a quick, doubtful look, then hurried away.

Steven leaned toward Mags. "Bow tie?" he asked.

"What a nerd," Duane said, laughing as if he'd made a private joke.

"I told him it was a fancy party," Mags said.

Steven blinked. He looked down at his own hoodie and jeans. "It's not," he said.

"I know." Mags laughed.

"Dafari," Steven said, "you haven't heard anything from Carlos, have you?"

Dafari shook his head. "Nothing. I have tried searching for him, even hired a detective firm. But no luck."

Steven nodded.

"It is ironic," Dafari continued. "Were you or Mister Pig to go missing, I could use Carlos's machinery to trace your Zodiac energy anywhere on the earth. As long as you were not using your wave blocker, of course. But Carlos is just a normal man, like seven billion others."

Over by the coffee machine, Liam and Ox seemed to be blocking Billy's way. Steven heard Liam say, "You want coffee? Hit me first. You heard me, posh boy. Hit me!"

"Maybe we better . . ." Steven began, starting toward the coffee machine. Duane and the others followed him.

When they got over there, Billy was backed up against the table. "I said *hit me*!" Liam insisted. He didn't sound cruel, just enthusiastic.

Ox stood nearby, watching the proceedings. His eyes flicked from Liam to Billy.

"I d-don't want to hit anybody," Billy said.

"Liam," Steven said, laying a hand on his shoulder. "I think you've had enough coffee."

Liam whirled to face Steven, then turned and clapped Billy on the arm. Billy winced slightly.

"Sorry, mate," Liam said. "Just playing around."

"If you want the latest equipment, you better be nice to this guy," Steven continued. "He's our new quartermaster."

Billy smiled.

Ox stepped forward. "Quartermaster, huh? Maybe we can talk about getting me outfitted."

"Outfitted," Duane said. He looked away, but there was an edge in his voice. "Like a soldier."

Ox turned to look straight at him. "I *am* a soldier. Or I was."

"H-have you killed people?" Duane asked.

Everyone went silent.

"I'd like to know that, too," Steven said.

"That's not who I am," Ox said, frowning. "It's definitely not why I'm here."

That wasn't an answer, Steven thought.

"Look, I can help you out," Ox continued. "That plane of yours, for instance—it used to belong to Vanguard."

"So?" Steven asked.

"So I helped the techs set up its programming. I could show you some tricks."

"*If* we program it to obey your commands," Duane said.

Ox turned and glared at Duane. For the first time, the former Vanguard operative seemed a bit angry. He was the same height as Duane, but he seemed twice as imposing.

"If I wanted to steal your *plane*," Ox said slowly, "it'd be gone by now. And so would I."

Duane quivered but stood his ground.

Thankfully, the sound of clattering heels broke the tension. Roxanne's mother was being pushed toward the group by her daughter—who seemed desperate for company. "*Maman!*" Roxanne exclaimed. "I wanted you to say *allo* to—"

"Steven!" Mrs. LaFleur dashed up and gave him a fierce hug, almost cutting off his breath. "Of course I remember you."

"Hello, Mrs. LaFleur," Steven gasped.

"I owe you a very large apology, young man." Mrs. LaFleur disengaged and looked him in the eye, very serious then. "When we met before, I fear I was not at my best."

"*Maman*," Roxanne cautioned.

"I understand, ma'am." Steven forced himself to smile. "The Zodiac powers can be a shock, at first."

"Of course, yes." Mrs. LaFleur nodded vigorously. "Your own mother and father must have gone through that, as well."

Something flipped upside down in Steven's stomach. He'd never had a close relationship with his parents, even before the powers came into play. Over the previous year, he'd texted them several times, making various excuses for staying overseas a little longer. They always replied with a brief message, saying they were proud of him and hoped he was well. He'd barely spoken to them.

No, he thought, *my parents don't even know about my Zodiac powers. They're too busy with their business, their fancy company, and their world travels.*

They never knew what to do with a son anyway.

Steven looked away. Mags and the others had drifted off again, taking Liam and Duane with them. Ox stood alone, off to the side. He seemed much less dangerous, almost uncomfortable. His drink looked comically small in his hands.

"In any case," Mrs. LaFleur continued, "I'm so glad my girl and I are talking again. I've missed my little Roxy." She grabbed Roxanne around the shoulders and hugged her tight.

Roxanne grimaced.

"And I'm very much looking forward to having her back home with me," Mrs. LaFleur added.

"I told you, *Maman.* I haven't decided anything yet."

Mrs. LaFleur smiled. "All in good time, *cherie.*"

"Mrs. LaFleur," Steven said slowly, "it's true that Roxy—that *Roxanne* has gotten much better at controlling her powers. But that's only one of the reasons she's here."

Roxanne frowned. "You mean Maxwell? But he's got no powers left."

"Jasmine thinks he's still a threat."

"Maxwell . . ." Mrs. LaFleur turned to her daughter. "That's that soldier man you told me about, yes, dear? The one you trounced down in China?" She smiled. "He doesn't sound very tough."

A deep voice cut in. "He's still a danger. Trust me."

They all turned to see Ox. He'd crept up on them without anyone noticing, including Steven. *Pretty sneaky for a big strong guy,* Steven thought.

"Ox," Steven began.

"It's Malik," Ox said.

"Malik." Steven planted himself directly before the imposing Zodiac and forced himself to look Ox in the eye. "Do you have something to tell us?"

"Just that you shouldn't underestimate Maxwell," Ox replied. "He'll never give up trying to steal the Zodiac power."

"That's . . . fascinating." Mrs. LaFleur pushed forward, smiling. "Roxy, you didn't tell me about this one. He's quite . . . muscular."

She ran her nails along Ox's exposed bicep. Ox raised an eyebrow.

"Oh, *Maman,*" Roxanne said, holding up a hand to cover her eyes. "Really?"

Mrs. LaFleur ignored her daughter. "I could use some more punch," she said. "Would you care to accompany me, Monsieur . . . Malik?"

"Ox," he said, impassive.

"Monsieur *Ox*. Ooh. Perhaps you could tell me more about this deadly, *mysterious* Maxwell fellow?"

Roxanne and Steven watched, wide-eyed, as Mrs. LaFleur led Ox toward the punch bowl. Ox seemed unsure, almost dazed.

Roxanne blinked. "Is that just nauseating? Or is it a *ginormous* problem?"

"I have no idea," Steven replied.

Roxanne leaned in close. She seemed uncharacteristically serious. "I meant what I said. I haven't made any decisions. But I do miss my music."

"And your mother misses you," Steven said.

"Yeah. That too."

"That must be nice," he said.

She looked at him, puzzled. "What?"

He turned away. "Nothing."

He felt a sudden need to get out of there. He mumbled an apology and started across the room. Roxanne watched him go, a strange expression on her face.

He edged past Duane and Dafari, who were arguing about some detail of the complex's computer systems. At the punch bowl, Ox was rather urgently introducing Mrs. LaFleur to Liam.

"It's true—nothing can hurt me!" Liam said. As Steven rushed by, Liam reached out and grabbed him by the arm. "Steven! Show the fine lady. Hit me!"

Steven wrenched his arm free and bolted for the door.

Outside, in the hall, he leaned against the wall. His heart was pounding; he was breathing much harder than usual. He closed his eyes and tried to calm himself.

Is this a panic attack? he wondered. *Mom used to get those. Maybe I have something in common with her after all.*

He squeezed his eyes shut, tight enough to see sparkling patterns. One of them looked like a tiger, roaring and growling something he couldn't understand.

Poof.

He opened his eyes, knowing what he would see. Kim stood before him, the Rabbit energy just fading around her tiny form.

"Hey," she said.

"Hey!" He shook his head to clear it. "It's good to—I mean, where have you been?"

"I just had to think for a while."

He peered at her. She seemed very tired, and her eyes looked as if she'd been crying.

"We were all worried," Steven said.

"I took a walk." She came right up to him, so her head was almost touching his chest. "Then I started packing."

"Packing?"

She turned away, very fast, and raised her hands to her eyes. He heard her sobbing.

Steven felt completely helpless. "What's going on?" he asked.

"My father had a stroke," she said.

He swallowed. "Oh."

Steven looked around. Through the doorway, he could still hear the sounds of the party: laughter, glasses clinking, Liam whacking himself over the head with something. But out there, they were all alone.

"When?" he asked.

Kim turned halfway around, not quite facing him. "He was admitted to the hospital a couple days ago. I knew that when we went on the mission."

"You should have told me. We could have managed without you."

"I didn't know if it was serious. Until I got the call today, right before class."

He stepped forward, thinking, *What should I do? Hug her?* Somehow, that didn't seem like the right move.

"How bad is it?" he asked.

"He's—he seems to be paralyzed on one side. He can talk, but he's having trouble with words. . . ."

She let out a terrible wail and started to cry again. Steven stepped toward her, but she waved him back.

"I'm okay," she said. "It's just . . . I've always kind of taken care of them, and now my mother *really* needs me."

Steven nodded. "Of course."

"But I hate it there. And I'm gonna hate not being *here*." She looked up at him. "With you."

He felt tears rising in his eyes.

"Don't *you* cry!" She smiled, wiping away her own tears. "If you start, I'll never stop."

He laughed. "Promise."

He fished in his pocket and pulled out a tissue. She accepted it gratefully and blew her nose loudly.

"Very ladylike," he said.

"Shut up." She laughed, then cried a little more.

He reached out, tentatively, and touched her arm. "What do you need?"

"Nothing. I'm all packed and I've got a ride."

"Want to come in and say good-bye to everybody?"

She shook her head. "I can't. I couldn't stand it. But I had to tell you."

They stood there for a long moment, sniffling. Steven thought: *Neither of us wants her to go.*

"Is Jasmine okay?" Kim asked, finally. "Can you handle her?"

"I'll have to." Steven grimaced. "Yeah, I can handle it."

"I'll come back," she said. "As soon as I can."

"Be careful," he said. "Maxwell's still on the loose. I worry about you out there alone."

She gave him a little smile. "I worry about all of *you* here without *me.*"

So do I, he realized.

She ran forward, not looking him in the eye, and hugged him tight. When she kissed him on the cheek, he felt a warm tear flowing down her face.

Then, with a faint *poof,* she was gone.

He stood alone for a long time, listening to the laughter

from the party inside. He thought about a girl he liked a little more than he should and a woman who'd walled herself off in a gleaming sphere. *This team,* he thought. *It feels like it's slipping through my fingers, one person at a time.*

He wondered how long he could hold it all together.

THE NEXT MORNING, Steven stood with

Duane in the high-tech war room, squinting up at the map of Europe on the big wall screen. It was zoomed in on the eastern half of Germany, with a bit of Poland and the Czech Republic visible, as well.

"I still can't see it," Steven said.

Dafari, the programmer, rose from his computer console and crossed over to join them. "Mister Pig," he said, holding out a hand to Duane. "Allow me?"

Duane frowned and handed over his tablet computer. Dafari took it, then pinched at the screen with two fingers and poked it several times.

Up on the wall screen, a faint red glow appeared next to the word BERLIN.

"That's Zodiac energy?" Steven asked.

"Yes," Duane said, snatching his tablet back. "But it's very faint."

"Some of Maxwell's agents are still at large," Steven said. "Snake, Monkey, Rat. Could it be one of them?"

"Maxwell's people can usually screen themselves from our scans." Duane shrugged. "But even if this is one of them, it doesn't match anything we have on file."

"We cannot yet tell what Zodiac sign it represents," Dafari explained. "I am attempting to obtain permission to use a NATO satellite, with the goal of acquiring more accurate data for Mister Pig."

At the words *Mister Pig*, Duane flinched slightly.

Steven tried not to laugh. Dafari knew the nickname annoyed Duane, but Duane was too shy to ask him to stop. Over the past months, the two had settled into a routine of constant verbal sparring. But they respected each other and worked well together.

Steven stared up at the screen, watching the red dot pulse and flicker. There were several possibilities, but none of them made much sense. It wasn't Kim; she'd already reached America. It could be a Vanguard operative—Rat, maybe, or Snake—with a defective screening device. But that seemed too sloppy for Maxwell.

"Is it Horse again, or Dog?" he asked. "They might not have Maxwell's screening tech anymore."

"We obtained new scans of Horse and Dog in Dubai," Duane said. "This doesn't match either of their signatures."

Then Duane started fidgeting, shifting from foot to foot. He was glancing at Steven with a desperate look in his eyes.

"Duane," Steven said. "You want to talk to me alone?"

Duane nodded.

Steven mumbled apologies to Dafari and led Duane away from the main cluster of computers. Over in the corner, a few old wooden desks stood beneath a bulletin board.

"What is it?" Steven asked, perching on a desk.

"About Dubai." Duane looked away. "I—I—I got knocked out. I failed the team."

"Are you still worried about that?" Steven sighed. Sometimes Duane needed a *lot* of reassurance. "It's not your fault. We didn't know Horse and Dog were going to show up— we didn't know there was going to be fighting at all!"

Duane didn't move.

"Your powers are just less physical than the others'," Steven continued. "But there's nothing wrong with that."

Duane nodded.

"Something else?" Steven asked.

When Duane spoke, Steven could barely make out the words.

"I miss Kim."

Steven paused, unsure what to do. He reached out a hand to touch Duane's shoulder, then remembered that Duane didn't like to be touched.

"Me too," Steven said.

Duane hung his head.

"Hang in there," Steven continued. "We have to hold this together. You and me, and Liam and Roxanne."

"If Roxanne doesn't leave, too."

Steven swallowed. "Yeah," he said. "If."

Roxanne wasn't answering Steven's texts, so he decided to try the lounge. The computer terminal sat empty, and the wall TV was dark. But a large figure lay sprawled out on the central sofa.

"Liam," Steven called. "Have you seen . . . ?"

Something in Liam's expression made Steven stop. The Irishman was staring at a pair of metal objects on a chain, shifting them back and forth in his hand.

"What are those?" Steven looked closer. "Dog tags?"

"Aye," Liam said. He didn't look up.

"Whose are they?"

"Mine."

Steven looked at him sharply.

Liam grimaced and straightened up on the couch. "They used to be, anyway."

"I didn't know you were in the army."

"I wanted to learn to fly planes," Liam said. "But I hated taking orders. The officers were so full of themselves."

"When did you get your discharge?"

"Ah. That, y'see, is the thing." He looked at Steven, and

his eyes seemed tired. "I wasn't exactly discharged."

Steven frowned. "You just . . . left?"

"Couldn't stand it a minute longer, so I walked right out of basic training." Liam sighed. "Aye, it sounds bad, I know. But I didn't leave anybody in danger or anything. I would've made a lousy soldier anyway."

Steven shook his head, struggling to process the information. He'd never suspected that Liam, of all the team members, had a secret in his past. He had always seemed unflappable, cheerful, and rock solid—in more ways than one.

"You never told us this before," Steven said.

"Aye, well. I'm not proud of it."

"Did they come after you, when you left? The British Army?"

"I went back home. People in my town protect me." He let out a little laugh. "I think the army were happy t' see me go."

A thought struck Steven. He hesitated before asking, "Is that *why* you joined up with us?"

Liam looked away. "It was a factor."

"Why now? Why are you telling me this now?"

"I dunno. It's just . . . the team seems pretty fragile." Liam fingered the dog tags. "Maybe it's time I gave myself up, faced the marching-band music."

"Liam, whatever you've done in the past, you're doing your service *now*. You helped save thousands of people back in Dubai."

"Jasmine saved the people, mate. We were just traffic cops."

"That's not true." Steven paused, then shook his head. "What's going on around here today? Is *everybody* ready to quit?"

"This isn't a lifetime job, Steven. Not necessarily. Ask our little Rabbit."

He misses her, too, Steven realized.

"She didn't even say good-bye," Liam said.

"She said she couldn't."

"Aye." Liam stared at the dog tags. "I get that."

"Look—"

Roxanne burst in, waving her phone in Steven's face. "Okay, man, I'm here," she said. "Enough with the texts!"

Liam rose to his feet. As he trudged to the door, he seemed different from his normal jaunty self.

"Don't do anything crazy, okay?" Steven called after him. "Okay?"

"Aye." Liam flashed Steven a sad smile. "Just feeling moody, I guess."

As Steven and Roxanne watched, he walked out.

"What was that about?" she asked.

"You don't want to know," Steven replied.

"What's so important? You interrupted my guitar practice."

"I need to know. Are you gonna leave or not?"

Roxanne's gaze moved from the door to the TV, then

all around the room. She looked at Steven, frowned, and plopped down onto the couch. She rubbed her eyes.

"I dunno," she said. "I showed my *maman* what I can do now, all the ways I've learned to use the Rooster power. She says I don't need any more training. She says I've got it under control." She looked up at Steven, almost pleading. "That's a big step for her. You were there—you remember how freaked she was, the first time she saw me blow a lamp apart with my voice."

Steven nodded. "She ran away. Practically left a *maman*-shaped hole in the wall."

Despite herself, Roxanne laughed. "She's . . . demonstrative."

Steven smiled.

"She might be right," Roxanne continued. "That I can control my power, I mean. But I didn't do so well against Horse and Dog."

"None of us were ready for that."

Just like Duane, Steven thought, *she's blaming herself. But this is tricky. I don't want her to lose confidence in herself, but I don't want her to leave, either.*

"Straight talk?" he asked.

She nodded. "Always."

"*Please* don't go."

Roxanne blinked. "Huh?"

"I mean, there're *reasons* for you to go. I know you want to get back to your music and your mom. But there're reasons for you to stay, too. We can all learn to use our powers better—and Maxwell's still out there. He might come after us again."

She frowned. "Is this supposed to be helping me make up my mind?"

"Yeah, because none of that matters. What matters is, I'm beggin' you. Don't go right now."

She looked at him, surprised. "Oh."

"Kim's gone. I just found out Liam's got some stuff to deal with, too. And Jasmine . . ."

"What?" Roxanne asked. "What about Jasmine?"

"She's absolutely determined to mount a head-on attack on Maxwell's headquarters."

Roxanne stared at him. "She *does* know about Kim? That we're shorthanded?"

"I don't think she cares anymore." Steven shook his head. "All that matters to her is finding Carlos."

"Yeah," Roxanne said. "I was thinking about him."

"The point is, I need you to back me up. I can't talk sense into Jasmine by myself—I tried a couple days ago and she practically turned her Dragon power on me."

She frowned. "What if we can't talk her out of this?"

"Then I need you to help make sure she doesn't get killed."

Roxanne exhaled loudly. She turned away and tapped her foot on the floor. She started to sing under her breath, very low. Steven couldn't make out the words.

"You gotta keep trying," Roxanne said finally. "To convince Jasmine, I mean. I wanna find Carlos as much as anybody, but Maxwell's got an army."

Steven nodded. He smiled gratefully.

"I'm not promising to stay forever," she continued. "But I'll see this Jasmine business through. Hey, how 'bout *you* tell my mother?"

Steven shook his head right away.

"Just kidding." She got up and started toward the door. "I'll take care of it."

"Thanks," Steven said. "I mean it."

"Don't worry, kid." She turned back and flashed him a wry smile. "After I take care of *Maman*, facing off with Maxwell oughta be easy."

That time, Jasmine wouldn't open the Infosphere. Steven struggled with the hatchway door; he even summoned the Tiger power to give him extra strength. But the door was locked tight.

He stepped back, frustrated, and stared at the gleaming sphere. It looked like an alien visitor in the old dusty basement.

Then his phone buzzed. He fumbled to answer it. "Jasmine?"

"Go away," she said. Her voice sounded faint, distant.

"I just want to tell you a few things," he said.

There was a long pause, so long he thought they'd been disconnected. He stared at the sphere bobbing lightly in the air before him.

"Well?" she said finally.

"Roxanne's staying," he said. "For now. But Kim's already gone."

"I know."

"Jasmine, maybe we ought to think about other ways to find Carlos."

Her laugh crackled in his ear, hollow and cold. "Kid, what do you think I've been doing for the past three months?"

"Well . . ." He thought frantically. "What about this energy signature that Dafari and Duane found? In Germany?"

"I've seen it. It's too faint to be a Zodiac wielder."

"It's gotta be something."

"Probably just trace energy." She sighed, as if she were tired of having the same argument over and over again. "Sometimes small amounts of Zodiac energy seep into ordinary people, but it doesn't give them powers or anything. Besides, it's Tiger energy. And *you're* the Tiger."

Steven's eyes went wide. He nearly dropped the phone.

"Tiger energy," he repeated. "How do you know that? Dafari said—"

"Dafari isn't the Dragon."

A halo of energy blazed out from the Infosphere. Steven stepped back in surprise. A moment later, the energy was gone.

"Jasmine. Shouldn't we—"

"I'm making plans for the assault, Steven. There'll be a large storm system coming in over central Australia in two days' time—that's when we'll do it." She paused. "It's when *I'll* do it. You can come or not."

Steven barely registered her words. His mind was racing. *Another Tiger?* He didn't even know why it was so important to him—but it was. The beast inside roared, nearly drowning out the rest of the world.

I have to find him. Or her. I have to find this Tiger.

Two days, Jasmine had said. Berlin was just a flight away. He could take Liam and Roxanne, maybe Duane, and be back before . . .

Suddenly, a phrase Jasmine had spoken echoed in his mind: *Maybe the Zodiac power is meant to be wielded alone.*

"Steven?" Jasmine said. "Did you hear me?"

"Yeah." He spoke slowly. "Two days. Got it."

The line went dead. He lowered the phone, still deep in thought.

He walked up to the sphere and looked into its reflective surface. His own face stared back, warped and sinister in the dim light.

Then he turned and started back through the stone hallway, toward the ladder to the surface. Almost absentmindedly, he raised his phone again and dialed another number.

"This is Billy."

"Quartermaster? I'm going to need some supplies for a trip." Steven paused. "And let's keep this between us, okay?"

PART THREE
TRAP A TIGER

CHAPTER ELEVEN

STEVEN RODE ATOP the Tiger's back, along the dusty plain. They passed boulders, dead trees, and a few animal skeletons he didn't recognize. The landscape seemed endless, covered with a low fog that hid the horizon from view.

I've been here before, he realized.

As if in answer, the Tiger let out a deep growl. And then Steven remembered where he was:

The Tiger's realm.

The beast continued on its way, powerful legs moving steadily across the level ground.

"Where are we going?" Steven asked. "Do you want to show me something?"

No answer. Just another growl.

He squinted ahead. He could see something in the distance: an animal, crouched down low. It had gray fur with faded black stripes down its back. It was turned away.

It's another one, he realized. *Another Tiger.*

The second Tiger's fur was matted and patchy, and a few of its claws were missing. When it saw them, it turned and let out a deep roar.

Steven's Tiger, the one he was riding, stopped and snarled. He felt it respond to the challenge, its blood rising. The second Tiger was old and gray but also dangerous. And there was something else in its roar—something that excited Steven's Tiger even more than the prospect of a battle.

Fear.

The old Tiger rose heavily to its feet and began to pace. It walked in a small circle, around and around again. Steven watched its progress, puzzled.

Then he noticed something else. A tiny form on the ground, just beyond the old Tiger—a shock of white, barely visible in the fog.

A *baby* Tiger, with fur as pure as new-fallen snow.

The old Tiger turned and let out a loud roar. Steven frowned. *Is it protecting the little one?* he wondered. *Or . . . or does it just want the young cub for itself?*

A terrible thought struck him. *Is it going to eat it?*

As if in answer, the tiny Tiger rose to its stubby feet. It turned and regarded them one by one: the old gray cat, the newly arrived Tiger, and the puzzled boy rider.

Then the little white Tiger opened its mouth and let out a roar so loud, the world shattered to pieces.

"Kid. *Kid!*"

Steven's eyes snapped open. Two flight attendants—a young man and an older woman—were staring at him from the aisle. The man looked concerned. The woman seemed to be trying to conceal her annoyance.

"What?" Steven asked.

"The plane's about to land," the male attendant said. "It's time to buckle up."

"And, uh, stop screaming," the woman added.

Steven shook his head, still disoriented. He flashed the attendants a quick, embarrassed smile and reached for his seat belt.

As they walked away, the woman shook her head. "Unaccompanied minors," she muttered. "Nothing but trouble."

Steven leaned over the empty seat next to him and peered out the window. He could just barely see the parks and skyscrapers of Berlin, the long river winding through and around them. The city grew larger, drawing closer as the plane descended.

He closed his eyes, trying to remember what he'd just

experienced. Visions were nothing new to Steven; ever since he'd gotten the Tiger power, they came to him occasionally. Sometimes they were easy to remember, and other times they seemed like dreams, fading away as soon as he tried to grab hold of them.

The visions usually came to him on airplanes. Carlos had told him a theory about that—something about rapid movement over the surface of the earth and the fields of ley-line energy below. Steven didn't really understand it.

He remembered the Tigers, the creatures from his vision. What did *that* mean? He'd gone on the trip because of the Tiger energy that Duane and Dafari had detected. Was that just his imagination running wild, conjuring up literal images of Tigers he might find?

He thought of the vision-Tigers, wild and untamed. Then he thought about Carlos, who was still missing—lost somewhere out in the world.

And then, for some reason, Steven's own words came back to him: *Are people your friends just because they're* like *you, because you share some experience?*

Or are they really just strangers?

The plane dipped sharply, and another jolt of panic hit Steven. Once again, he felt like the floor had dropped out from underneath him. As if the roar of a newborn beast, or the sudden descent of an aircraft, could undo everything he'd ever accomplished in his life.

Get ahold of yourself, he thought. *You're on a mission. Whatever's out there, it's time to find it.*

If you're ever going to be a hero, now's the time.

Steven straightened up in his seat and stared ahead. But his hands gripped the armrests tightly until the plane was safely on the ground.

CHAPTER TWELVE

IT WAS ALMOST DARK by the time Steven reached the city. He rented a bicycle—using Jasmine's credit card—and parked it in Kreuzberg, the area where the Zodiac signature had been detected. Then he set off down a long street called Oranienstrasse in search of his objective.

CHAPTER TWELVE

The air was growing colder as night fell. The Tiger energy kept Steven warm, but he still wished he'd remembered to bring a coat. Tourists and students bustled past him, all bundled up in jackets. The sidewalk was crowded with tables from cafes and restaurants, spilling out almost to the street. The stone walls were covered with street art: graffiti, cartoons, elaborate portraits of politicians and historical figures.

Steven frowned at the Zodiac energy detector in his hand. Its screen showed a map of the immediate area. A few blocks ahead, a red dot glowed faintly: the Tiger energy.

A big man brushed by Steven, glared at him, and muttered something in German. Steven didn't understand the words, but he figured they meant "Watch where you're going."

When he looked down at the tracker, the red dot was gone. Panicked, he shook the device in the air. The dot flickered back on, vanished again, then reappeared.

Jasmine's right, he thought. *It sure is a faint energy signature.*

Suddenly he wondered: *What am I doing here?* He'd flown more than 2000 kilometers, without telling anyone where he was going, on the faintest hunch. Something had drawn him here, he realized—something bigger than himself, maybe bigger than the whole Zodiac team.

What if this is a trap? What if someone's tracking me, *just like I'm tracking this Tiger—or whatever it is?*

He shook his head. *Stay focused.* He realized he was tired. Hungry, too.

Maybe I just need some food.

He bought a curry and ate it as he walked. There was no time for panic, no room for second thoughts. He had to find the Zodiac wielder—or if there wasn't one, the source of the energy. Then he had to get to the airport and fly back to Greenland. He wanted to get home before anyone noticed he was gone—and he *had* to be back before Jasmine launched the assault on Maxwell's base.

But it was too late to fly home that night. And he wasn't sure anyone in Berlin would rent a hotel room to a fifteen-year-old kid, even if that kid had a credit card.

The curry tasted good. He started to walk faster, keeping one eye on the tracker. He crossed a busy street and then stopped dead, staring at the building on the corner.

One brick wall was completely covered with an elaborate painting. It showed a boy, about Steven's age, holding out his hands to ward off an attacking monster—a mythical creature, half man and half ram, with a sharp coiled horn on its head. The painting looked worn, chipped, much older than the graffiti surrounding it.

Around the boy, a halo of energy rose up. It might have originally been in the shape of an animal: a pig, a rabbit, even a tiger. But the image was too faded to make out.

Steven walked up to the wall and touched the painting. Inside him, the Tiger surged. There was energy there, traces left behind from an ancient battle. That painting could be a depiction of some past Zodiac user, a boy who'd wielded the power in an earlier time.

Steven felt newly energized. The painting proved he was on the trail of something important. *The Zodiac power is all around, in the air. I'm not just chasing after some phantom. This is real.*

When he looked down at the tracker, the red dot was gone again.

That time it wouldn't come back. He shook the tracker, held it up in every direction, even took out the batteries and put them back in again. The device seemed to be working fine. The signal was just gone.

Steven looked back up at the wall painting, and a wave of doubt passed over him. Maybe it wasn't a Zodiac user after all. It could be just a kid, playing around with his friends—or maybe a character from some '80s video game.

Am I just seeing what I want to see? Like . . . like Jasmine?

No. The Zodiac energy was there; he could feel it. And he'd gone that far . . . he had to see it through.

But the tracker was still dark.

The red dot, he thought. *Before it disappeared, where was it?* He closed his eyes and tried to visualize the spot where it had been on the map: about a block and a half from where he was. Halfway between the next intersection and the one after that, on the right side of the street.

He stashed the tracker in his pocket and resumed walking.

When he reached the spot, one building was boarded up. The house next to it was dark from the first floor up, but a small flight of steps led down to a black glass door with a rope set up before it.

A young couple brushed past Steven, heading down the steps. As he watched, a doorman in a stylish jacket appeared, shrugged, and pulled the rope aside. The couple went inside.

Steven took one step down, but he couldn't make out what was inside the door. He checked the tracker again: still nothing.

Taking a deep breath, he walked down to face the doorman.

"I'm supposed to be inside," Steven said.

A condescending smile crept across the doorman's face. He placed a hand on the rope, not moving it. *"Nein,"* he said.

A man in an ugly sport jacket pushed Steven aside and started arguing with the doorman. Steven whirled toward the man, angry—then had a better idea. He quickly slid around the corner, glanced up, and launched himself towards a landing above him.

Below Steven, the doorman said *"Nein"* again. He hadn't even seen Steven; he was too busy arguing with sport-jacket man.

Steven smiled. Sometimes the Tiger powers were a life-saver. Other times, they were just *fun*. He found a fire door that had been left propped open and jogged down a small staircase, ending up just behind the main entryway.

A short stone hallway led to an archway with blinking

lights over it. Steven passed through it, brushing by two girls with drinks in their hands. They turned to watch him, amused.

"They're getting younger," one of the girls said.

Then he was inside the main hall. It was dark, with gray stone walls and a crowded dance floor. Up on a raised platform, a DJ darted back and forth, spinning records. A pounding beat filled the room.

Steven made his way around the edges of the dance floor to a slightly quieter area. A few people in tight jeans lounged in chairs. As he approached, a college-age man with cropped hair turned to look at him, raising one eyebrow.

Suddenly, Steven realized: *I have no idea what to say.*

"I, uh . . . have you seen anybody *strange* around here lately?"

The man turned back to his friends. One of them, Steven saw, was a very thin woman clad entirely in rubber, with a gigantic afro. The other, a man, had the tallest, sharpest Mohawk hairstyle Steven had ever seen.

"Nope," the first man said.

Steven mumbled something and left. Their laughter followed him.

This isn't gonna work, he thought. *Even if the Zodiac is here, I'm never gonna find him. Nobody's even going to take me seriously!*

"Boy," came a soft female voice.

Steven whirled around. A tall, beautiful woman with striking pink hair was just walking out from behind the bar, heading toward him. For a moment, Steven thought about running. But he decided against it.

"I'm the manager," the woman said. She placed a hand on his shoulder and smirked at him. "Are you old enough to be in here, *liebchen*?"

Steven swallowed. "Yes?"

She stared at him for a long moment. The woman spoke English with a slight accent and had dark green eyes. She seemed vaguely familiar, but Steven couldn't remember where he'd seen her before. Maybe on TV? She was pretty enough to be an actress.

Inside him, the Tiger growled.

"Relax, kid," she said. "I'm just playing with you. This is Berlin. Everybody's welcome at the party." The woman gave him a provocative look. "And the parties last forever."

Steven frowned. He remembered what Roxanne had said: *Nothing lasts forever.*

"You want a beer?" the pink-haired woman asked. "On the house?"

"I . . ." Steven frowned. "I better not."

She turned to frown at the dance floor, apparently misinterpreting his hesitation. "I know," she said. "It's a pretty lame crowd so far. Later it'll get crazy."

He nodded.

"You don't want a drink. You don't seem to want to dance. Why are you here?" she asked.

"I—I'm looking for someone."

The woman laughed. "Everybody here is looking for someone."

"I mean a *specific* someone."

Steven made a decision. He took the woman by the arm and led her past the bar, into a dark corner near the men's room. She followed, amused.

"You're a little young for me," she said, a teasing note in her voice.

He closed his eyes and concentrated. The Tiger image rose up around him, roaring above his head.

The woman watched, her green eyes growing wide. A couple of clubbers stumbled off the dance floor, watching, but as the Tiger faded away, they lost interest.

"Someone who can do that," Steven said.

The woman was staring at him. She brushed pink hair out of her eyes.

"Assuming I knew this person," she said, "and assuming I told you where he was, what are you gonna do when you find him?"

Steven's pulse quickened. *She knows,* he thought. *She's seen the Tiger!*

"I just want to meet him," he said.

"You're not trying to hurt anybody?"

"No," he said, trying his best to sound convincing. "I'm . . . I'm a hero."

She stared at him.

Steven swallowed. He replayed his own words in his head. *Did I overdo it?*

Then she pointed a thumb upward. "You want the guy upstairs," she said.

"Upstairs?"

"Top floor. He lives in the attic apartment. He's been there since *way* before this club opened."

Steven stared at the woman. Something inside him, some Tiger instinct, seemed to roar in her presence. *Why?* he wondered. *Is it a warning of some kind?*

Is it her? Or this place?

Something buzzed in Steven's pocket. He pulled out the tracker. The red dot was back, brighter than ever.

"There's a staircase in back," the woman said, pointing toward an alcove.

"Thanks," he said.

He headed for the stairs, pushing through the crowd. The music rose up around him, growing louder.

"Hey!" the woman called.

He stopped and turned back. Past the crowd of dancers, she stood smiling at him. There was something in her eyes—those dark green eyes—that he couldn't read.

"After you find your friend," she yelled, "come on back down. We'll have that drink."

Inside Steven, the Tiger roared even louder. He felt anxious, jumpy, and nervous for reasons he couldn't understand.

He nodded quickly, then hurried on his way.

CHAPTER THIRTEEN

THE STAIRCASE CREAKED under Steven's
feet. The walls were bare wood, stained and discolored. A
few patches of peeling paint still clung to them.

How old is this building? he wondered. Steven had grown
up in America, where nothing had been built more than
two or three hundred years before. In most of the world,
there were far older places.

And some of them held very old power within them.

As he climbed, the club music faded to a dull throb.
By the time he reached the fourth-floor landing, he had to
strain to hear it.

On impulse, he pulled out his phone and hit a speed-dial number. The call went straight to voice mail.

"Hi, this is Kim. I don't know what I'm doing right now, and neither do you. Leave me a message and we'll figure it out together."

Beep.

"Hey," Steven said. "I, uh, I just wanted to make sure you're doing okay in America. You wouldn't believe where I am! Oh, this is Steven. Duh." He paused, feeling awkward. "I think . . . I've got a weird feeling I'm on the trail of something big, something that might change my life. Crazy, huh? I guess I just wanted to talk to you. . . . Man, that sounds lame. Oh! I hope your dad's doing better. Stupid, should have said that first. . . . Anyway, I guess I was . . . thinking about you. Okay, bye."

He clicked the phone off, shaking his head. "Stupid," he said again.

Then he heard a high-pitched moaning. It wasn't loud, but somehow it filled the stairwell. His Tiger senses reached out, locating the source: the door up ahead, at the top of the stairs. It had no buzzer, no nameplate or window. Just a knob.

It wasn't locked.

He stepped inside, treading lightly as a cat. The door opened directly into a small kitchen with old cast-iron pans hanging from the walls. The ceiling was low, not more than six feet high. The shelves were bare.

The moaning grew quieter.

Steven slipped around a corner and down a short hall-way. Sepia-tinted photos lined the walls, some of them in ornate frames. The people in the photos appeared to be Chinese, many of them teenagers.

Once again, he sensed he was drawing close to something—as if he were running down a hill, stumbling faster and faster toward his destiny.

He came to a door, partway open. A sickly smell, like mildew, wafted from inside. He pushed open the door and gasped.

Over by the wall, in a rickety bed, an incredibly old Chinese man lay propped up on a stack of pillows. A cable with tubes attached to it led from a medical moni-tor mounted on a metal stand to a disk-shaped machine clamped to the man's bare chest.

The old man's head was turned away, toward the win-dow. Steven couldn't tell whether or not he was awake.

The man moaned.

"Oh!" Steven said, involuntarily.

Very slowly, the man turned his head. He had tubes in his wrinkled neck, and moving seemed difficult for him.

"Winnow," the man said.

Steven stepped into the dark room. "What?"

"The *window*. Shut it," the man barked, waving an arm. "It's cold!"

Steven hurried to the window and pulled it closed. The

noise from the street vanished, muffled by the glass.

"Curtains," the man grumbled. Steven pulled the curtains, shutting out the lights of Berlin. Then he turned back to face the old man.

"Who are you?" Steven asked.

"I was gonna ask you that," the man replied, "since you're in my house."

Steven frowned and pulled out his tracker. The red dot glowed bright, almost filling the screen.

"You're Zodiac," Steven said.

The old man turned away. "Haven't heard that word for a long time," he said quietly.

Steven's mind was spinning. He didn't know what he'd expected to find, but the idea of an *old* Zodiac had never crossed his mind. Still . . . what had Jasmine said, back in the Infosphere?

There are legends about the Zodiac power . . . stories about its former wielders. A lot of them didn't end up very well.

"It's true," Steven said.

Then he remembered something else. Steven and his team had gained their Zodiac abilities at the Convergence, a rare time when the power of the mystic pools could be focused and concentrated into human hosts. That point in time—the conditions that made the Convergence possible—came around only once every 144 years.

Steven peered at the old man. His eyes were barely visible under the wrinkled folds of his skin.

"How old *are* you?" Steven whispered.

The man coughed. Then, slowly, a smile stole over his face. He opened his mouth wide and laughed.

"You—" he began. "You wouldn't belie—"

He burst into a coughing fit. Steven stepped back, unsure what to do. The man paused, tried to catch his breath, and burst out coughing again.

"Wa'er," he gasped, pointing at a nearby table.

Steven grabbed a glass of water and held it up to the man's mouth. The man coughed again, swallowed some, and jerked his head. A small stream ran down his chin.

Eventually he stopped coughing. He turned his head to stare straight at Steven.

"Don't get old," he said. "Never get old."

Steven felt a chill run through him. He was rooted to the spot. He had no idea what to do next, or even why he was there. But the old man might hold the answers to a *lot* of his questions.

"Where did it come from?" Steven asked. "The Zodiac power?"

The man gestured at the table again. Steven frowned, then pulled open a small drawer. It took him a few moments to recognize the objects inside.

"Oracle bones," Steven said.

The old man grunted in agreement.

Steven lifted two of the flat disks, holding them up to the light. They were brittle and discolored with age, their surfaces covered with tiny Chinese writing.

Steven had seen oracle bones before—well, sort of. Someone had sent him a modern-day version of one, filled with circuitry, the previous year. When it arrived, its message had been written in Chinese, a language Steven couldn't read. Before his eyes, the writing had morphed into a cryptic warning in English.

Steven had never found out who sent him the warning.

Those oracle bones, the ancient artifacts he held in his hands, were different. They were the real thing.

"These must be three thousand years old," he said.

"Give or take a few hundred," the old man said.

The man took another drink of water. Then he motioned for Steven to pull up a chair and began to speak.

"There was a man," he said. "His name was *Xu*, I think. He longed to become king."

"Of China?" Steven asked.

"Yes, yes. Don't interrupt. . . . I need to get through this. Xu came up with the idea to harness the lines, draw magic from the stars. He built the pools, combined the power from above and below. It's all written on those bones." The man paused, gasped in a breath. "He made the first Zodiacs."

Steven nodded. He remembered the mystic pools, filled with unknown liquid.

"The Zodiacs were beloved," the man continued, "in the time of the first emperor. During the Han dynasty, they helped explore the world. They served the emperor, they guarded the Silk Road. Those were glorious days. But even then . . ."

The man erupted in another coughing fit. Steven rose to help, but the man waved him away. The fit passed.

"Even then," the man said, "there were those who didn't trust people with such power. They created weapons . . . artifacts designed to contain the Zodiac energies, if any of its hosts should ever run amok.

"Those weapons were used, in the time of the Three Kingdoms. The Zodiacs were distrusted, even hunted. When the Mongols came, the Zodiacs fought them. But the Mongols' numbers were too great. They slaughtered our people. The last Zodiacs, the few that remained, went underground.

"Nothing was heard of them for a very long time. Some of them left China, following different paths. After the Opium Wars, there was briefly a Zodiac team based in England."

Steven's mind was whirling. *England?* Where else had the Zodiacs spread, over the centuries?

"The Zodiacs trusted no one," the old man continued, "not after what had been done to their brothers. When Sun Yat-sen founded the republic, some of us—of *them*—they hoped it would be a new beginning. But that didn't last, either.

"Then came the Sino-Japanese Wars . . . the first salvos of the Second World War. We Zodiacs rose up to defend our homeland from the invaders. I tried to warn them . . . tried to see the big picture. But I didn't imagine—couldn't even conceive of how horribly that would . . ."

The man began to make small gasping noises. For a moment, Steven thought it was another coughing fit.

Then he realized: *He's crying.*

"I'm sorry," the man said. "Oh, Horse, my brother. Rabbit, Snake, brave little Monkey. And Dragon, my love. I am so, so sorry."

Steven felt paralyzed. He couldn't follow the whole story, but clearly the man was caught up in some unimaginable grief.

"Dog," the old man continued. "You turned against me, betrayed us all. But I forgive you. I still love you."

Did he lose his whole team? Steven wondered. *To what?*

And then, the inevitable thought: *Will the same thing happen to me?*

The old man straightened up. He looked around at the bare room.

"After the war," he said, "I woke up here. Half the city was in ruins. But in Berlin . . . they're used to that. Always, they rebuild." He shrugged. "It seemed a fitting place to stay."

The man reached out then and grabbed Steven's arm with surprising strength. The cable attached to his chest stretched taut, rattling the machine at the other end.

"The cycles," the man said. "The cycles know no mercy.

The Convergence is the beginning, but the end is always the same. After the power enters the world, it must eventually be purged. And when it is gone . . . *no trace of its hosts remains."*

Another chill ran through Steven. He wanted to pull his arm back, but he couldn't look away from the man's eyes. They seemed filled with sadness, with infinite pain.

A shudder ran through the old man. He closed his eyes, and for a moment Steven was afraid he was dying. But his grip remained firm.

A familiar glow began to radiate outward from the man's frail body. It rose up, shifting and changing above his head. Slowly it resolved into the shape of a tiger.

A gray tiger with old, tired eyes.

Steven concentrated. His own Zodiac halo blossomed, forming a young, vital tiger. As Steven and the old man sat with their hands clasped, the two tigers exchanged looks of mutual respect.

Then Steven noticed something odd. A tiny machine, like a listening device, sat on top of the heart monitor clamped to the old man's chest. It looked extremely high-tech, unlike the rest of the medical equipment in the room.

Steven reached out and carefully plucked the device free. Orange lights winked along its length.

He turned to the man. "What . . . ?" He held up the tiny machine. "What is this?"

"It's a signal booster," said a woman with a familiar voice.

Steven whirled around—and blinked. It was the woman from the club—the tall one with pink hair who'd told him about the old man. She stood there smiling at him, a knowing look on her face.

For a moment he thought he was hallucinating. *Am I dreaming again, like on the plane? Is this another vision?*

"What are you doing here?" he asked.

The old man's Tiger energy was gone, faded away. The woman crossed over to him and placed a hand on his forehead. The man shuddered.

"Poor thing," she said. "He's almost gone. Only the barest trace of Zodiac energy left in him. Not enough to lure you here, from thousands of miles away." She gestured at the device in Steven's hand. "We needed some help."

Steven looked up at the woman, tried to speak—and found he couldn't. That time he really *was* mesmerized, held in the grip of some ancient power. He couldn't even look away.

"Use a Tiger to trap a Tiger," the woman said.

"Sorry," the old man mumbled. "I'm sorry."

As Steven watched, unable to move a muscle, the woman reached up and tugged at her pink hair. *It's a wig,* he realized. She pulled it off and shook out long dark hair.

Then he recognized her.

"Snake," he whispered.

The signal booster slipped from his hands, clattering to the floor.

Snake was one of Maxwell's Black Ops agents—the

most treacherous Zodiacs of all. Her power was hypnosis. Back at Dragon's Gate, she'd turned Duane against the team and nearly killed them all.

Snake smiled with self-satisfaction. "Should have taken the drink, kid."

Steven felt the Tiger roar inside him. It flared bright, struggling against the hypnotic compulsion that held him still.

I've got to break free, he thought. *The Tiger is strong inside me. It can do anything!*

But Snake's hold on him was firm. Like most of Maxwell's operatives, she'd been trained extensively in the use of her power.

Distract her, Steven told himself. *Say something. Anything!*

"Why?" he asked.

She shrugged. "You'll have to ask Maxwell about that. The good news is, I think you're gonna get the chance."

The Tiger surged and roared. It prowled around the inside of Steven's mind, searching for a way out.

"No. I mean why wait? Why not just take me down in the club?"

The Tiger growled. It was growing stronger. Just a few more minutes . . .

"Too many witnesses," Snake replied. "Besides, I had to wait for my backup."

A sharp blow knocked Steven forward. His skull exploded in pain. The Tiger howled.

When he looked up, the leering figure of Monkey—another Vanguard agent—was staring down at him. Monkey held up a wooden club, waving it around.

Monkey turned to Snake. "Sorry I'm late."

"You're always late." She didn't sound pleased. "I had to practically lure this kid up here with a trail of bread crumbs."

As soon as Snake's eyes left him, Steven seized his chance. He jumped up, willing the Tiger power to come forth. He leaped through the air, roaring mightily, straight toward Snake—

—then stopped in midair as Monkey grabbed him by the neck from behind. For a moment, Steven flailed in his grip. Then Monkey clubbed him on the head again, hard.

Before he could recover, Monkey grabbed his head and twisted it around. Steven's face was aimed straight at Snake.

Her eyes were cold: unblinking, unforgiving. She stared at him—and not just *at* him, but *into* him. The Tiger fell before her power-stare, along with its host.

"Please don't move," Snake said. Her voice was soft and pleasant.

Steven fell to the floor.

The next few minutes passed in a haze. Snake gestured to Monkey, who picked up Steven's unmoving body and slung it over his shoulder.

Steven knew he was in trouble. This wasn't like sparring with Horse and Dog; Monkey and Snake were two of Maxwell's toughest operatives. They'd beaten him, rendered the Tiger useless.

They were going to deliver him to Maxwell. And whatever Maxwell had planned, it couldn't be good.

Snake paused. She turned toward the old man, a cold look in her eye. His own eyes were closed; his lips moved rapidly, making unintelligible sounds. He seemed lost in a dream—or a vision, maybe.

A vision of two Tigers? Or three?

Snake wandered over and touched the machine on the man's chest. "Bad heart," she said, almost idly. "He should have died years ago."

No, Steven thought. *No, no. Please, no!*

"What did he say to you?" Snake said. "'After the power enters the world . . . it must eventually be purged.'"

She reached out and switched off the machine.

There was no surge of power, no flash of lightning. The man simply hissed out a final breath and slumped back, dead.

"No," Steven whispered.

As Monkey carried him out of the room, Steven felt himself starting to lose consciousness. He knew he should keep fighting, should summon the deepest reserves of the Tiger's ferocity. Maxwell's forces might defeat him in the end, but he knew what Jasmine would say: *Don't give up. Never give up.*

But Jasmine seemed very far away, along with the rest of the team. And when Steven thought about the old man, all he felt was an enormous sense of loss. That man had been the only other Tiger in the world, the only other person who knew what it was like to wield that power. And he was gone.

I never even knew his name, Steven thought.

Then he sank into the blackness.

CHAPTER FOURTEEN

STEVEN SHOT AWAKE. Fading dream
images flickered away: a small blond girl being menaced by
a bear; a giant blowtorch blasting away a snowy landscape;
an army of powered people, all wearing identical uniforms,
spreading like ants to cover the world.

The Tiger, he realized. *The Tiger is screaming.*

He was lying on a hard, curved surface. He tried to sit
up—and discovered he couldn't move. His arms, his legs,
even his head were all held tight. Some strange metallic
binding curved around his body like a mold, leaving only
his face exposed.

Two faces loomed into view. The first belonged to a grim square-jawed man in a Vanguard uniform. His expression was neutral, but there was something in his unblinking eyes that made Steven shiver.

The other face was thin and pale, with stringy hair half-covering the eyes. *A girl,* Steven thought. *Not much older than me.*

The girl snorted. "Big deal," she said, pointing her thumb at Steven.

The man continued to stare.

Steven fidgeted. The metal mold held him faceup, restricting his view of the room. The walls were also made of metal and angled inward, coming together in a single point on the ceiling high above. The room reminded Steven of something, but he couldn't remember what.

Don't freak out, he told himself. *Concentrate!*

He closed his eyes and tried to summon the Tiger. It roared back—a low, cautious noise. But it refused to come out.

That was strange. Normally, the Tiger hated confinement—and it always welcomed a challenge. Steven usually had to fight to keep it *inside*, not to coax it out.

It knows something, he realized. *It knows something I don't.*

That was a frightening thought. If the Tiger didn't want to act, there had to be a reason. Until Steven could figure out that reason, there was nothing to do but stall.

He opened his eyes and turned his head as much as

he could, staring at the square-jawed man. "Dude," Steven said. "You work for Maxwell?"

The man said nothing. The girl leaned her head toward Steven and laughed, a short nasty laugh.

"Maxwell's crazy," Steven said, a tremor creeping into his voice. He could already tell he wasn't going to win them over.

"I've been called worse."

That was Maxwell's voice: deep, confident, and arrogant. A jolt of fear ran through Steven. He squirmed, rattling the mold confining his body.

The man and the young girl stepped back, out of view. Then all Steven could see were the bare metal walls.

"Oh, you're panicking," Maxwell said. "Sorry about that. I suppose we can let you see what's going on."

A soft hum filled Steven's ears. The mold receded from his head, retracting into the table. The formfitting prison still held the rest of his body, but he could move his neck.

The room, he saw, was round and filled with freestanding machines. The uniformed man stood a few feet away, still studying Steven with an unnervingly steady gaze. And beside him, as expected, was Maxwell himself, tall and imposing in his crisp military uniform.

Inside Steven's mind, the Tiger grew a little stronger. He could sense it sniffing around, exploring the slight increase in physical freedom. But it still wasn't ready to show itself.

Maxwell turned away, toward a cluster of computers a few feet away. The stringy-haired girl was just seating herself on a stool, facing a dizzying array of high-tech equipment. Steven noticed his wallet and phone sitting on a table, next to a large monitor.

"Thank you, Mince," Maxwell said.

The girl gave Maxwell a self-satisfied smirk, then started tapping at a touch screen.

Steven tried to stay calm. The last time he'd seen Maxwell, the Vanguard leader had attempted to leech the power out of Steven with his bare hands. More than a year had passed since then—but sometimes Steven could still feel Maxwell's fingers gripping his shoulders, the fierce Dragon-blasts searing into his flesh.

The other man, the one with the square jaw, spoke up for the first time. "Steven Lee," he said. "The boy who would be a Tiger." He didn't sound impressed.

Maxwell turned to the man. "Don't underestimate him, Malosi. Steven does indeed hold the Tiger power within him."

Steven flexed his arms; still nothing. *Stall,* he thought again. *Keep him talking.*

Give the Tiger time.

"I beat you twice, Maxy," Steven said, smirking. "Want to try for three?"

Maxwell smiled back. The other man—Malosi—clenched his fists.

"Correction," Maxwell said, like a teacher gently coaching a student. "You *escaped* me once. The second time, you dealt me a setback."

"So arrogant," Malosi said, glaring at Steven.

"What are you, the waiter?" Steven said. "Get me a beer."

Malosi's eyes went wide with anger.

Maxwell laughed. "Young Mister Lee," he said, "you truly have the heart of a Tiger. If things were different, you might have become my finest soldier. Better than all of them." He turned away and seemed to look off in the distance, as if remembering something that had happened long before. "Better than Jasmine, even."

"Hey, I'm not going anyplace." Steven shrugged, rattling the mold slightly. "Make me an offer."

"Don't trust him," said Malosi.

"Oh, he's just playing for time," Maxwell replied. His voice was deep and steady. "I had young Steven by the throat last year, his life hanging by a thread, and he defied me. He's not going to join me today, or tomorrow. Or ever."

So much for stalling, Steven thought.

"What now?" Malosi turned to look at Steven again, and a flicker of doubt seemed to cross his face. "Are you going to alter his mind?"

"That would require the Dragon energy," Maxwell replied, "which is not currently in my possession."

Malosi nodded slowly. He seemed thoughtful, maybe a bit troubled.

"Besides, I've sworn never to use the Zodiac power that way again," Maxwell said. "I prefer my friends to be true friends, and my enemies to hate me as they choose. The Dragon's mind control is . . ."

He hesitated.

"It's *wrong*," Maxwell finished.

Steven let that sink in for a minute. *Maxwell, worried about what's wrong?*

"We'll proceed as planned," Maxwell continued. "Mince?"

The pale girl swiveled away from her computer screens.

"Please activate the qi transfer generator," Maxwell said.

For the first time, Mince looked startled. "Me?"

"Why not? The Operator has trained you." Maxwell took a step toward her. "You understand the equipment, don't you?"

A slow, greedy smile crept across Mince's face. "*Oh,* yeah," she said.

She turned away. Her fingers flashed from one touch screen to another. A low hum began to rise throughout the room.

The Operator? Steven wondered. *Who's that?*

"Don't worry," Maxwell said, turning back to Steven. "Mince is a prodigy. She knows what she's doing."

"Yeah?" Steven replied. "She kind of looks like a psycho."

"I've got three advanced degrees, buttface," Mince said. "How 'bout you?"

Maxwell laughed. "Children, children. We're all here for the same reason."

"I don't think *I* am," Steven said.

"Of course you are," Maxwell replied. "You just may not enjoy it as much."

The hum was getting louder. *Come on, Tiger,* Steven thought. *Come on!*

"It'll take a few minutes for the generator to warm up," Maxwell said. "That gives us time to continue this enlightening conversation." He loomed over Steven, turning the boy's head to stare into his eyes. "Do you know the very first thing I ever learned about waging war? When I was just starting out?"

"Always act like a big dumb tool?" Steven asked.

Malosi took a step toward Steven, fists clenched. Without even looking, Maxwell held out a hand and stopped him.

"Never rush a campaign." Maxwell's voice was calm. "Plan every step carefully, adjust as you go, and keep a measured pace." He paused, frowning. "I forgot that lesson last year. I allowed myself to become greedy, careless. That's how Jasmine was able to steal the Dragon power from me."

Steven closed his eyes. He tried again to coax the Tiger out, to force it to understand the urgency of the situation. But the Tiger just sat, crouched in some dark corner of Steven's mind, as Maxwell droned on.

"Being defeated is a valuable experience," Maxwell said. "It's humbling. It forces a person to take stock, to examine what's really important. To focus more directly on his goals and take careful steps to reach them.

"Would you like to know the steps I took?"

"Please, teach me, *Yoda*," Steven muttered, his eyes still closed.

"Step one: recruit the help you need."

Despite himself, Steven opened his eyes. Maxwell was staring up at a small rectangular window set high on the wall. The space beyond the window was lit up like a projection room, but Steven couldn't make out anything inside it.

"Step two," Maxwell said, "fashion the proper tools. That prison holding you tight, the equipment Mince is using. Everything down to the design of this chamber itself, here at Vanguard headquarters. Do you recognize it?"

Suddenly, with a shock, Steven did. *It looks like the Convergence chamber,* he realized, *the place where we first got our Zodiac powers. Only it's smaller, scaled down, without the pools of Zodiac energy.*

"Step three: divide your enemies." Maxwell smiled. "All I had to do was separate her from the only teammate who might be able to help her . . ."

"Me," Steven said.

"It was incredibly easy to lure you to Berlin. Just a hint that you might learn more about the Tiger . . ." Maxwell laughed. "Don't worry. You will, soon enough."

"Get a little closer to me and *you'll* learn about the Tiger," Steven sneered. "Jarhead."

Before Steven knew what was happening, Malosi punched him in the face. Steven's head exploded in pain. He caught a quick glimpse of Malosi's face, twisted in rage.

"Have some respect," Malosi hissed.

Steven tensed up. The mold clattered around him. He felt the Tiger rise up inside, roaring and howling, responding to the attack.

Maxwell grabbed Malosi's arm and pulled him away. "Watch," Maxwell said. "This will be instructive."

At last the Tiger burst forth. The ghostly cat form took shape in the air, roaring and swiping out against its enemies. Steven felt the mold around him bend, starting to give way—

—and then fire ignited all around him. Hidden gas jets, concealed within the confining mold, flared to life, raising small flames around the outline of Steven's body. He looked at the inferno and felt a bone-deep terror.

The Tiger, he realized. *It's afraid of fire!*

He struggled and squirmed within his prison. The flames licked his skin, singeing his arms, but he stayed calm. *I could shatter the mold and break free,* he thought, *if the Tiger would just act. . . .*

But the Tiger was terrified. Its power was intact, still strong within Steven, but it was paralyzed with fear, helpless. All its instincts told it to flee for its life.

Steven flexed his muscles, but it was no use. The trap, the bizarre ordeal, seemed to have been designed for him and him alone.

He felt the Tiger recede, hiding inside him once again. Without its power, its assistance . . .

. . . *I'm just a kid.*

It knew, he realized. *The Tiger sensed the fire trap as soon as we got here. That's why it didn't want to come out.*

Maxwell waved a hand in the air. The flames died down, disappearing into the molded prison.

Steven slumped back, exhausted.

"You know nothing about your power," Maxwell said, "and Jasmine knows nothing about hers. She may have taken the power from me, but she'll never hold it." He paused, looking off in the distance. "Only I can control the Dragon."

Then another person spoke, the voice amplified and distorted by some hidden speaker system: *"Keep your eyes on the boy. He's still dangerous."*

Malosi frowned. Mince looked up, irritation on her pale face. Maxwell turned toward the lighted window high on the wall and nodded.

Is that the Operator? Steven wondered. *Is he up there?*

He realized he was breathing fast. The flame ordeal had drained him physically, but worse than that: he was really afraid. His only hope of getting out of there was the Tiger—and it had failed him. Maxwell, or someone working for him, had known exactly how to defeat it.

Something else was bothering Steven, too. The voice of the hidden Operator . . . it struck a vague chord in his memory. Something he couldn't quite remember. Maybe something he didn't *want* to remember.

Malosi stood at attention, rigid and contrite. Maxwell walked over to him.

"You shouldn't have struck young Steven," Maxwell said. "You are my child, too—more than him, more than any of them. You must be worthy of the gift you are about to receive."

"I'm sorry," Malosi said.

"We are brothers," Maxwell said. "Brothers-in-arms. This is a war we're fighting, make no mistake. We all obey orders . . . from other soldiers, from forces within ourselves, from the stars themselves."

Malosi nodded.

"You're a good soldier," Maxwell said. "A good son."

Steven twitched his arms, testing the mold again. His head was still free, but the prison held the rest of his body even tighter than before; he could barely wiggle his fingers. The Tiger had dwindled to a tiny presence in the back of his mind.

The hum in the room shifted tone, becoming a high whine. Mince whirled around in her chair.

"All systems dope," she said, then grinned. "I mean go."

"Very well," Maxwell said.

"Wait," came the amplified voice of the Operator. *"Stem seven is blocked."*

"Mince?" Maxwell called.

"I flushed out all the branches. . . ." The girl peered at her screens. "Oh. Yeah."

"Run the qi cleanse protocol," the Operator said.

Mince turned away from her station, her finger hovering over a touch screen. For just a moment, she glared up at the lighted window on the wall. "I *know*," she said.

Maxwell moved to look over her shoulder. His expression was hard. "Mince, you are the second most brilliant scientific mind in all of Vanguard."

Mince kept her face turned away from her boss. Steven saw her clench her fists. She seemed possessed by some sort of rage.

" '*Second*,' " she repeated.

"Yes," Maxwell continued. "But you're only sixteen years old. Learn from your mistakes."

Mince started to breathe hard. Her fists trembled. She was almost as young as Steven and physically small. But Steven had the feeling that, if she'd had something sharp in her hand right then, Maxwell would be dead.

"Maybe . . ." Mince still didn't look at Maxwell. "Maybe I should be going to the *prom* instead."

"If you fail me, that's not where you'll be going."

Mince inhaled sharply. Then she blinked twice and whirled back toward her screens.

"Running cleanse protocol," she muttered.

"Don't force the energy," the Operator said. *"Let it flow along the lines."*

That voice, Steven thought. It was distorted, masked by the speaker system, echoing off the metal walls. But . . .

No. No, it can't be.

The whining in the room rose to a high pitch, then settled to a steady drone.

"Got it," Mince said. Then she looked up at the lighted window, as if waiting for the voice to correct her again. But the Operator said nothing.

"Well," Maxwell said, striding back over to Malosi, "shall we?"

Malosi followed Maxwell to the table where Steven lay. "That equipment," Malosi said, pointing at the molded prison. "Is it for the transfer?"

"Oh, no." Maxwell smiled. "That's just to hold him in place."

"Transfer?" Steven asked. "What transfer now?"

Maxwell leaned down and smiled at him, an almost fatherly smile.

"This is your lucky day, Steven," he said. "You've never met another Tiger before."

"Your guys killed the other one!"

"Oh, him. True." Maxwell gestured at Malosi. "Good thing there's a third."

Steven turned to stare at Malosi.

"He's a Tiger?" Steven asked.

"*The* Tiger," Malosi said. "I was meant to have the power that you stumbled into during the Convergence."

Malosi seemed hungry, filled with pride. A fiery rage burned behind his eyes.

Suddenly, Steven remembered his vision. *Three Tigers,* he thought. *An old one, gray-furred, whose time had passed. Mine, of course.*

And a baby, newly born.

Maxwell reached into his coat and pulled out two small metal objects. He lunged forward and clapped them onto Steven's forehead. Steven cried out and squirmed, but some sort of glue kept the devices affixed to his temples. And the mold held him tight.

He felt the metal devices clamping tighter, pushing tiny tendrils into his skin. He scrunched his eyes shut and twitched his head back and forth in panic.

"Now," Maxwell said, "the final piece of the plan."

He held up a small bronze sphere. It was dented and very old, but Steven could feel the Zodiac power radiating from it. He remembered the old man's words:

They created weapons . . . artifacts designed to contain the Zodiac energies.

Steven struggled to keep his cool. He cocked his head at the sphere. "For me?"

"In a way." Maxwell smiled. "Malosi, take your position—"

A phone rang.

Everyone looked around, confused. A flash of anger crossed Maxwell's face.

Mince hopped off her stool and ran, puzzled, to a nearby table. She picked up Steven's phone.

"It's the kid's," she said.

"Ignore it," Maxwell ordered.

The phone rang again.

Mince peered at the screen. "No name on the caller ID," she said. "Number is 812-555-5424."

Steven's eyes grew wide. *Kim,* he thought. *That's Kim's number. She must have gotten the message I left, back in Berlin, and finally called back.*

Panic surged through him. Steven's team carried wave blockers, which prevented an enemy from detecting their Zodiac energy signatures. Kim still had her blocker; under normal circumstances, Maxwell couldn't track her. He wouldn't even know she'd left the team.

But if they answer that call, Steven thought, *if they figure out who it is . . . they'll know she's in America. They'll know she's alone. And they'll go after her!*

Maxwell's eyes narrowed. He glared at Mince. "I said ignore it."

Mince looked up from the phone, as if snapping out of a trance. She shrugged and tossed it back onto the table.

When the ringing stopped, Steven exhaled in relief. He slumped back down on the table.

Then he stiffened as the two metal objects clamped to his forehead lit up. For a moment, he'd almost forgotten about them. They started to hum, pulsing with energy.

Steven thrashed, suddenly frantic. *They'll go after Kim soon anyway,* he thought. *And Roxanne and Liam and Duane . . .*

My whole team. The team that's falling apart . . . that I can't manage to keep together.

Maxwell held up the bronze sphere. It seemed to wobble in his hands like a water balloon—as if its surface were shifting, turning to liquid.

"The *jiānyù,*" Maxwell said. "It's ready."

Jiānyù, Steven thought, struggling to remember the bits of Chinese his grandfather had taught him. *That means prison—*

Then the power drain began. It wasn't like back at Dragon's Gate, when Maxwell had tried to steal the Tiger power from Steven. That had felt like needles, like pinpricks all through his body. Like searing heat and burning cold, ripping him apart.

This was different. This was surgical, precise. A hand seemed to reach straight into Steven's mind, feeling around for something—for the Tiger, crouched in its hidden lair.

The Tiger hissed. It growled. And then, to Steven's horror, it whimpered.

It knows it's helpless.

Steven closed his eyes. He marshaled his mental defenses, the meditation techniques Jasmine had taught him. But it was no use. The invader, the seeking energy-hand, seemed to know everything about him. As soon as he twitched one way, it mirrored his movements.

In one shockingly quick moment, it grabbed the Tiger and pulled it out of him.

"*NO!*" Steven cried.

"Oh," Maxwell said.

Steven opened his eyes—and blinked in shock. He strained his neck against his confinement, unable to believe his eyes.

The sphere in Maxwell's hands—the *jiānyù*—was morphing, changing shape. One by one it sprouted four legs, a tail, a thick bronze head, sharp staring eyes, and even sharper fangs.

A tiger, Steven thought. *It's a tiger now.*

Without a word, Maxwell turned and held out the *jiānyù* tiger to Malosi. Malosi hesitated for a moment, eyeing the artifact.

"Take it," Maxwell said.

Malosi reached out a hand and touched the tiger.

The *jiānyù* seemed to surge with energy. It flashed and shifted, changing form rapidly. Steven wasn't sure when he remembered it later, but he thought he saw it transform briefly into the shape of a bronze horse, then a dog—

—and then Steven felt something stab through his mind, as if he'd been slapped. Stars flashed before his eyes. He clattered back against the table.

When he looked up again, Malosi stood before the table. He looked taller, more powerful than before. Maxwell held the *jiānyù* loosely at his side. The artifact looked just as it had at first: an ordinary bronze sphere, tarnished and dented with age.

Mince pulled out a small analyzer device and started running it up and down Malosi's body. The analyzer, like the room itself, looked horribly familiar.

As Steven watched, a glowing cat shimmered into existence in the air above Malosi. But it was a different tiger form than Steven's. It was thicker, fiercer, with snow-white fur and rage-filled red eyes.

It turned to him and growled.

Steven looked away. He felt utterly defeated. He wanted to cry.

Maxwell paced slowly around Malosi.

"The Tiger is unique," Maxwell said. "That's why we're taking no chances with it. That's why I lured young Steven here. And it's why Malosi is so crucial to my plans."

Malosi clenched both fists. The white Tiger swept its head through the air, roaring with power.

"I can feel it," Malosi said. "The power . . ." He stared up at the swirling energy. "It feels right."

"Power," Maxwell repeated. "It justifies many things."

Footsteps echoed on the metal floor—a steady tapping, growing closer.

"Ah! The Operator," Maxwell said. "The man who taught me the secrets of the Tiger."

Steven didn't want to look. He knew what he'd see. He'd figured it out: how Maxwell had solved the problem of the Zodiac power and where all the new equipment had come from. Only one person in the world could have accomplished that.

A delicate masculine hand grasped Steven by the chin, wrenching his head around. Despite his best efforts to resist, Steven found himself staring into the face of the Operator.

The face of Carlos.

Carlos turned Steven's head one way, then the other. He touched the two metal devices on Steven's forehead, peering at them through thick glasses. His movements were careful, unhurried, and his expression one of pure scientific detachment.

Maxwell walked up behind Carlos, looking over his shoulder at Steven. Mince and Malosi followed, keeping a respectful distance from their boss.

"Is it done?" Maxwell asked.

Carlos turned slowly toward Maxwell. A cruel smile spread across the scientist's face, making Steven's blood run cold.

"Perfect," Carlos said.

CHAPTER FIFTEEN

STEVEN'S UNDERGROUND CELL was

small and dark. Thin glowing energy rods stretched from
floor to ceiling, forming bars around three walls of the cell.
Only the back wall was solid, with a half-screened area
leading to a toilet and sink.

Steven paced back and forth, his mind whirling. He
walked to the sink and splashed water on his forehead.
It was still sore, with small red marks where the energy
drainers had been.

But that wasn't what bothered him. For the first time in more than a year, the Tiger was completely silent. Steven hadn't realized it, but he'd grown accustomed to its low roar, the constant fire in his blood. Without it he felt weak, hollow.

And something else was bothering him. Something awful, an image he couldn't banish from his mind:

Carlos.

Jasmine and Carlos had founded the Zodiac team together. By the time Steven joined up, the two of them were inseparable. They planned and executed operations as a unit, with Carlos planning the technical details and Jasmine leading the strike team.

But before that—before there even *was* a Zodiac team—Carlos had worked for Maxwell. It was Carlos who'd perfected the Convergence technology that had allowed Maxwell to loose the Zodiac powers on the world.

And then Carlos had turned against Maxwell, sabotaging the Convergence. Steven had been there—had seen it with his own eyes. That was when he'd received his own powers, through whatever accident of fate had taken him to that strange chamber deep beneath Hong Kong.

But what if . . .

Steven closed his eyes. He didn't want to think it.

What if Carlos had never *really* turned against Maxwell? What if he'd been working for Maxwell all along, spying on Jasmine and Steven and the others? Maybe Carlos had just

been biding his time, waiting to return to Vanguard and continue his work. Maybe he'd played them all, deceived them, for more than a year.

Jasmine was back in Greenland right then, depriving herself of sleep and human contact, devoting all her energies to her obsessive search. Meanwhile, the object of that search was *there*—doing Maxwell's dirty work.

Carlos's smile, Steven thought. *The way he looked at me . . .*

He wandered to the side of his cell and studied the energy bars. Hesitantly, he reached out and touched one. A painful electric shock ran through him. Where his finger was making contact with the bar, images pulsed in the energy, flickering like a sped-up film. They were all Zodiac images: a ram, a snake, a rooster. Rat, tiger, dragon.

Outside the cell, two guards sat at a small central command post. They studied screens showing various camera angles of the Vanguard headquarters: an access road, a guard tower, an aerial view of the eerie white domes.

They're not even paying attention to me, Steven realized. *Without my power, I'm nothing to them.*

He was still touching the bar. The pain grew stronger, spreading like daggers up his hand and into his arm. He yanked his finger away.

"Kinda hypnotic, huh?" someone said.

Steven squinted past the bars, into the darkness. He could see, for the first time, a man standing in the next cell. He was tall and blond, and as he approached he pointed toward the spot where Steven's finger had been.

"Hurts like crazy. But when they first put me in here, I still stared at it for a long time. Ten minutes, maybe. Almost fried my pinky finger."

Without the pressure of Steven's finger, the energy appeared solid again. The Zodiac images were gone.

Steven looked up. Now that the man stood directly on the other side of the bars, Steven recognized him. He was another Zodiac wielder, the only one whose body changed significantly when he used his powers. Steven had seen him only briefly in human form—but the mangled ear and missing eye were a dead giveaway.

"Dog," Steven said.

"Not anymore," came a deep female voice. "Now he's just Nicky."

Steven whirled around. In the cell on the opposite side of his, a muscular woman stood watching. Even before he saw her clearly, Steven knew who she was: Horse.

Horse pointed at the energy grid. "These bars," she said. "They're some particular combination of qi/ley-line energy. I don't understand it. Long story short: they'll give a normal person a nasty shock, but they're specifically designed to stop Zodiac power users."

Steven frowned. "But I don't have my powers anymore."

"Maxwell ain't takin' any chances," Nicky replied. "That's why we're here."

Steven looked from Nicky to Horse. Nicky's body

showed no trace of his Dog fur, and Horse—Josie, that was her name—seemed slightly smaller and weaker. They didn't look like the same people who'd teamed up with him to move that truck in Dubai, mere days before.

"He took your powers, too," Steven said.

A quick flash of memory came to Steven: the *jiānyù* sphere shifting briefly into the shape of a horse, then a dog. So he *had* seen that, after all.

"That's right," Josie said. "But he wants to make sure we don't have any trace of Zodiac energy left. So he's holding us here till . . . I don't know how long, actually."

"He's gonna lock us all up eventually," Nicky said, a gloomy expression on his face. "Your loser friends and guys like Ox who ran out on him. Even the Vanguard agents like Monkey and Snake."

"Why are they still working for him, then?" Steven asked.

"They don't know." Josie shook her head in despair. "They don't know what's gonna happen to them."

Steven moved closer to her. "Did he trap you, too?"

"Ha!" Nicky laughed, shaking his head. "He didn't have to. We crawled right back to him after Dubai, looking for work."

"Stupid. Stupid," Josie said. She turned away, clenching her fists. "Last year, I swore I'd never work for him again."

"It's *their* fault," Nicky said, pointing at Steven. "The

kid here and his friends. They made us look like idiots—"

"No," Josie said. "It's not their fault. If we looked like idiots in Dubai, we did it to ourselves." She paused. "Guess I got what I deserved."

Steven looked at her, then back over at Nicky. He remembered working with them in Dubai, the three of them sharing Zodiac energy to do something none of them could accomplish individually. That had been just a few days before, but it seemed like an eternity had passed.

Since we all had powers.

He felt a wave of despair. *They seem so weak,* he thought, *so defeated. And me . . .*

. . . I'm a hero. Remember?

"No," he said. "We're getting out of here."

Dog laughed. "How exactly are we doing that? With no powers?"

"I have powers," Steven said.

He closed his eyes and concentrated. The world outside faded away: the cells, the guards, the Zodiac-proof bars. All that remained was Steven . . .

. . . and his grandfather.

Steven remembered Jasmine's coaching, the meditation techniques she'd taught him. *Find a spirit guide,* she'd said, *some person or animal that can help you dig deep. Someone who knows you and can lead you to the hidden parts of yourself.*

Steven's late grandfather had raised him, taken care of him while his parents were busy building their corporate empire. Grandfather had always been his guide, as well as his link to his Chinese heritage. The old man had been an easy choice.

Steven looked inward. His grandfather's wrinkled face smiled at him. Grandfather pointed a withered finger downward, then took Steven's hand and leaped.

Together, they dove deep into Steven's mind. They passed faces and buildings, sounds and smells. Steven caught a glimpse of Jasmine and Carlos, smiling as they assembled the Zodiac team for the first time. Then he saw his high school class, milling about the New China Heritage Museum, unaware of the Convergence energies bubbling under their feet.

A sound was rising—a faint growl. Still smiling, Steven's grandfather turned toward the sound. In the darkness below, Steven could see an animal, coiled into a tight ball to protect itself.

The Tiger.

As Steven approached, the beast turned its head toward him. Its eyes seemed to flare, its courage returning at the sight of its host. It opened its mouth, but instead of the usual deafening roar, only a low snarl came out.

Steven staggered, suddenly exhausted. He opened his eyes. Nicky and Josie were staring at him from either side of his cell, through the bars.

"Well?" Steven asked.

"The Tiger appeared above you," Josie admitted. "But only for a second."

"The Zodiac power is still inside us," Steven said. "We all had it, even before the Convergence. The hard part is *using* it."

Josie shook her head, keeping her voice low. "I've fought the Tiger—fought *you*—before. It looked like a shadow of itself, just now."

"I can do this," he insisted. "I can get us out of here."

"You'll never keep it up," Nicky said. "Not long enough to take out those guards."

Steven turned toward the guard station. One man was snoring, and the other one laughed at a cartoon in his magazine. They hadn't noticed the prisoners talking.

"I don't have to take out the guards," Steven said. "All I have to do is get through these bars, and then I can let you two out."

Josie frowned, considering.

"But I need a distraction," Steven continued. "If the guards see me doing this, they'll stop me."

"Two guards," Josie said. "We'll need to distract both of 'em."

She hesitated.

"What?" Steven asked.

Josie turned to face him directly. "How do you know you can trust us?"

Steven shrugged. "I don't, I guess. But you have to start trusting sometime."

He thought he saw doubt on her face.

She was quiet for a long moment, then nodded. "I can take one guard. Nicky?"

Nicky gave her a nasty smile. For the first time, he seemed almost like his old self. "Just watch me," he said.

The three of them stood at the front of their respective cells, each facing the bars leading to the guard station.

"Ready?" Steven whispered.

Josie nodded sharply, looking straight at the guards. Nicky shifted back and forth like a boxer getting ready for a match. Then he gave Steven a crooked smile.

"Go," Steven said.

"Hey!" Josie called.

The sleeping man opened one eye. The other guard looked up from his magazine, shrugged, then went back to reading.

"*Hey!*" she yelled.

The guard sighed and threw the magazine down on the monitor console. He crossed over to Josie's cell. "What is it?"

"I'm not supposed to be in here," she said.

The guard shrugged again. "That's not my call."

"You don't understand," Josie insisted. "I work *for* Maxwell. I was trying to save him when these two maniacs attacked!"

"It's true," Steven said, keeping his distance from the

bars leading to Josie's cell. "She's not on *my* team!"

The guard shook his head. "I don't get involved in Zodiac business," he said. "That's up to Maxwell."

Just then, Nicky let out a howl of pain. He dropped to the floor and clutched his stomach.

"My gut," Nicky cried. "It's on fire!"

The guard at Josie's cell started to move past Steven, toward Nicky's cell. But Josie snapped at him, stopping him in his tracks. "Hey. I'm talking to you!"

The guard turned to her. "Lady, there's something wrong with your boyfriend."

" *'Boyfriend'?* Listen, buddy. When Maxwell hears about this, he'll hang you in his garden and use you for target practice!"

The second guard reluctantly roused himself. He crossed over to Nicky and crouched down to peer through the energy bars. The now-furless Dog was writhing around on the floor, moaning.

"What's wrong with you?" the guard asked.

"I dunno," Nicky gasped. "But it hurts!"

Steven cast quick glances from side to side. The first guard was still arguing with Josie. The second one dropped to his hands and knees, trying to examine Nicky through the barrier. Neither of them was looking at Steven.

He sucked in a breath, gritted his teeth, and walked into the bars.

The electric charge lanced through him at every point

of contact: his arms, his legs, his torso and face. The pain was sharp and biting, and it seemed to come from everywhere at once. He ground his teeth together, muffled a cry, and marched forward.

"Lady," the first guard was saying, "I can*not* let you out of here."

"Do you need a Milk Bone?" the second guard asked Nicky.

The pain from the bars seemed to surge, growing even stronger. Steven gasped silently, knowing he had to remain quiet. Nicky and Josie were still distracting the guards, but sooner or later all eyes would turn to Steven. If that happened too soon, his escape plan would be ruined.

Zodiac images seemed to flash and flicker before Steven's eyes. A bright red rooster, trumpeting the arrival of day. A fierce ox, head lowered to charge. A flash of searing dragon breath.

Steven concentrated, using Jasmine's meditation techniques to block out the pain. Again he sought out his grandfather, using the old man's calm face as an anchor. Together they sank down again, retreating deep inside Steven's mind, seeking refuge from the searing agony.

I can't do it, Steven thought. *It's too much pain. I can't pull this off.*

An image of the Zodiac's rabbit flashed before his eyes.

Kim, he thought. *I've got to do this for her. If I don't stop Maxwell—she'll be—*

The Tiger roared.

Zodiac energy flared up around Steven. He reared his head back and let out a scream, long and deep and primal. All the pain, all the rage and regret and loneliness inside him, seemed to erupt, expelled from him in one explosive moment.

When he shook his head and returned to his senses, he was standing outside the bars.

The guards whirled around to look at him. For a moment, everyone stopped. The guards blinked, stunned.

That moment was all Steven needed. He launched himself into the air and kicked out, striking the first guard a fierce blow on the neck. The guard lost his footing and stumbled into the energy bars leading to Josie's cage. He screamed.

Josie reached between the bars and grabbed the guard's collar. She pulled him close, jamming his head against the electrically charged bars. The guard let out a series of sharp gasping noises.

The other guard drew his weapon, advancing slowly. Steven could feel the Tiger energy fading; he wouldn't be able to hold it for long. He dropped to all fours and loped over to the startled guard. He swept out one hand like a paw, knocking the energy weapon out of the guard's hand. Then he clenched his other hand into a fist and slammed it into the man's stomach.

The guard dropped to the ground—and the Tiger

winked off, as if a switch had been thrown. Steven staggered backward.

He shook his head, trying to clear it. The energy was gone; no trace of it remained. He felt exhausted, spent, more tired than he could ever remember being in his life.

Josie's voice cut through his mental fog, rousing him. "Well?" she said. "Let us out!"

Steven looked over at her. The first guard, the one she'd pulled against the bars, lay unconscious on the floor. Steven ran to him and pulled an electronic control key off of the guard's belt, then aimed it at Josie's bars.

A doorway-size gap appeared in the energy. Josie stepped out, took a long look at Steven, and smiled. She gave him a friendly punch on the arm, which hurt more than it should have.

"Hey," Nicky called. "Over here?"

Steven crossed to his cell, with Josie just behind. Nicky lay on the floor, grinning.

"I'm not really sick!" Nicky said. "Good acting, huh?"

Josie rolled her eyes. Steven shrugged and pointed the remote control at the cell, deactivating the bars.

"I'll alert the Golden Globes," Josie said dryly. "Now let's get the hell out of here."

CHAPTER SIXTEEN

"SO," ROXANNE SAID. "That's it."

Next to her, Liam let out a long sigh. "Aye," he said.

"This is a very poor idea," Duane said.

The three of them stood shoulder to shoulder in the war room, staring up at the big screen. It showed an aerial view of Maxwell's compound in the desolate Australian outback. The compound's large central building, white and featureless, squatted on the red sand. Similar smaller buildings, all of them round or oval, fanned out around it in a regular pattern. Two access roads curved in from opposite sides, breaking through patches of sparse scrub and leafless trees.

"And Jasmine wants us to attack that?" Liam asked.

"In less than twenty-four hours," Roxanne replied.

"I love a good brawl, but we're shorthanded." Liam turned to Duane. "Any word from Steven?"

Duane shook his head.

Roxanne frowned. Steven had been missing for more than a day—which wasn't like him at all. *And it leaves us with a big hole in the team,* she thought. *If we're really planning to assault our worst enemy in his home . . .*

"Dafari," she said, turning to the console where the computer expert sat. "Can you zoom in on the complex?"

Dafari nodded and typed in a few commands. Up on the big wall screen, the strange dome-like buildings grew larger. They looked like plastic toys, meticulously arranged along the sandy red plain.

"What about Ox?" she asked, turning to Liam. "You really think we can trust him?"

"I'm gettin' tired of answering that question," Liam said. "I like the bloke, but I'm not his brother and I'm not his sponsor. Like I said, the only way to know is to test him in battle."

Just then, Ox walked in. His face was grim. Roxanne couldn't tell whether he'd heard them talking about him.

"A meeting?" Ox said. "I must have missed the e-mail."

Duane glared at him. "Perhaps there *was* no e-mail."

"You're here now," Liam said.

Ox looked around. "Where's Steven, anyway?"

"Steven? He's in Berlin." Billy, the new quartermaster,

had just entered the room. He looked around nervously as everyone turned to stare at him at once. "Something wrong?"

"Berlin?" Roxanne asked. "Steven told you he was going there?"

"He followed the Tiger energy!" Duane said.

Liam marched up to Billy and pointed a finger in his face. "Why didn't you mention this before, mate?"

"H-he told me not to?" Billy said.

Duane frowned. "We told him to wait. For more data—"

"It is gone," Dafari said.

They all walked over to Dafari's station. His screen showed a map of Berlin, with no overlays or winking lights.

"He's right," Duane said. "The Tiger energy I located . . . there is no trace of it now."

Liam frowned. "Is the word *trap* popping into anyone else's mind?"

Duane leaned down to tap on Dafari's keyboard. "If Steven were there," he said, "he'd be shining like a bright light on this board. B-but there's no sign of him, either."

"Maybe he has his wave blocker on?" Roxanne asked.

"That'd block him from Maxwell's tracking devices but not ours. I'm not getting a ping from his phone, either."

"We should do a wide-range search," Dafari said. "I am setting the scanners specifically to detect Tiger energy."

Duane sat down next to him. "It'll take a few minutes to cover the—oh, wow. That was fast."

Roxanne leaned down to look over their shoulders. The computer screen showed a flashing tiger icon.

"Is that Steven?" she asked. "Where is he?"

Duane pointed up at the wall screen. The image of Maxwell's Australian headquarters, white buildings against red soil, was still displayed. In between two of the buildings, a tiger icon flashed.

Roxanne let out a long sigh. "Guess we better tell Jasmine."

"Jasmine? She's gone, too."

Again, they all turned to look at Billy.

"Billy, mate," Liam said, "you have got to start leading with the important stuff!"

"Sh-she asked for a basic field supply kit and took off." Billy swallowed nervously as Roxanne and Liam closed in on him. "I think she said something about moving up the timetable."

Roxanne gestured up at the screen. "She's already on her way. Without us."

"Are ye surprised?" Liam asked. "Jasmine's barely said three words in the past month. She doesn't think she needs us anymore."

Billy shook his head. "I shouldn't have let her go. I shouldn't have let either of them go."

Roxanne smiled at him. "You're a hell of a quartermaster, Billy. But I don't think you could have stopped the Tiger."

"Much less the Dragon, mate!" Liam said.

A movement up on the screen caught Roxanne's attention. "Steven's icon is moving," she said, crossing back over to Duane's station. "Are they transporting him somewhere?"

"I—I don't like this," Duane said. His eyes flashed from screen to screen, his fingers flying across his keyboard and then Dafari's. "Maxwell can screen Zodiac signatures from our scans, can't he?"

"Yes," Ox said. "If he didn't want you to know Steven was there, we wouldn't be seeing this."

"Again," Liam said, "that word *trap*."

"Yeah, but we can't just leave him there." Roxanne sucked in a deep breath. "Now we have to go."

She looked around the room. Liam was right: they were shorthanded. Duane was already absorbing data, planning the attack, but his powers weren't suited to a head-on assault. Liam would fight until he dropped, but his abilities were mostly defensive. Roxanne herself could break through force fields and walls, but she was no match for an army.

So that leaves . . .

"Malik," Roxanne said. "You in?"

Ox smiled and cracked his knuckles. "About time," he said. "I won't let you down."

"We should get moving, like, *yesterday*," Liam said. "Jasmine's already got a big head start—"

A sharp beeping noise rose up from the console in

front of Duane. Everyone froze. Duane looked at the screen, swept his hand across it, then turned sharply to stare at Ox.

Ox cocked his head and stared back.

Duane reached out and, in a quick motion, snatched up a handheld analyzer from its cradle. He held it up, listening as the piercing *beep-beep-beep* continued.

"What is it?" Roxanne asked.

"The Zodiac power scan," Duane said. "It's focused on Australia. But something is . . ."

He stood up and waved the analyzer in the air. He moved it toward the wall screen and the beeping noise softened. Then he held it up to Ox and the beeping grew louder—almost deafening.

Ox just stared at him. Everyone else gathered around Duane, watching.

"In his forehead," Duane said, waving the analyzer around Ox's head. "Just beneath the skin. Something's transmitting a signal."

"A signal?" Roxanne asked. "A signal to where?"

"To the same point in Australia."

Liam stared in disbelief. "Maxwell's headquarters?"

"Within a kilometer, anyway."

Roxanne felt her Zodiac power flaring. "What kind of *signal* is it?"

"I can answer that," Dafari said.

They all turned toward him. Still seated at his console,

he punched a few buttons and then gestured up at the wall screen.

The view of Maxwell's headquarters was gone from the screen. In its place was a washed-out real-time image of the Zodiac team: Roxanne, Liam, and Duane, with Billy standing just behind them. Their necks were craned around, and they were looking away.

That's us, Roxanne realized. *It's the view from Ox's forehead!*

"It is a camera," Dafari said.

One by one, the team turned back toward Ox. Up on the screen, their images mirrored their movements, staring straight out at the room.

"Well," Ox said, his face stony, "I guess that's that."

In a dark cave on the other side of the world, the same image shone out of an old CRT screen. The monitor was recessed into a stone wall, as if some deranged interior decorator had installed it in the rock wall.

A small man raised his eyebrows and reached out a sharp finger, pointing in turn at each Zodiac member. Rooster. Ram. Pig.

The man smiled. "Looks like our little game may be up," he said.

Other small men gathered around him. They lurked in the shadows, waiting for his instructions.

An alarm rang out.

"Ah! We have places to be," the man said. "Let's move."

He cast one last look at the Zodiacs staring out of his video screen. Then, with a crook of his finger, he led the others down the hole and away.

CHAPTER SEVENTEEN

WITH JOSIE'S HELP, Steven managed to
unlock the elevator in the center of the prison chamber,
using the unconscious guard's palm to unlock the mech-
anism. There were buttons indicating the ground floor
and an intermediate security level. Steven reached for the
ground-floor button, but Josie stopped him.

"Better idea," she said.

She reached down and pressed an unmarked button
underneath all the others. The elevator lurched and started
to move—not up but down.

"There's a level below this one?" Steven asked.

"This facility dates back to World War Two," Josie explained. "Our best escape route is the old evacuation tunnels beneath the holding cells."

"I didn't know about that," Nicky said.

"You might try reading the mission briefs."

"We're in the middle of the desert," Steven said. "Where do the tunnels go?"

"Not far—just out to the checkpoint on the access road, at the entrance to the compound. We'll either have to fight our way out from there or slip past the guards. But at least we'll have a head start."

"What do we do then?" Nicky asked. "We don't have our powers. How are we gonna survive in the desert?"

Josie grimaced. "One problem at a time."

The elevator door opened. Steven stepped out and sucked in a breath of stale air.

The tunnel was low and narrow. Bare pipes ran along the stone ceiling, dripping water onto the sludgy floor. The air was humid, the desert heat seeping in to merge with the moisture from the pipes.

The passageway curved around; it was hard to see more than a few dozen meters ahead. One wall was piled with old decaying stone blocks. "What are those?" Steven asked.

"Remains of a temple," Josie replied. "From somewhere in the Middle East, I forget where. Maxwell collects treasures from all the places where Vanguard fights its wars. . . . I guess he piles up the extra inventory down here."

Steven peered down the passageway. Past the temple blocks, he could see a pile of African masks and what looked like an American Civil War cannon.

"Vanguard gets around," he murmured.

"Hey," Nicky growled. "Can we get a move on?"

Josie nodded and started down the tunnel. "Shouldn't be far to the checkpoint," she said. "Maybe three-quarters of a mile."

Steven followed, dodging a puddle on the floor. "So Maxwell just stole your powers?"

"Well, we did run out on him in the middle of a battle," Nicky said.

Josie turned to glare at him.

"I'm just saying," Nicky added.

They rounded a bend in the corridor. Steven slowed to look at a life-size statue of a Mayan warrior, in a crouching position on the tunnel floor. It looked as if the Mayan had just settled there, a hundred or a thousand years before, and never bothered to get up.

Steven hurried to catch up with Nicky and Josie. "I guess Ox was right. He said Maxwell would throw anybody under the bus—"

"Ox?" Josie stopped and whirled to face Steven. "Malik? You've seen him?"

"Uh, yeah."

Should I have said that? Steven wondered. But Josie's face didn't look angry, just concerned.

"He came to us," Steven said. "Ox—I mean, Malik. He wanted to join up."

"Did you say yes?" Josie asked.

"When I left, he was on some kind of probation." He frowned. "Why? Do you not trust him or something?"

"It's—" Josie turned away. "Ah, it's nothing."

Nicky grinned. "Josie likes Malik."

"No!" she exclaimed. "Not—not like that. It's just, we were friends. I thought I could rely on him, trust him to have my back. And then, in the middle of the Dragon's Gate battle, he disappeared."

"We disappeared, too," Nicky added. "Again, just saying."

"I tried to find him," Josie said. "Put out the usual feelers, contacted everyone we'd worked with together. But he'd just vanished."

Nicky laughed—a dry, angry laugh. "Malik always thought he was better 'n me. Now he's crawling to our enemies for help."

Both Josie and Steven turned to glare at him that time. Nicky held up a hand. "I'm just—"

"—just saying," Steven said. "Got it."

"Anyway, kid," Nicky said, "your team doesn't look like it's doing much better than ours. We hear you're losing members."

"That's none of your business."

"No Rabbit anymore," Nicky continued, "and you might lose your Rooster, too, huh?"

Steven clenched his fists. "Shut up."

But Nicky kept pushing. "And then there's Carlos."

Steven frowned. "What do you know about him?"

Josie's laugh surprised him. It was sharp, hard, and completely humorless.

"Believe me, kid," she said, "Carlos is Maxwell's creature now. Maybe he always was."

An alarm rang out, filling the tunnel. A series of sharp electronic tones, repeated at regular intervals.

"I think we ought to run," Josie suggested.

Steven nodded. They took off at a steady pace, fast but not fast enough to tire out. Still, Steven had to strain to keep up. *These guys are trained soldiers,* he thought. *Good thing I'm younger than them!*

"Carlos is a brainiac, all right," Nicky said as they ran. "But it's that little girl Mince that scares me."

"Yeah," Steven said. "Mince. What's her deal?"

"She's one of the smartest people in the world," Josie said. "But she's also a complete sociopath—it's in her file. Girl's got absolutely no concept of right and wrong."

"Oh, yeah?" Steven said. "What's in *your* file?"

Josie opened her mouth to snap at him—then stopped dead, almost losing her balance. Nicky skidded to a halt just behind her. Steven almost stumbled into them.

Up ahead a heavily ornamented cannon from Tsarist Russia stood against one wall, next to an Egyptian statue. An ancient Viking longboat, chipped and faded, stood opposite them.

In the narrow space between the artifacts, Snake stood blocking the passageway. Monkey crouched on the rim of the Viking boat, his elongated toes gripping its edge.

Steven suddenly felt very tired. *I can't fight them,* he thought. *I have no power left.*

The Tiger is gone.

Snake stepped forward, a smirk playing at the corners of her mouth. She walked up to Josie, who looked away.

"Her file," Snake said, "is about to read 'Deactivated.'"

Josie stood in the dank tunnel, keeping her eyes averted. Snake, she knew, could hypnotize anyone—even another Zodiac—in a matter of seconds.

And I'm not even a Zodiac anymore, Josie thought.

Steven, the kid, was hanging back, watching. Nicky made a subtle move, edging around the Viking longboat. *He's gonna make a break for it,* Josie realized. *The idiot.*

Sure enough, Monkey leaped into the air and landed right in Nicky's path. "Don't try it," Monkey said. "We got orders from Maxwell."

"Dude," Nicky replied, "you've really changed."

That's true, Josie thought. Maxwell had done something to Monkey, altered his mind with the power of the Dragon. Now Monkey was utterly loyal. There was no hope of reaching him, of persuading him to let them go.

Snake on the other hand . . .

"What's the matter, Josie?" Snake asked. "Afraid to look me in the eye?"

Josie didn't look up. "You're backing the wrong horse, Celine," she said. "Uh, no pun intended."

Snake—Celine—cast an amused glance at Steven. "So you're on *his* side now?"

"No!" Josie clenched her fists. "It's like I told you last time we met. Maxwell is dangerous."

"Dangerous to *you*," Snake said.

"You don't know what he's capable of."

"You ran out last year," Snake hissed, "leaving me and Vincent—Vincent!—to pull Maxwell out of Jasmine's clutches. I let you go then. Now you come crawling back and you want me to do it *again?* You want me to turn traitor just so you can save your own skin?"

"We ain't traitors," Monkey said.

"Nope," Steven said. "You're just losers."

Monkey turned toward Steven, his grin growing even wider. He loped over and stared Steven right in the eye.

"You don't look like a Tiger no more," Monkey said.

Snake was still staring at Josie. Josie squirmed, avoiding her hypnotic glare.

"You want to go free?" Snake said. "Then fight me. Come on, Josie. Let's see some of that famous Horse action."

Josie shook her head. "I'm not the Horse," she said. "Not anymore."

"Not . . ." Snake frowned. "What happened?"

"Maxwell happened," Josie replied. "And he's not gonna stop with us. Sooner or later he'll take your powers, too."

Snake was silent. For the first time, her face showed a flicker of doubt.

Can I get through to her? Josie wondered. *Maybe so. Maybe—*

"No powers?" Monkey asked.

He leaped up on top of the Russian cannon, swinging his feet around a large growling lion's head carved beneath the barrel. Then he jumped off and swept out a long arm to cuff Nicky on the side of the head.

"Ow," Nicky said.

"No *powers!*" Monkey repeated. "That's gotta hurt."

"Vincent," Snake called. "None of your game, just subdue them. Let's wrap this up."

Josie saw her chance. While Snake was distracted, Josie chopped her in the throat. Snake let out a strangled yell and fell to the ground.

"Run!" Josie yelled. She took a step—

—and then Monkey was on top of her. His huge bare feet kicked out, his enormous fists jabbing into her face

and ribs. As Josie dropped, she looked up and saw a simian energy-form rise up to surround its smiling host.

He's powerful, she thought. *But he's sloppy—always has been. And I was a fighter long before I had Zodiac powers.*

She shot upward and slammed her head into his solar plexus. Monkey flew into the air, yelping and grabbing at his stomach. He bounced hard off the ceiling and dropped back down, limbs flailing. He reached out with his feet and grabbed on to the head of the Egyptian statue, wobbling until he came to rest.

The statue depicted a crouching dog god, with long ears and elegant paws. *I remember that mission,* Josie realized. *That was back before I had powers. Before any of us did.*

Back when we were all friends.

Monkey glared down at her. He didn't look amused anymore. His grin had turned to a sneer of pure cruelty.

"One shot," he said. "That's all you get."

Josie flinched, but it was no use. Monkey leaped toward her, punching again, kicking and slashing. She cried out and tried to scramble backward, to find some space to move. But this time he was giving her no quarter, no room. No opportunity to get the upper hand.

"You ain't Zodiac, lady," Monkey said. "You ain't one of us. Not anymore."

It was true. And in the end, it made all the difference.

When Monkey finally stopped hitting her, Josie lay limp on the floor. With a great effort, she raised her head and wiped the blood from her face.

A bleak mood came over her. *This couldn't have ended any other way,* she thought. *We were doomed, lost, from the minute we defied Maxwell. My whole life . . . it's just been one defeat after another.*

Over by the Viking longboat, Nicky was down on his knees. He stared straight up into the face of Snake, who stood haughty and imperious above him. Her green eyes glowed with Zodiac power, holding her prey motionless before her.

And Steven . . .

Oh, kid, Josie thought. *Kid. Well done.*

Josie coughed blood. Despite the pain, she started to laugh.

Monkey glared down at her. "What's so funny?" he asked.

Josie smiled. "He's gone."

Steven sprinted down the tunnel, legs pumping. His muscles ached, his lungs cried out for breath. He wasn't used to exerting himself without the Tiger power. Now he was just an ordinary kid.

An ordinary kid with superpowered villains on his tail.

He didn't look back. He didn't dare. He thought of Josie and Nicky and felt a pang of guilt. *I abandoned them. They helped me escape, and I left them back there. Who knows what Maxwell's gonna do to 'em?*

CHAPTER SEVENTEEN

He knew it had been a rational decision. Josie and Nicky were soldiers, and even *they* were no match for Snake's and Monkey's powers. One kid, one *ordinary kid*, wouldn't have made any difference in that fight.

Besides, Josie and Nicky hadn't helped him out of the goodness of their hearts. They'd used him to escape as much as he'd used them.

Still, leaving them wasn't the right thing to do. It wasn't the *heroic* thing.

Maybe I can rescue them later, he thought. *Maybe I can bring back help.* But even in his mind, the idea sounded weak, like he was trying to make himself feel better about doing something bad.

The tunnel was particularly dark there. A lot of the lights had burned out. Steven's foot landed in a puddle, making an audible splash. He rounded a corner, edging past a Sherman tank that had somehow been crammed into the passageway.

Then he stopped.

A Vanguard tactical team faced him. Six—no, seven soldiers in full body armor, with helmets that covered their faces, blocked the passage, from the left wall all the way to the edge of the tank on the right. And every one of them held up a big glowing energy rifle, aimed straight at Steven.

The leader's voice sounded metallic, filtered through his helmet. "Playtime's over, kid. Stand down. Now."

Steven shook his head, almost compulsively. *No,* he thought. *No, it can't end this way. Not after all that. I just escaped ten freaking minutes ago!*

"Don't make us hurt you," the leader said.

"'Cause we *can* hurt you," another soldier added, hefting his weapon. "A lot."

Steven clenched his fists in frustration and closed his eyes. *Tiger,* he thought, *I really need you now. I summon the power. I summon the power of the Tiger!*

Nothing.

The tac team leader lowered his weapon. He stepped forward and reached out a hand for Steven. Steven stepped back against the Sherman tank, shaking his head. He was outgunned, defeated, helpless.

In the corner of his vision, he saw something swoop through the air.

He whipped his head around and gasped. A dozen small men, maybe more, had descended on the tac team, whipping and soaring around them on ropes hanging from the ceiling. The men moved soundlessly, landing blows on the tac team's helmets and then leaping back upward to vanish briefly in the shadows.

The tac team stumbled, waving their weapons around. But the little men were too fast, too agile. They pressed on with their assault,

swinging up and down on their ropes, not giving the tac team room enough to aim their weapons. A familiar glow appeared around the men whenever they struck a blow.

Zodiac energy, Steven realized. *That's a Zodiac glow. But how?*

Then a small man was at his elbow. He wore a long cloak with a hood that covered the top of his head. A high collar apparatus stretched over his nose and mouth, leaving only his beady eyes visible.

"Come on," the man said.

He ushered Steven behind the Sherman tank, to a small space up against the tunnel wall. Steven shook his head; there was barely enough room for the two of them. And the tac team was sure to find them hiding there, once they'd fought off the little men.

But the hooded man reached out and touched a spot on the wall. A small door slid open silently. The man crouched down and started to crawl through the opening.

Steven hesitated.

The man turned and stared at him. "You want to live?"

Steven nodded and followed him.

The crawl space was low, barely high enough for Steven to fit inside. He followed the man down, around sharp turns and into narrow areas they both had to squeeze through. The air grew even hotter, more humid than in the outside tunnel. Steven found himself sweating.

The tunnel seemed endless. After a while, Steven couldn't tell how far they'd gone. He hardly even knew which way was up.

Eventually, they came out in a larger chamber, about the size of a small bedroom. A ragged sofa and a couple of folding chairs sat before a bulky CRT monitor set in the stone wall. The furniture looked as if it had been scavenged from a Dumpster.

By the time the little man lowered his hood and collar, Steven had already figured out who he was. A Vanguard agent, the only Zodiac Steven had never met. The man in the shadows.

"Rat," Steven said.

Rat's mouth stretched into a smile, and he made an elaborate bow.

"My friends call me Thiago," he said. "Or they would if I had friends."

Thiago stepped forward. Steven backed up, keeping his distance. Rat was rumored to be the least trustworthy of the Zodiacs. Steven had no idea what his intentions might be.

"Easy," Rat said. "I just saved you, remember?"

"Yeah," Steven replied. "But why?"

"I could answer that," Rat replied. "But it's better if someone else does."

He reached into his pocket and pulled out a flat white disk. He held it forward. Steven hesitated, but Rat shook the disk, insisting. Steven stared, suddenly recognizing the object.

"An oracle bone?" he asked.

He accepted the disk, holding it gingerly. For a moment,

he thought it was one of the ancient writing tablets he'd seen in the old man's room back in Berlin. But no—this was the modern version. It was a high-tech object, like the one he'd received anonymously the previous year.

"Read it," Rat said.

As Steven watched, small gray lines appeared on the white surface. Driven by circuitry inside the oracle bone, the lines resolved into letters, forming a message:

DEAREST STEVEN,

I KNOW YOU HAVE QUESTIONS, AND IT'S TIME FOR ANSWERS. PLEASE ALLOW THIAGO TO BRING YOU TO SYDNEY. I PROMISE I'LL TELL YOU EVERYTHING YOU NEED TO KNOW.

When he read the signature below the message, Steven felt cold. He turned to Thiago. The Rat lay lounging on the couch, reading a magazine.

"Okay," Steven said.

Then he looked back down at the oracle bone, wondering if he'd read it correctly. Yes, the message was still the same. And at the bottom, the gray lines spelled out a single unmistakable word:

MOM

CHAPTER EIGHTEEN

"YOU'RE WASTING TIME," Ox said.

"Either take me with you or lock me up and get out of here."

Liam glared at him. "Tell me the story."

"I've already told you. A dozen times."

"Then let's make it thirteen."

They sat together in a small interrogation room. Ox leaned forward against the table, his hands clasped. His face was rigid, unreadable.

Liam tipped his chair back, bracing his feet against the bottom of the table. He wanted to seem casual, in control. But he was anxious.

I vouched for this guy, Liam thought. *I convinced the others to trust him. And now . . .*

"You've got a camera, mate." Liam pointed at Ox's forehead, just above his eyes. "Right behind your bloody dermis. It sees everything you do."

"Looks that way," Ox replied.

"Care to explain how it got there?"

"What's the difference? You've already made up your mind." Ox gestured up at the wall, which they both knew concealed a surveillance camera. "Or at least, your friends have. They're watching right now, aren't they?"

Liam rose slowly to his feet, clenching his fists. "I stood up for you," he said, "and you played me."

"*Played* you?" Ox shook his head violently. "You're like children. Little kids tangling with adults. Maxwell's gonna squash you."

"And you'd like that."

"If I wanted that, I wouldn't be here." Ox paused. "You're already down two members. You go after Maxwell, you're gonna need every ounce of Zodiac power you can get. You need me."

Liam glared down at Ox's defiant face.

"As for the transmitter . . ." Ox jabbed a thumb into his own forehead. "For the last time, I don't know anything about it. I don't know how it got there. I don't know how long I've had it. I had no idea it existed until your friends found it."

Liam felt a rage building inside him. In his past, back home in Northern Ireland, that kind of anger had usually led to violence.

"You're a bloody liar," he spat.

Ox jumped to his feet. The two men leaned toward each other, their fingers gripping the sides of the table. Their faces almost touched.

"I'm not a liar," Ox said, his voice very even. "Whatever else you think of me, you know that."

Liam looked away. "Dragon's Gate," he muttered.

Ox peered sideways at him. "What about it?"

"What happened, a year ago? Down in the caverns?" Liam sat back down, forcing himself to be calm. "You were fighting us, and then you disappeared."

Ox frowned. Suspicion and doubt seemed to alternate on his face.

"You gonna tell the truth *now?*" Liam asked.

Ox pulled his chair closer and sat down. "I don't know," he said.

"You don't know? Don't know what?" Liam gestured wide with his arms. "Whether you've told me the truth?"

"I don't know what happened! In the caverns." Ox looked away, troubled. "Last thing I remember is you. Slamming into me with that crazy cannonball move of yours."

Despite himself, Liam smiled. "That was one of my better moments, aye."

"I woke up hours later," Ox continued.

"Not possible, mate," Liam replied. "The whole chamber collapsed. We barely got out alive."

"I wasn't *in* the main chamber. I was in a narrow side cavern." Ox pressed his fingers against his temples, as if trying to force a memory to the surface. "It was reinforced with metal beams, like somebody had prepared it specially. Took me most of a day to tunnel my way out."

"And you were alone? There was nobody around?"

"That's ri—" Ox stopped. His eyes went wide, and he blinked twice.

"What?" Liam leaned forward, staring at him. "What is it?"

"I was groggy from the fight," Ox said. His voice was almost a whisper. "I must have been drugged. So I didn't remember this until just now. . . ."

"Spit it out, man."

"I think I saw Rat."

It was Liam's turn to blink in surprise. He cast a glance up at the hidden camera, knowing that Roxanne and the others were watching.

"Rat," Liam repeated. "Where was this? In the side cavern?"

"No. Before that, in the main cave." Ox turned toward Liam now, as if asking him for help. "Somebody . . . someone was dragging me across the stone floor. I woke up for just a second—I remember now! I looked up and I saw his beady little eyes."

"Rat!" Liam paused, thinking. "Was he along on your mission that day?"

"Yeah. But we didn't see much of him after we arrived." Ox frowned again. "You got to understand, we never knew what Rat was up to. Even before he had Zodiac powers, that guy was running schemes within schemes. Maxwell allowed it, so long as he was useful, that's what the Vanguard Black Ops team was there for."

"And then what? What happened?"

"He leaned down—Rat—he put some kind of gun in my face and squirted gas at me." Ox exhaled heavily. "That's all I remember."

"Until you woke up in the little cavern."

Ox looked at Liam and nodded.

Liam studied him for a moment. At the beginning of the interrogation, Ox had seemed sullen, defiant. All that was gone now. He seemed spent, almost relieved, as if he'd purged himself of something he'd been carrying around for a long time.

I should keep pressing, Liam thought. *I should intimidate him, pepper him with questions, poke holes in every story he tells me. Not let up the pressure till I know everything he knows.*

But that's not me, is it?

Liam leaned back in his chair. When he spoke again, his voice was gentle. "Why did you do it? Work for Maxwell?"

Ox shrugged. "Money was good."

"Nah. That's an excuse, a reason you tell yerself."

Ox sighed and turned away.

"We used to talk about this," he said. "Me and the others, Josie and Nicky in particular. Back when we were ordinary soldiers, it was easy to go along. Easy to obey orders."

Liam reached into his pocket and fingered his dog tags. *Not so easy for some of us,* he thought.

"But once we got the Zodiac powers," Ox continued, "everything changed. It was like we had some greater responsibility. Like we had to look at ourselves and ask, 'What am I doing? How am I using this power to change the world, myself, my friends?'"

Liam frowned. "Go on."

"Josie and me, we talked about it the most. We knew Maxwell was off the rails, that this power was more than he should be trusted with. One time, we even talked about doing something about it."

"But you were afraid."

"*I* was afraid. Josie . . . with her, it was something different." Ox turned away, as if remembering something painful. "She's a good person. And she's a great fighter—there's nobody better to have at your side. But inside, she's weak. I knew whatever happened, whatever we decided, sooner or later she'd go crawling back to Maxwell."

He turned, then, and stared earnestly at Liam. "Not me. *Mate.*"

Liam stared back. There wasn't a trace of deception, of guile on Ox's face. And yet . . .

"I believe you, man." Liam grimaced. "But you've still got a bloody transmitter in your head!"

Liam's eyes flickered to the spot on the wall where the camera was hidden. Ox followed his gaze and stared at the wall for a long moment.

Then Ox reared back in his chair, whipped his head back, and slammed his forehead onto the table.

The table cracked under the impact. Liam shot to his feet, alarmed, and started to move forward.

But Ox held out a hand. He looked up through a haze of energy, through the fierce ox avatar flashing into being all around him. He glared at Liam through the blood starting to drip down his forehead. "Don't," he said.

Then he smashed his head down again.

Liam stepped back, forcing himself to watch as Ox bashed his own forehead against the surface of the table two, three more times. Ox was one of the most powerful people on the planet; each impact shook the room. The table's surface cracked again, then split in half. The ox form above his head snorted and howled in pain.

With the sixth impact, the table's legs gave way. It crumbled to the ground.

Ox staggered to his feet. Liam jumped up and circled the ruins of the table. He grabbed Ox by the arm to steady him.

Ox shook his head, dazed. Above his eyes, in a pool of dripping blood, Liam could see mangled wires and tiny circuits protruding from the skin.

" 'S'all right, mate," Liam said. "I got you."

The door burst open. Duane stopped dead in the doorway, his eyes darting from Ox to Liam to the small analyzer device in his hand. "Transmission ended," he said.

Roxanne ran in, with her mother just behind. Mrs. LaFleur gasped at the sight of Ox's bloody forehead, then clutched her daughter's arm tight. Roxanne patted her mother's hand, disengaged, and moved forward to stand with Duane and Liam.

"Plane's fueled and ready," she said.

Ox tried to speak. He coughed and stumbled. Liam caught him again. Ox nodded and pulled away. He stood upright, as if coming to attention, and turned to face the group.

"When do we leave?" he asked.

ALL DURING THE FLIGHT to Sydney,

Steven peppered Rat with questions. But the little man just smiled and refused to answer them. "You'll have a nice long mother-son chat," he said, "while I catch up on my TV."

Rat's helpers, the small shadow men, accompanied them on the private plane. The men bustled around, checking equipment and bringing Rat food and drinks. When Steven asked who they were, Rat paused before answering.

"I call 'em my Ratlings," he said. "They're like me, all born in the Year of the Rat."

"But they're *not* like you," Steven said. "You have the Zodiac power."

"So do they. A little of it, anyway."

Steven wondered how that was possible. He asked a few more questions, but Rat changed the subject every time.

After they landed, the little men hustled them into a van. Steven caught only the briefest glimpse of Sydney through the van's window: clean streets, modern buildings, and a big bridge that looked like a stretched-out Slinky toy.

The hotel was old but neat. Rat asked the little men to wait outside. Then he ushered Steven into a large open suite. The living room area had a couch and a TV, and a small kitchen was furnished with a table and two chairs.

His mother sat at the kitchen table, elegant as ever in a business suit and low heels. She was drinking from a set of old Chinese teacups, but the table was dominated by an elaborate modern coffee maker. She looked up and nodded at Steven, as if he were an employee who'd been summoned to her office.

Steven shifted back and forth on his feet, nervous. He hadn't spoken to his mother in person for more than a year.

Rat went straight to the sitting room and plopped himself down on the couch. He turned on the TV, which showed only static. He frowned at it and leaned forward, watching the screen closely. He didn't change the channel.

"Steven," Mrs. Lee said. "You look a bit ragged."

Her voice was completely level, every word modulated. *Does she even know I've been away?* he thought. *Does she have any idea where I've been, what I've gone through?*

He approached her, feeling awkward. The liquid in her teacup, he noticed, was dark brown. "Still don't like tea, huh, Mom?"

"I had endless arguments with Father—your grandfather—about that. Rest his soul."

At the mention of his grandfather, Steven's anxiety turned to sadness. He'd spent months trying not to think about that loss. Grandfather had basically raised him while his parents were occupied making business deals for LeeCo, their company. His mother had barely paid any attention to him the whole time he was growing up.

And now here she is.

"Why?" he asked.

Mrs. Lee looked up, and for a moment he thought she was going to ask him to explain the question. But instead she gestured at the second chair. "Sit," she said. "You're old enough for coffee, aren't you?"

"I'm old enough," he replied. "But I don't like it."

A humorless smile spread across her face. "Your father's child."

She took a sip of coffee and waited.

Steven looked around. Rat lay sprawled on the couch, staring at the muted TV. Its screen still showed raw static.

Steven walked over and sat down across from his mother. He felt six years old again.

"I have a lot of things to tell you," Mrs. Lee said, "and not much time. So I need you to listen and, if you can manage it, hold your questions until the end."

"I can *manage* it," he said. He felt his temper rising. "Do you think I'm still a kid?"

"Is that a question?"

He sat back in his chair, fuming.

"We've been watching Jasmine's operation," Mrs. Lee said. "To be blunt, it's falling apart."

"You know about Jasmine?" Steven asked.

She shot him a look. But he couldn't stop himself. "You haven't called me for months," he continued. "I never even told you where I was."

"We knew. We know all about Jasmine, and about Maxwell, too." She paused and took a deep breath. "Do you know why we've spent so much time building LeeCo? Why we dedicated ourselves to it to the exclusion of all else, including our son?"

Was that a quaver in her voice when she said *son*?

"LeeCo started small," she continued. "Your father had connections back in China, and we manufactured high-end meditation devices: crystals, white-noise machines, that sort of thing. What they used to call 'New Age.' When you were born, we were making a modest but steady living.

"Then we discovered qi energy."

Steven looked up sharply. He'd heard that term several times—most recently when Maxwell and his minions had extracted the Tiger power from him.

"I see you're familiar with qi. It runs through the earth, through all living things. We discovered it could be harnessed, used to focus thoughts and enhance meditation. We started incorporating low-powered qi amplifiers into several of our products.

"This attracted the attention of a man called Maxwell. He offered to fund our research, in exchange for access to the results. As part of the deal, he also agreed to fund our expansion into a multinational corporation."

"Maxwell," Steven repeated.

"Yes. He was quite generous—and extremely charming. We knew of his reputation; we'd heard rumors of his destructive tendencies. But the opportunity was too great to resist." She exhaled and took a deep draft of coffee. "In Western terms, you could say we sold our souls to the devil."

Steven nodded. The missing pieces of his childhood were beginning to fall into place.

"That was eleven years ago," Mrs. Lee continued, "when you were still very small. We expanded our research, and we diversified our operations. Maxwell didn't care what other business we pursued, as long as the qi-energy research continued. And whenever we needed money, he was there."

Steven grimaced. "He's reliable, all right."

"We didn't know that he was already planning what came to be known as Project Zodiac. Maxwell had researched the history of the Zodiac wielders, and he knew the time of the Convergence was coming. He was planning to use this to build an army of superpowered warriors."

"And . . ." Steven paused and looked his mother in the eye. "And you helped him."

"Unwittingly." She returned his gaze without flinching. "But we had many late-night discussions about this, your father and I. And we decided that Maxwell is too unstable, too dangerous to be trusted with the Zodiac power."

"Good decision," Steven replied. "But a little late. Are you *still* in business with him?"

"Again, if you could hold your questions . . ." She shrugged. "Yes. Or so he thinks, at any rate. Maxwell has many unreliable allies."

Rat spoke up without turning around. "My ears are burning."

"We also developed the technology that allows Rat to share a small part of his power," Mrs. Lee said. "His little army has been very useful to us."

Steven glanced over at Rat. For just a moment he thought he saw, on the blurry TV screen, an image of Liam—Ram. Liam's face was contorted with rage. Then the image faded and the screen returned to static.

"As the Convergence approached," Mrs. Lee continued, "we determined that we had to act. We couldn't defy Maxwell openly—he would simply crush us and take our company away. So, after much discussion, we chose another path."

She turned away from him, toward the coffee maker. As she poured another cup, he saw that her hands were trembling.

"Mom?" he asked.

"This is difficult," she said.

Something in her voice sent shivers through him.

"In that chamber, beneath the surface of Hong Kong," she said, "Maxwell hoped to concentrate all the power of the Zodiac into himself."

"I know," Steven said. "I was there."

"Do you know *why* you were there?"

He opened his mouth to reply, then stopped dead. His mother was still turned away, not looking at him.

A recent memory flashed into his mind: Jasmine in the Infosphere, staring at him suspiciously. *I always thought it was odd,* she'd said, *the way you happened to stumble into the Convergence chamber, just in time to get charged up with Zodiac power.*

And suddenly he knew.

"You," he whispered, barely able to look at his mother. "You sent me there."

Mrs. Lee nodded. "We arranged it all. The class trip to Hong Kong, the tour of the museum. Everything was timed to coincide with the Convergence." She turned, finally, to look at him with eyes that seemed older than her years. "Something—some*one*—had to stop Maxwell from absorbing all the power. We knew the only thing that could do that was a Tiger."

"You used me." He stared at her, struggling to comprehend. "I was your tool."

"You are our *son*." Her gaze burned into him. "And I know—both your father and I have known, since you were very small, that you were destined for greatness. But our life back home was too comfortable . . . too American. You needed a push."

He shook his head. "Most parents force their kids to play Little League or something."

"We are not most parents," she replied, "and you are no ordinary boy. You are a Tiger—perhaps the fiercest, most powerful Zodiac the world has ever known."

"So . . . wait. Hold up a minute." He turned away. "You arranged for me to be present at the Convergence, and then . . . what? Did you tell Jasmine and Carlos to scoop me up and take me with them, too?"

"No. We were aware of Jasmine, but we didn't know about her plans. When she sabotaged the Convergence, that caught us by surprise." She frowned. "But when you decided to go back to Greenland with her, we decided that was best. Where better to learn about your new power than with others of your kind?"

"Yeah," he said. "At least there I had a family."

Mrs. Lee's composure broke for just a moment as a look of pain passed across her face. Steven thought: *So I can hurt her, after all.*

He felt a surge of self-satisfaction. Then, immediately, he hated himself for it.

"You left me alone for a year," he said. "Why step in now?"

"Because, as I said, things are falling apart." She grimaced. "The Rabbit has left your team. The Rooster may depart soon. Jasmine has lost all perspective. Maxwell managed to capture you, and he might well have killed you after he was sure your power was gone."

Steven shook his head. He wanted to listen, wanted to give his mother the benefit of the doubt. But this news, this revelation—it was too much. All he wanted right then was to hurt her.

"So you do care about me," he said, his voice brittle and shaky. "A little anyway."

"There's nothing we care about more," she said. "And you must believe me: we would not have placed you in this situation if we didn't think you could handle it."

He frowned.

"Even now, your father believes we should see how events play out." She turned away. "He doesn't know I'm here."

Rat turned toward them, grinning. *"AWWWK-*ward," he said.

Mrs. Lee ignored him. "You must act soon," she said to

Steven. "Maxwell gained an almost unbeatable advantage when Carlos returned to him."

"Carlos," Steven said. "Is he really working with Maxwell again?"

"Oh, yes." Mrs. Lee shook her head sadly. "Back at Dragon's Gate, Carlos and Jasmine managed to drain the Dragon power from Maxwell. But the power never completely leaves a Zodiac wielder. I think you learned that today, when you escaped from Maxwell's cell."

Was that a note of pride in her voice? Despite himself, Steven felt his heart swell.

"Maxwell arranged to have Carlos kidnapped," his mother continued, "and then, with his last shred of Dragon power, he altered Carlos's mind. He's done this before, when his own operative Monkey defied him."

"So Carlos *is* working for Maxwell," Steven said, "but not because he wants to. He's been brainwashed?"

"That's right. But it's not good news. The Dragon's mind-wipe power is ruthless, absolute, and permanent. Carlos is now Maxwell's unquestioning ally." She looked him in the eye. "The process is irreversible."

"Poor Carlos," Steven said. He turned away. "Poor Jasmine."

"Poor human race," his mother said.

Steven shook his head. His mind was reeling. He'd need a week just to come to terms with everything his mother had told him.

But he didn't have a week. "Jasmine's planning an assault on Maxwell's headquarters," he said. "It's set for tomorrow."

"Actually, she's already on her way," Rat said. "She changed the plan after you got snatched up in Berlin."

Steven shot him a questioning look.

Rat grinned. "I planted a camera inside Ox," he said. "He had no idea. But it gave me live breaking-news type info to hand off to your mom here." He gestured at the static-filled TV screen. "They found it and blocked the signal a couple hours ago. Now it seems to have stopped transmitting entirely."

Steven nodded. *So that's why he's been staring at that blank screen.*

"Maxwell will know that Jasmine is coming," Mrs. Lee said. "We don't have much time."

"Malosi," Steven said. The pieces were falling together in his mind, almost faster than he could process them. "He's the key. The Tiger power links the other Zodiacs together. When I use it, it helps the team, strengthens all of our powers. Maxwell's going to use it the *opposite* way— to defeat Jasmine and the others!"

Mrs. Lee nodded. "Plans within plans." She turned away and started rummaging in a bag on the floor.

"I've got to go," Steven said. "I've gotta help them."

"Of course you do," she replied. "You're our Tiger."

"You don't tell me what to do!"

She stopped and stared at him. For just a moment, everything that had ever passed between them seemed to hang in the air: all the arguments, the neglect, the deceit. Everything that kept a mother and son apart, no matter how much they might love each other.

Then Mrs. Lee's expression turned hard again.

"You're right," she said. "But maybe I can help you do it."

She held out a small metallic object shaped vaguely like a heart. It was perfectly smooth except for a single button built into the top. Steven took it from her and ran his fingers over its cold surface.

"This is a qi amplifier," she explained. "It's kind of a . . . helper, a way of bringing out a person's inner gifts."

"Or inner Zodiac power," he said.

"Exactly. We were developing it for Maxwell, before we learned of the Convergence. After that, we managed to keep it from him."

Steven stared at the device. "So Maxwell doesn't have this."

"If you find yourself in danger, it may allow you to draw on your inner resources. But use it sparingly. It's still experimental. After two or three uses, the circuitry will fuse permanently, rendering it useless."

He nodded and pocketed the device.

"Also," she added, "it draws its energy directly from the stars. So try to use it outdoors."

"Great," he replied. "Does it only take name-brand batteries, too? Or high-octane gas?"

She shrugged. "It's all I can offer."

Steven stood and walked away from the table. Out of the corner of his eye, he saw his mother watching his every move. He believed what she'd said, the revelations about his power and about Jasmine and Carlos. And yet . . .

I can never trust her, he realized. *Not completely. She and Dad . . . they always have their own agenda.* He turned toward Rat. *For instance, why are they in league with* this *guy?*

So many questions.

"Steven?" Mrs. Lee said. "Your friends need you."

He didn't look at her. He turned to Rat and asked, "Will you take me?"

Rat nodded, smiling. "I got another toy for you, too."

"Then let's go." He turned back toward the kitchen table. "Mom."

She stood up. He had the strange feeling she wanted to hug him—though he couldn't remember the last time she had done that.

He held up the qi amplifier. "Thanks for this."

She nodded.

Then he rushed out the door as fast as he could. He didn't want her to see him cry.

PART FOUR

THE FALL

CHAPTER TWENTY

JASMINE SOARED through the sky, her fists clenched before her. The Dragon blazed all around, its tongue whipping and hissing. It stared straight into the setting sun, as if challenging nature itself to some primal battle.

Ahead of Jasmine, spread out across the red sand of the Australian outback, lay the Vanguard complex. An old dirt access road wound toward it, ending at a small checkpoint flanked by two guard towers. The white central building was spherical, with a couple of bumps protruding on opposite sides. It was surrounded by smaller white buildings, numbered one through eight and connected by thin paved pathways.

According to Ox's intel, the small buildings were barracks for soldiers, supply depots, and weapons caches. Two larger, oval-shaped buildings bracketed the main building. One was a recreation hall, and the other held detention cells.

That might be where Carlos is, Jasmine thought. *Steven, too.*

The complex was clearly on alert. Vanguard soldiers, in their distinctive uniforms, hustled from one building to another, brandishing fierce-looking energy weapons.

At the checkpoint, a single agent spoke into a phone. He pointed up, at the fearsome Dragon blazing through the sky.

Jasmine let out a fierce screech, like the cry of an ancient, wrathful god. The Dragon whipped around in the sky, then turned and swooped toward the first guard tower.

At the tower's base, the last Vanguard agents scurried inside. Its twin cannons began to glow bright, and a pair of energy beams stabbed into the sky.

Jasmine didn't flinch, didn't veer. Her face was a mask of determination and rage. The Dragon surged bright, even brighter than before. It opened its mouth, snapping and snatching through the air—

—and *ate* the Vanguard energy beams.

Then it let out another noise, a horrible noise—one that might have been laughter.

Jasmine unleashed a blast of fire. The tower's first cannon disintegrated in a shower of glass and metal, raining

down on the road below. Jasmine turned to the second cannon and, once again, breathed fire, a prolonged barrage that bathed the guard tower in an inferno of unimaginable heat. Glass cracked. Steel liquefied. Soldiers fled, retreating toward the heart of the Vanguard base.

She followed their path, pausing in midair to survey the small domes. They bore large numbers on their roofs, counting down as they arced around the main dome to her right, like pebbles around a lake. Eight. Seven. Six.

Inside her, the Dragon screamed, an ancient power reveling in its own release. It had *enjoyed* blasting those soldiers, along with their weapons of destruction. Now it wanted more: more combat, more enemies, more devastation.

Jasmine swooped low, reared back up into the air, and let loose with a full-strength Dragon blast. Dome eight cracked wide and exploded, plastic and metal flying. Soldiers poured out like ants, scattering toward the rear of the complex. A small group of them paused, pointed up at the sky, and struggled to aim their energy rifles at the moving target.

Jasmine didn't even notice. She was already hovering over dome seven, unleashing another deadly Zodiac burst.

I'll blast them wide open, she thought. *Every one of them. Until I find—*

Her earpiece crackled to life.

Jasmine frowned; that should have been impossible.

She'd set her comm system to ignore most incoming calls. There was only one frequency that could get through—and only one man who would know to use it.

A faint voice came through. "Help."

Jasmine went cold. It was him. It was Carlos.

"Help," he repeated. "Building five—"

The channel went dead.

She looked down at the carnage, the smoking crater that had been dome seven. Small rooms—bunks and barracks for soldiers—lay exposed, wrecked and burning. A few Vanguard agents sprayed foam on the fires while others spoke urgently into their wireless comms.

When she turned to look at the main dome, the Dragon surged. *There,* it seemed to say. *There is our enemy. Let me loose!*

No, she told it, *not yet.*

Not until we find him.

But the Dragon kept screaming. Its power was almost too much to bear. She'd gotten used to it those previous months, learned to live with the constant burning in her brain. But there was something different about it now. It almost sounded like a warning.

Jasmine knew she'd been distant from the others. She'd cut them out of her life, obsessed with her private crusade. *They think it's because of the Dragon,* she thought. *They think I can't handle it—that it's too overwhelming for any human to wield and still maintain sanity.*

But that's not it.

Keeping the Dragon at bay had been a constant battle. But what really weighed on her—what made her uneasy and constantly pushed her away from her teammates—was what it could do to her friends. The harm it might do if it were unleashed, free of her control, at the wrong time.

Her own words returned to her mind, the words she'd spoken to Steven less than two days before: *Maybe the Zodiac power is meant to be wielded alone.*

Was that what the Dragon meant, why it seemed to be screeching a warning inside her mind? Jasmine thought of the research she and Carlos had done into Zodiac users of the past. There were very few records to be found. It was almost as if, when their time was up, the hosts of the Zodiac power just . . . vanished.

She looked up at the blazing Dragon surrounding her, at its sinewy snakelike body and hissing jaws. *When all this is over,* she wondered, *will it consume me, too?*

Does having more power only make the end more certain?

Jasmine swooped over the main building, watching the Vanguard soldiers flee for cover. Dome six slid by beneath her. And then—

Five.

She paused for a moment, hovering above the small structure. Energy welled up in her hands, forming a blazing ball of fire. *Do it,* the Dragon seemed to say. *Unleash our power!*

No, she told it. If Carlos was inside, a frontal attack might hurt him. It could even kill him.

After all, he's human. And I'm not—not quite.

Willing her power to fade, she wafted down to make a soft landing. There were no soldiers in the area—they had all fled, seeking reinforcements.

Building five, like the others, was perfectly round and unnaturally white. Even that close it seemed smooth and featureless, as if it was made of a single sheet of high-tech plastic. She squinted, noticing something odd: as the sun set, the dome was beginning to emit its own radiance. A barren eucalyptus tree stood up against it, silhouetted like some gnarled demon in the eerie glow.

She walked slowly around the dome until she came to a door built into the side. She pushed it lightly, and it swung inward.

Again, the Dragon's warning screamed in her mind.

Jasmine walked inside, into darkness. Something moved up ahead, and her power flared up involuntarily. She edged forward and jumped as the motion repeated itself.

It was a mirror.

She concentrated, radiating just enough Dragon energy to light her way. Images of herself reflected the light back: ahead, beside, and above.

She was in a hall of mirrors. One mirror showed her clenched fist, glowing bright. Another reflected her ankle.

A third showed the back of her head, whipping around as she turned to look.

She glanced down warily, frowning. The floor was mirrored, too, reflecting the soles of her boots as she walked.

She heard a faint cry from up ahead.

Jasmine reached out, feeling her way. The corridor curved around, an endless succession of warped images. She moved forward, flinching at the constant echoes of her own movements.

It was hard to tell how far she had walked. But eventually the mirrors spread out; the corridor widened into a larger chamber. And in the center of that chamber . . .

Carlos stood on a low dais, tied to a pole with his back against a freestanding complex of mirrors. His face was turned partially away from her. As she approached, he craned his neck around, straining against his ropes. He looked stressed, almost panicked, and there were bruises on his cheeks.

Then he saw her and his eyes closed in apparent relief.

"Jaz," he said softly. "Sorry I didn't make it home for dinner."

She walked up to him slowly, cautiously. At last she'd found him, battered but alive. She should be happy; she should be bursting into tears, rushing into his arms.

But the Dragon was screaming. *Wrong,* it seemed to say. *This is all wrong!*

"Jaz?" Carlos asked.

She paced in a circle, studying Carlos. She had a strange urge to touch his bruises. She raised a hand to his face, and he flinched. She felt embarrassed, ashamed.

"Maxwell—he brainwashed me," Carlos continued. "He—he reached right into my head and made me do things. Terrible things." He shivered. "But I fought it off. I threw off his conditioning."

"You must have been through hell," she whispered.

"You know what kept me going? The thought of getting home. To everyone, but . . . but mostly to you."

Her hands were shaking, she realized. She grabbed one with the other, forcing herself to be still.

Carlos managed a weak smile. "Can we continue this with me untied?"

She took a step toward him. But again, something made her stop.

"I don't blame you," he said. "I don't blame you for being suspicious. But listen, Jaz." He turned to stare into her eyes. "These past few months, I've witnessed every side of Maxwell's operation. Things we never saw before, either of us, when we used to work for him. Maxwell's soldiers— they still think I'm working for him. But I know how to stop him. I can bring him down. I can *end this madness for good.*"

She gestured at the mirrors on the walls. "He tied you up here? In this sadistic little fun house?"

"Yeah. When you attacked," he said. "He wanted me out of the way."

"Maybe he wanted you as bait?" she asked. "To draw me here?"

"I don't—maybe. But you're still the Dragon, aren't you?"

Slowly, she nodded. "I am."

"Jaz, this is it. This is everything we've worked for, right at our fingertips. Ever since the day we first met, in that dive bar. Remember? You showed me those stolen papers labeled 'Project Zodiac.' It was in Oakland, California."

"It was Palo Alto," she said sharply.

Confusion crossed his face. "No. It was Oakland."

"I know," she said. "I was testing you."

"Smart. I would have done the same thing."

She frowned and turned away. Every human bone in her body yearned to release him, to trust him and help him and be with him, the way she had been before. He was Carlos; he was the man she'd spent the previous three months searching for, to the exclusion of everything else. She'd sacrificed sleep, food, and friendships, all so she could find and rescue him.

But it's all wrong.

"Jaz, it's me. It's really me." He struggled against his bonds, gazing at her with those earnest, pleading eyes. "Just let me down? And we'll go save the others. Together."

She stared back for a long moment. Memories flashed through her mind, a thousand images of the times she'd spent with him. Founding the Zodiac complex, holding hands and shivering in the cold as they watched the foundation being poured. Teaming up to sabotage Maxwell's Convergence plans. Recruiting Roxanne, the first of the new Zodiacs, in a castle in France.

Defeating Maxwell in the caves beneath China.

"I'm the Dragon," Jasmine said softly.

She reached out a finger and zapped the rope around Carlos's neck. Then she freed his arms and legs. He stumbled down off the dais, into her arms.

"Thank you," he said.

She reached out to embrace him. He felt warm and welcoming. His smell was masculine, familiar.

Then something caught her eye. In the mirror behind Carlos was a reflection of his hand. As she watched, he reached into his back pocket and pulled out a small, unfamiliar device with a single large button on it.

She pulled back and stared at his face. It was twisted into a nasty, conniving grin. She backed away, but it was too late.

He pressed the button.

All around, the mirrors began to whir and move. With astonishing speed, the corridors vanished, the walls folding up like chairs after a party. The mirrors swung back and snapped into place—*klik-a klik-a klik-a*—against the outer walls of the dome.

She stood in the exact center of the dome-shaped building. Mirrors shone from every wall, every surface, stretching up to the ceiling and down across the floor.

"Surprise," Carlos said.

Jasmine summoned the Dragon. It flared bright, reflected in every mirror. She swiveled to face Carlos, her hands blazing.

"Careful, Jaz," he said. "Close range like this, you might kill me by accident."

His voice was different: taunting, cruel. But he was right.

She turned and aimed a Dragon blast at the side wall. It struck a mirror—

—and rebounded at her, striking her in the stomach. The impact knocked her off her feet and sent her skidding across the floor.

She lay still, clutching her stomach and struggling for breath. For a moment, she wasn't sure what had happened. She'd wielded the Dragon power a hundred times, but she'd never felt it turned back on her.

Carlos strode around her in a wide circle, keeping his distance. He was still grinning. "That worked better than I expected," he said.

"How?" she gasped.

"Ah! Good question." He continued to pace, gesturing like a professor addressing a lecture hall. "The Zodiac energy is theoretically infinite, and the Dragon can access more power than any of the other signs. You know that, right? Don't bother to answer, just lie there twitching.

Anyway, the Zodiac was nothing until one man figured out how to harness it. And who was that man?"

"You," she said.

"Right! Me. And now I've done it again . . . figured out the ultimate trap for a Zodiac wielder." He looked around, pleased with his handiwork. "Took a lot of stress testing before I was sure it would work. But it's true: the only thing that can stop the all-powerful Dragon is the Dragon itself."

She glared at him. The Dragon was quiet, receded within her—gathering its strength.

"Of course," Carlos continued, "much as I hate to admit it, I couldn't have done it without Maxwell. This sort of work requires equipment and resources. He was *very* generous."

"But . . ." She struggled to her knees, watching him. "But you turned *against* Maxwell."

"Did I? Or was I working with him all the time?"

She knew that wasn't true. It couldn't be. But his words sent a chill through her.

He turned away, shrugging. "It's not important. What matters is, Maxwell is right. You can't be trusted with the Zodiac power—none of you."

"And he can?"

"Maxwell is a visionary. And I'm going to help him fulfill his destiny."

Carlos's demeanor had changed. He sounded wholly

rational, perfectly assured. He seemed to truly believe what he was saying.

Jasmine felt the Dragon rising inside her again. *Keep quiet,* she told herself. *Don't let him know you're getting your power back.*

"What about the things you said before?" she asked. "All the plans we made, to stop Vanguard and take Maxwell down?"

"Oh, Jaz." The cruel grin crept back onto his face. "You're so easy to trick."

"No." She shook her head. "You're—it's like you said before. He brainwashed you."

"That's irrelevant. If the conclusion is correct, the method of deriving the answer doesn't matter."

She frowned. "That doesn't sound like the scientific method."

"Besides, he's given me all these toys!" Carlos stepped back, gesturing around at the mirrored chamber. "And once again, I have come up with a new variation on the Zodiac power. In this case: the inescapable trap."

"You can't trap the Dragon," she said.

"Oh! That's your *dangerous* voice. It's all low-pitched and throaty. I know *that* Jasmine."

"Don't do this, Carlos. I'm begging you."

"Good." He looked across the room at her. "I like it when you beg."

She struggled to rise. *One moment,* she thought, *he seems like the Carlos I know—with maybe a few things wrong in his head. The next moment, he's a complete monster.*

"This is only the beginning, Jaz. I'm going to take the others down, too, one by one." An even deeper coldness seemed to creep into his eyes. "Maxwell and I have it all planned. We're going to drown Liam. Roxanne, we'll crack in half. I'm not sure about Duane. Maybe we'll beat him to death . . ."

"No. *No.*"

Despite herself, Jasmine felt the Dragon power growing. It surged along with her alarm, her horror at Carlos's words. Her hands pulsed with energy.

"That's it, Jaz." He watched her hungrily. "Show me what you think of me."

"You're insane," she snarled.

"Am I? Maybe." He seemed honestly surprised. "Mostly I just feel free. As if a lot of useless rules that held me back are gone now, leaving my mind free to wander."

The Dragon roared inside her.

"It feels good, Jaz," Carlos continued. "Letting things go. Letting go of stupid ideas like loyalty, friendship. Love."

The energy built, bubbling up inside her like lava in a volcano. All around her, the Dragon rose, whipping its savage head. Its jaws, its ancient eyes shone back at her from a thousand mirrored surfaces.

"Let it go, Jaz," Carlos urged. "Let it out. Let it all out."

She turned on him and spat fire. He ducked, laughing.

White-hot energy burst out of her, flashing over his head and slamming straight into the mirrored wall. Jasmine barely had time to think: *He* wanted *me to do that*—

And then the fiercest energy blast of all, the ultimate expression of the Dragon's power, rebounded back on her. Pain surged through her, unimaginable agony slicing through every nerve ending in her body. She staggered and fell to the slick mirrored floor.

A shadow fell over her. Jasmine shook her head, struggling to remain conscious. She could barely move. Every bone, every muscle burned with pain.

When she looked up, Carlos was staring down at her. On his face was an expression of deep concern, reflected in the mirrored panes around him. For a brief moment, she dared to hope he'd broken Maxwell's conditioning.

"Beg me, Jaz," he said. "Beg me again."

As she slipped into oblivion, the last thing she heard was the sound of his cackling.

CHAPTER TWENTY-ONE

"JASMINE," ROXANNE SAID. "She did *that?*"

"M-maybe she *doesn't* need us," Duane said.

Roxanne sat with Liam and Ox, staring at the hologram rising from Duane's outstretched hands. It showed Maxwell's Australian base—and the base had seen better days. Two domes and a guard tower had been smashed flat. The central dome seemed intact, but smoke rose from a dozen little fires scattered around it.

Duane was wired into the plane's computer and comm systems by a dozen cables. He blinked, absorbing information from some unseen source. As he used his power, the ghostly image of a giant boar flickered above his head.

"Her power readouts are off the scale," he said. "I've never seen Zodiac energy of this magnitude."

"Aye," Liam replied, "but where *is* she?"

Roxanne touched her earpiece. "Jasmine," she said, "do you copy? Do you read?"

Nothing.

She looked at the hologram again. One dome was fully on fire, blazing into the air.

Ox ran his eyes across the scene. "I don't like it," he said. "We're less than half a click away now—well within their scanning range. Why aren't they mobilizing to meet us?"

"We're in stealth mode, mate," Liam replied.

Ox raised an eyebrow at him. "Vanguard *built* this plane. You think they don't know we're here?"

As if in answer, the plane lurched sharply. With a dull whine, all its systems went dead. Duane's hologram winked out.

Liam and Ox ran for the controls together.

"What happened?" Liam yelled.

Duane blinked. "Complete power loss," he said. "Some sort of command has been entered into the system, shutting down all systems."

Roxanne's eyes went wide. "All systems?"

"Yes. Including the engines."

"So we're dead in the air."

"It l-looks that way," Duane replied. "Only a few cameras and comm channels are still online."

"Vanguard," Ox said. "They sent a remote shutdown command. I should have anticipated it."

"We all should have," Roxanne said.

"I know the plane's software," Ox said. "I might be able to override the command." He crouched down below the console and wrenched open an instrument panel, revealing circuits and switches beneath.

Liam planted himself in the pilot's seat and grabbed at the stick. He punched a few buttons, then threw up his hands. "No response," he said.

"Try it now," Ox said.

The plane lurched again.

"Power restored," Liam said. "Wait—it's partially down again."

Ox tumbled sideways, swore, and crawled back over to the instrument panel.

"Make it fast, mate," Liam said, struggling with the stick. "Fast would be good."

"Do we know where we are?" Roxanne asked.

"Directly over Vanguard," Duane said. "And they are powering up energy cannons."

Duane stabbed at a touch screen several times. The hologram reappeared, staticky and wavering. It showed the plane shaking, its nose tilting dangerously toward the ground. As a guard tower passed directly underneath them, its two big guns swiveled to aim at their airborne target.

"H-hang on," Duane said.

The guns fired, twin energy beams stabbing into the

sky. Roxanne tensed—but the impact didn't come.

"A target this—uhhh—wobbly is hard to hit," Liam said, bouncing and jolting about in the pilot's seat. "Only silver lining we've got, I reckon."

"It's not gonna be much of a silver lining when we smash into the ground," Roxanne said.

"Aye, the glass is lookin' less than half-full." Liam craned his head down toward the access panel. "Malik?"

Ox's head was buried inside the console. "Working on it," he said.

"Rox," Liam called, whipping his head around. "You better strap on a chute."

"Got it," she said, and moved toward the pile of parachutes next to the jump door. "You too, Duane."

Duane shook his head. "I have to keep monitoring."

He ran his hand over the flickering hologram, panning across the scene outside. The plane was almost out of the guard tower's range, but not quite. The guns swiveled and fired another high-powered energy blast—dead on target, this time.

The plane jolted. Duane's chair slid across the floor; a few of his inputs pulled free of their sockets. He grabbed onto the table, frantically trying to steady himself.

Roxanne strode over and yanked him to his feet. He started to protest, but she paid no attention. She reached out and pulled free his wires, then shoved a parachute into his arms.

"Can't monitor anything if you're dead," she said.

He pulled the parachute on and fastened the buckle.

A faint hum filled the cabin. "Back to two-thirds power," Ox called.

"Aye," Liam said, pulling hard at the stick. "Right rudder's responding again, but she's sluggish. And no autopilot. Turning into the wind now. But we're not gonna be in the air for long." He whipped his head around to face Roxanne and Duane. "Everybody bail out. Now."

Duane turned to him, stunned. "Wh-what about you?"

"I'm gonna stay with the plane." Liam grunted, struggling with the stick. "Maybe I can take out a few of those bloody domes on the way down."

Roxanne led Duane to the jump door and thumbed it open—just as the plane veered sideways. She lost her footing and almost tumbled out. She caught a quick glimpse of the central Vanguard dome, passing dangerously close as the plane wove its crooked course through the air.

A small line of soldiers filed out of one of the small domes, which crowded around the main structure like young creatures protecting their mother. The soldiers pointed up at the sky, struggling to aim their weapons at the wobbling plane.

"That's a lot of soldiers," Duane said.

Another dome loomed close, not more than five meters away. Liam swore again, pulling up hard on the stick. Then he leaned down and kicked Ox's shoulder.

"You too, mate," Liam said. "Make like a sailor and bail."

Ox scuttled back out of the access panel. When his face appeared, it was grim.

"Can't do it, *mate*. You need me here."

"The devil I do. I'm an ace bloody pilot."

"Vanguard's sending a constant series of kill signals," Ox explained. "I'm rerouting the systems on the fly, but they've changed a lot of the access codes. You're lucky I know this plane better than anyone else."

"And *you're* lucky I've got my hands full, or I'd kick you out that door."

At the jump door, Roxanne touched Duane on the shoulder.

"I'll take the soldiers," she said, pointing toward the ground. "You take cover *there*—past the main building. Wait for Jasmine, and see if you can get near the big dome—"

"No," Duane said. "I'm coming with you."

She looked at him. "No way. There's too many of them."

"That's why I'm coming." He sucked in a deep breath. "I won't let you down this time. I *can't*."

She started to argue, then thought better of it. She nodded, her eyes wide.

The plane lurched sharply forward, its nose turning toward the ground.

"Ox!" Liam yelled. "Get the hell out. I'll take me chances alone. I'm indestructible, remember?"

"You need me," Ox replied. "Besides, nobody's indestructible."

"Maybe. And maybe nobody's unstoppable, either."

"A lot of people have tried to kill me," Ox said. "It's gonna take more than your crap flying to finish the job."

He stood up and clapped a grease-covered hand on Liam's shoulder. "Besides, I got a lot to make up for in my life. Maybe this is where I set things right."

Together, they turned to stare out the forward windows. One of the small white domes was growing larger and larger in their view. It bore the number 2 on its roof. The plane wobbled and dropped, heading straight for the structure.

"Guess we're gonna find out," Liam said.

Then he turned toward Roxanne and Duane. Roxanne had never heard Liam's voice so sharp, so angry.

"What are you two starin' at?" Liam barked. *"Get out already!"*

Roxanne glanced out the jump door. On the ground, the soldiers were gathering in a circle, locking their weapons. One of them barked orders to the others, his words lost in the roaring, rushing wind.

"Here we go," she whispered.

She touched Duane on the shoulder, and they jumped together.

CHAPTER TWENTY-TWO

IT WAS THE burning smell that roused Liam. He shot awake, looking around wildly.

The cockpit was a mess. The plane's nose had caved in on impact, smashing the forward instrument panel into Liam's chest and pinning him to his seat. The window was a spiderweb of cracks, obscuring his view.

Liam groaned. He flexed his arms, then his legs and was surprised to find he wasn't hurt at all. It took him a moment to remember: *Right. The Zodiac power.*

A little fire was burning in the empty copilot's seat. He waved at it, batting at the flames until they went out. Then he pushed hard at the instrument panel until it creaked and gave way. Slowly, he squeezed his way up and out of the pilot's seat.

The plane had crashed nose-down, leaving the whole cabin tilted forward. Instruments lay strewn and broken everywhere, and furniture had flung across the compartment. The big table stood on its side, and just past it, toward the back of the cabin . . .

Ox lay beneath a large collapsed bulkhead. His eyes were closed.

"Aw, no," Liam said.

He launched himself through the air, bounced once off the ceiling, and made a three-point landing right beside the fallen Zodiac. He planted his feet on the ground, then reached down and grabbed at the bulkhead, lifting with all his might.

It didn't move.

Neither did Ox.

"Come on, you numpty," Liam said, his voice trembling. "I vouched for you. Don't die on me now."

He touched Ox's neck. The man's pulse was slow but strong. He was still alive. Liam let out a heavy sigh of relief.

He turned Ox's head to the side. Ox coughed and gasped.

"Malik," Liam said. "Mate!"

Ox opened his eyes in alarm. He looked briefly around the plane, then at the massive beam pinning him down. Finally, he turned to Liam.

"You suck at landings," Ox said.

They grabbed at the bulkhead together. Liam tried lifting it, pushing it to one side, then the other. But even their combined strength couldn't budge it.

"Must be wedged against the wall," Liam said. "Hang on, I'll get a—"

"No," Ox said. "Get out there."

Liam blinked at him. "What?"

"Roxanne and Duane are outnumbered," Ox said. "Badly. They need your help."

Liam rose to his knees. "Mate, I can't just leave you—"

"I'm fine. Strong as an . . ." Ox winced in pain, then gave Liam a weak smile. "Just go!"

Liam looked him in the eye for a long moment, then nodded. "You're all right, mate."

Ox grimaced. "Just don't get cocky," he said.

Liam turned to face the front window. Only the safety-glass coating was holding its shattered surface together. Through the prism of tiny cracks, he could see a mostly empty supply depot piled with crates and boxes.

He leaped into the air, curled into a ball, and punched straight through the window, smashing it to pieces. Seconds later, he was outside and running across the dark Vanguard compound.

From the shadows, two figures watched him go. Then

they crept their way into the dome, climbed up the wing, and entered the crashed plane. . . .

For Duane and Roxanne, things went wrong from the very start. They landed off course, farther from the main building than they'd intended. As soon as they touched down, in a clearing between the domes, a squadron of Vanguard soldiers appeared, brandishing energy rifles.

Duane sucked in a breath. *Soldiers,* he thought.

But Roxanne gave him a quick smile. "We got this," she said.

He nodded, shrugged off his parachute, and assumed a back-to-back defensive stance with her. Above the two figures, the bright-plumed Rooster and the raging Pig rose up together.

Roxanne let out a massive screech, sweeping wide. Her sonic wave blasted into the first three soldiers, knocking them off their feet.

Duane gestured, the Zodiac energy trailing from his hand. The last two soldiers recoiled in shock as their energy rifles exploded.

"Good work!" Roxanne said. "I always forget—your power can disrupt machines, too."

"Machines are easy," Duane said. "*People* are hard."

"The important thing is, you did it."

He looked down at the soldiers, lying unconscious on the ground, and smiled. "I did it," he agreed.

Then he looked past Roxanne, and his heart sank.

Roxanne followed his gaze. Another squad of soldiers was pouring from one of the domes and running toward them. And from the other side of the clearing, a second squad was headed toward them, as well.

Then he turned toward the main building. A *third* group of soldiers was circling around the wall. They were staying close to the building, their movements careful and unhurried. They hadn't seen the first two squads yet.

Duane glanced at the squad edging around the main building. That had been his and Roxanne's objective, but it was impossible. They'd never make it past all those soldiers.

"Okay," Roxanne began.

"What's your plan?" he asked.

"In a word: run."

Duane followed her, sprinting along the curving path. The darkness was complete, broken only by the eerie white glow of the domes themselves.

The clatter of footsteps echoed through the night. At least twenty soldiers were behind them, maybe thirty.

As they rounded one of the small domes, the path straightened out. Duane frowned, remembering the layout of the complex. They were headed toward the rear, past the main building. Soon the domes would thin out and be gone.

Then there'd be nowhere to hide.

Glancing back, he saw the soldiers round a bend,

pointing at him and Roxanne. A volley of energy bolts filled the air.

Roxanne grabbed Duane's sleeve and yanked him around a corner. A bolt sizzled against the dome where he'd been standing a second before.

"Interesting," Duane said. "The Vanguard weapons don't even leave a scratch on the domes. The building materials must be specially designed."

"Interesting *later*," Roxanne snapped. "Right now it's—"

Someone slammed into her, knocking her off her feet. Roxanne cried out and fell to the ground.

Instinctively, Duane took a step back. As he watched, Roxanne's attacker landed, unfolding his limbs to reveal—

"Liam?" Duane asked.

Liam turned to stare at him. The Irishman's eyes were blank, glassy. Hypnotized.

"Welcome to Vanguard," came a low female voice.

Duane whirled around. Snake stood at the end of the path curling around the last dome in the complex. Her eyes were glowing with Zodiac power, looking past him at . . .

"Roxanne!" Duane called. He turned just in time to see her climb to her feet. Her eyes were blank, too. Her mouth opened, and a single high-pitched note came out.

Pain lanced through Duane's head; he dropped to his knees. Before he could recover, a trio of Vanguard agents grabbed him tightly by the arms.

"Don't move, pig-man," Snake said. "I think *you* know what my power can do."

He shook his head, groggy. Duane had experienced Snake's hypnotic control back at Dragon's Gate. She'd used him the way she was using Liam and Roxanne, as a weapon against his friends. He was still ashamed of that.

Snake gestured toward the back of the complex. Roxanne and Liam started to move, both of them walking stiffly. The soldiers followed, ushering Duane along in front of them.

As they passed the last dome, the landscape turned to red earth. There were no trees there, just sand and rock. In the distance, another access road curved around the back of the complex, but that one was unpaved. It didn't look like it had been used for a long time.

Duane glanced back. From his viewpoint, three of the small domes were visible, all still intact. The large central building rose up beyond them.

Still no sign of Jasmine, he thought. *Where is she?*

Snake led them into the cleared area between the complex and the arc of the access road. A small shack, made of bare wood, stood alone on the sand. It was unlit—barely visible in the darkness.

But as they drew closer, Duane could make out three figures clustered around the shack. Monkey leaned against one side, scarfing down a banana. Three banana peels lay on the ground at his feet.

Snake raised an eyebrow at him. "Thanks for the *assist*," she said sarcastically.

Monkey grinned and chewed. "We been busy," he said.

The second figure was a tall, serious-looking man in Vanguard uniform, holding a third, limp man by the collar. Duane squinted and managed to make out the unconscious figure: Ox.

Snake turned sharply to the soldiers. "That's far enough," she said. "Give us room."

The soldiers fanned out, forming a semicircle. They raised their weapons, keeping the Zodiacs in their sights.

Duane, Liam, and Roxanne were penned in, facing the shack. Duane glanced at Roxanne. She stood silent, utterly obedient. Her eyes looked like big blank circles.

Snake walked slowly up to the tall Vanguard agent. She peered at him with . . . suspicion, maybe? Duane wasn't sure. He wasn't good at reading emotions.

"You must be Malosi," Snake said.

The Vanguard agent nodded. The two of them stood for a moment, appraising each other awkwardly.

Then the agent—Malosi—pointed a thumb at Monkey. "He wasn't much help to *me*, either," he said, "but we managed to scoop this one up." He hefted Ox's limp body.

Monkey shrugged. He tossed away his peel and pulled out yet another banana.

I'm the only one left, Duane thought. He pulled himself up to his full height and turned to face Snake directly.

"What now?" he asked.

Snake stared back at him for a moment. Her eyes flared, as if she were considering using her power on him. But instead she just turned and called out to Monkey. "Vincent?"

Monkey stood at the door to the shack, finishing off his last banana. He threw away the peel and rapped twice, fast, on the door of the shack. "Yo, Operator!" he called. "Time to place a call!"

Duane watched, puzzled. *Operator?* Slowly, the door opened.

Carlos stepped out of the shack, his movements calm and unhurried. He cast his eyes across the group, as if taking the measure of each player in turn. Snake, her eyes glowing with power. Liam and Roxanne standing rigid at attention. Monkey smirking.

Duane gasped.

Carlos paid no attention. He turned to Malosi and gestured at Ox, unconscious on the ground. "Over there," he said.

Malosi reached down and lifted Ox by the collar again. A faint Zodiac glow rose up from Malosi as he tossed Ox toward Duane and the others. Ox crashed to the ground and groaned.

Duane helped him to his feet. Ox gestured at Liam's rigid, unmoving form. "If this guy knew how to land a plane, I could have taken both Vincent *and* that new Tiger."

"New Tiger?" Duane asked.

But before Ox could answer, Carlos stepped forward and smiled. "Everyone's here," he said. "That makes things easier."

"Carlos?" Duane asked. "What are you *doing*?"

Carlos whipped out a small dart gun and fired—four times, in rapid succession. The first dart struck Roxanne on the neck. She cried out and staggered back.

Ox slapped at his throat as the second dart made contact. The third one struck Liam, whipping his head around.

Duane tried to duck, but there was no time. The dart struck his neck and stayed there, attached by some kind of adhesive. He scrabbled at it, but it wouldn't budge.

Then he felt thin metal probes break his skin. They jabbed into his neck, sharp and hard. "What is it?" he cried, trying to turn his head to see. "What's it doing to me?"

"They're . . ." Ox winced in pain. "They're burrowing into our skin. Little . . . nanotendrils, I think they're called."

The metal feelers dug into Duane's flesh. He tugged at the device, but it was no use. It had taken root, and it wouldn't budge.

"It's a power drainer," Carlos said. "My own design."

"Yeah?" came a female voice.

Duane turned. Roxanne and Liam stood together— both clear-eyed, glaring at Carlos. *The dart,* Duane thought. *It broke Snake's hypnotic spell!*

"Drain this," Roxanne said.

She opened her mouth to let out a sonic cry. But all that emerged was a weak, strangled screech.

Carlos laughed. "The Zodiacs," he sneered. "You know, I never thought much of this team. Without Jaz and the kid, you're nothing."

Duane clenched his fists. He didn't know why or how, but Carlos was definitely working for Maxwell again. He had figured that out, intuitively, a few moments before Carlos fired the darts. Sometimes Duane could do that—put together the pieces of a puzzle on a nonrational level.

For all the good it does me, he thought.

"You forgot somethin', brainiac," Liam said. "Your little dart might be stuck to my neck with superglue—"

He launched himself through the air, leaping toward Carlos. The Ram burst forth, snorting and roaring above his head.

"—but nothing can break my skin," Liam finished.

Carlos watched calmly. At the last moment, he stepped to the side—just as the Ram started to fade. Liam flailed in midair, tumbled, and landed in the dirt.

Carlos leaned down, speaking to Liam like a patient teacher. "The dart doesn't *need* to penetrate your skin," he said. "That just makes the process faster. Your power lasted a whole thirty seconds longer than your teammates'—I hope you made the most of it."

Snake, Monkey, and Malosi moved closer to Carlos. *We could rush him,* Duane thought. *Carlos isn't much of a fighter.*

But without our powers, we'd never beat them all. Not to mention two dozen armed Vanguard agents.

Duane could feel the drainer doing its work, sapping the Zodiac energy within him. He was helpless; so were Liam, Roxanne, and Ox. They'd been tricked, outmatched. Defeated.

Liam staggered over to rejoin his teammates. He dabbed at a cut on his lip and stared for a moment at the small drop of blood on his finger.

Duane had never seen Liam bleed before.

They stood together, along with Roxanne and Ox, opposite the Vanguard forces—and Carlos. Two groups facing off like gunslingers in the Old West.

"What now?" Duane asked.

Carlos grinned and held up a small cylinder. "I'm glad you asked," he said.

He pressed a button, and the world seemed to tip on its side.

CHAPTER TWENTY-THREE

ALL AROUND the little shack, the ground began to rumble and shift. A circular plot of land rose up, tilting slightly. The red soil began to crack apart, sliding away to reveal a carefully engineered artificial platform.

The soldiers took another step back. As they watched, the platform began to rise into the air.

On the platform, Roxanne struggled to maintain her balance. A sudden lurch knocked Duane off his feet. He fell into Liam, and the two of them tumbled to the surface.

"Ow," Liam said. "Not invulnerable anymore, remember?"

Roxanne stumbled. "What's *happening?*" she asked.

She looked up, dazed, and saw Carlos standing over her. Snake and Monkey flanked him. Malosi stood just behind, frowning as always.

Carlos held up the cylinder, the device he'd activated just a moment before. "Surprise," he said.

Roxanne just stared at him.

"You'll excuse us," Carlos added. "We have a few preparations to make." He gestured toward the edge of the platform. "Go ahead. Take a look."

He turned away and motioned to Snake, Monkey, and Malosi. They followed him toward the shack, away from the depowered Zodiacs. They seemed totally unconcerned with Roxanne and her friends.

And why should *they be concerned?* Roxanne thought. *We're trapped and powerless!*

The Vanguard agents, she noticed, seemed surer on their feet. They'd been expecting Carlos's trick, the rising plot of ground that had thrown their enemies off balance.

Liam touched her shoulder. "What now?" he asked.

"You heard the man," she said. "Let's check out the view."

She led him, lurching and stumbling, over to the edge of the huge disk. Now she could see: the airborne area covered a circle about twenty meters in diameter. The shack had risen along with them, but the domes and the access road were still down on the ground. She could see the soldiers, too, staring up at attention from below.

They were still rising. *We must be about ten meters in the air,* she thought. The ground shifted and cracked beneath their feet, revealing the transparent plastic surface of the platform.

For the first time, the enormity of the situation struck Roxanne. *This isn't some military base we're assaulting,* she thought, *or a criminal mastermind with a secret hideout. It isn't a mindless sandstorm or a couple of rogue agents.*

This is the most dangerous man in the world. With his private army—and a near-infinite box of toys.

She turned to look back at the shack. Monkey was fumbling with a device on his wrist.

"Vincent," Carlos asked, "do you have the holo-link set up yet?"

"Almost," Monkey muttered. He shook the device in the air.

The disk stopped rising. The soil had thinned out, leaving a layer of thick transparent plastic holding them in midair. Red earth crumbled off the sides, falling like snow to the edges of the glowing Vanguard complex—twenty meters below.

Roxanne crouched down and cleared the last bits of dirt away, making a bare patch on the disk's surface. Through the plastic, the Vanguard domes looked like luminescent marbles scattered across the ground. The guards were tiny pixels of light, their energy weapons glowing in the dark.

It's like a game, she thought. *But what are the rules? And where's the main player—Maxwell?*

Then Duane was at her elbow, speaking low. Liam and Ox had crouched down, too, casting occasional glances over at the Vanguard operatives.

"They're using gravity-negation equipment to keep us in the air," Duane said. "I think it's in the shack. I might be able to slip inside and sabotage it, if someone can distract our opponents."

The shack, Roxanne noticed, was at the exact center of the platform. Inside it, machinery hummed and whirred, dropping in pitch as the disk stabilized in midair.

"Well, we're fresh out of Zodiac power," Liam said. "But Ox and me are still fighters. If he tackles Snake low, I might be able to—"

Ox motioned for silence. Carlos was striding toward them, with Snake right behind. Celine's eyes glowed like warning lights.

Carlos stopped a few feet from Roxanne and her team. He began to pace back and forth like a college professor, glancing at each of the Zodiacs in turn.

"Let me explain what's going to happen," Carlos said. "Each of you has a drainer on your neck. Right now they're inhibiting your powers—but I *could* use them to drain the Zodiac energy out of you, one at a time, until nothing is left. That would work. It would do the job.

"But," he continued, "it would be inefficient. It would take time. It would increase the possibility of sloppiness, of error. For instance, while I was draining *you*"—he pointed at Roxanne, then at Duane—"*you* might be tempted to try to deactivate this lovely antigravity platform. Which, I might remind you, would lead to a pretty big fall for those of us—like me and *you*"—he pointed at Liam—"who do not currently possess extra powers."

"I'll take me chances," Liam growled.

"I'm sure you would. Which is why *I* am taking none."

Carlos turned and motioned to Malosi. The young man stepped forward.

"You're familiar with the special properties of the Tiger," Carlos said. "When Steven wielded it, he made a fascinating discovery. The Tiger is the only Zodiac sign that can connect with the other powers, drawing them together and enhancing their strength. That ability turned the tide at Dragon's Gate, enabling you to defeat Maxwell."

"Enabling *us*," Roxanne said. "You fought with us, Carlos."

"I did," he acknowledged. "That was a long time ago."

For just a second, Carlos seemed to waver. A confused expression crossed his face. *Huh,* Roxanne thought. *Could there be some of the old Carlos left inside him?*

But he had already snapped out of it and seemed his new, cruel self again. "At Dragon's Gate, the Tiger was your salvation," he said. "Here, it will be your—"

"Dammit," Monkey said. "I can't get this to work."

Carlos glanced over, annoyed. He strode across the platform and grabbed Monkey's arm. With a harsh twist, he clicked the device free of Monkey's wrist.

"Ow," Monkey said.

Carlos marched to the shack and mounted the device on the outer wall, securing it with a magnetic latch. Then he ran his fingers expertly along its tiny touch screen.

A hologram rose into the sky, three or four times life-size. Maxwell's glowing dark-eyed face looked down sharply at them. He stared around, surveying the group in an unhurried, almost casual way.

"*I think he was going to say 'your doom,'*" Maxwell said.

Roxanne studied the enormous hologram. Maxwell sat in a dark room, holding only a tarnished bronze sphere in both hands. The sphere glowed, casting an eerie light on his face.

The Maxwell hologram turned to face Malosi. "*My Tiger,*" Maxwell said, with a hint of pride in his voice. "*You may begin.*"

Malosi smiled up at the looming face. For a moment, Malosi looked less like a warrior and more like a child. *A child,* Roxanne thought, *receiving a rare word of approval from his parent.*

Then Malosi's face went hard again. He nodded, closed his eyes, and clenched his fists. The white Tiger began to rise up around his body, raging fierce and wild in the night.

Not many options, Roxanne thought. *Carlos is Maxwell's creature now; so is Malosi. And Monkey is absolutely loyal.*

That only leaves . . .

"Snake," she said softly. "Celine?"

Snake frowned at her, then looked away.

Malosi's eyes were closed; he seemed to be in a trance, gathering his strength for some battle to come. Carlos was tapping on a small analyzer device. Monkey just stared up at Maxwell's image with pure adulation.

Roxanne leaned in closer to Snake. "You're next, you know," she whispered. "Once Maxwell has our powers, he's gonna take yours, too."

Snake glared back. But her eyes didn't glow.

"That's ridiculous," she said.

"Roxy's right," Liam said, leaning in. "Ye know it's true."

"It is what *I* would do," Duane said, "if I were a power-hungry madman." He paused. "Which I'm not, of course."

"No. No," Snake replied, her voice low. "I'm loyal to Maxwell. I'm not a traitor, like Josie and Nicky." She pointed at Ox. "Or like *him*."

"Maxwell doesn't care about loyalty," Ox said. "He has no allies. Only tools."

Snake cast a nervous glance at Carlos and Monkey. They hadn't heard the conversation. She turned and stared off in the distance, as if remembering something from long before and far away.

"Berlin," she said quietly. "I miss Berlin."

The Zodiac energy continued to build up around Malosi. He spread his arms, drinking it in.

"Let me ask you something," Roxanne said. "This should be your moment of triumph. Do you feel triumphant?"

Slowly, Snake shook her head.

It's working, Roxanne thought. *She's listening!* Roxanne opened her mouth to continue—

—and then a sharp stab of pain ran through her neck. She raised a hand and touched the power drainer. The pain was focused there, spreading rapidly through her neck and chest, into her entire body.

"Aye," Liam said, staggering. "I feel it, too."

Roxanne winced. She dropped to her knees, and Ox and Duane fell with her. She looked up at Snake and held out a hand.

Snake's eyes still weren't glowing. But she shook her head.

"Too late," she said sadly.

Then Carlos was beside her. "Too late indeed." He cast a cruel smile down at Roxanne. "But that was a good last try."

"What's—happening?" Roxanne gasped.

Carlos gestured at Malosi.

The Tiger bloomed and blossomed white-hot around Malosi, brighter than ever before. Its claws scratched at the air, feral and deadly. Energy flared in all directions, forming tendrils of Zodiac power in the air.

Then the tendrils reached out to the captive Zodiacs. As Roxanne watched, a single energy strand touched Liam's neck. He cried out.

A second power-tendril made contact with Duane, and

a third with Ox. When the last one struck Roxanne, she felt a searing pain all through her body. A sharp, deadly agony that made the former effects of the power drainer seem like a gentle caress.

It's like Carlos said, Roxanne realized. *This is how we share power with Steven—like when we all helped move the truck, back in Dubai. But this time, the power is being leeched out of us!*

Roxanne peered up at Carlos through a haze of pain. Malosi stood on one side of the scientist, blazing bright, his eyes wide open. On the other side, Monkey jumped up and down, watching with eager eyes.

"As I said," Carlos began, "my technology could drain each of your powers individually. But by harnessing the power of the Tiger, I can do it all at once."

"Where—" Roxanne struggled for breath. "Where does the power *go?*"

But even as she asked the question, she realized she knew the answer.

In the hologram, Maxwell's eyes were wide. The sphere in his hands glowed brighter. It flowed like mercury, like liquid metal. Roxanne knew that glow: it was Zodiac energy.

Our energy, she thought.

She struggled to her feet and turned to address Maxwell directly.

"You can't—hold that much power," she said. "It almost destroyed you once."

Maxwell's giant visage smiled down at her. He pointed

at Carlos, and although it was impossible, Roxanne could swear Maxwell's arm reached right out of the hologram.

"That was before I had him," Maxwell said.

In Maxwell's hands, the sphere continued to change shape. With a shock, Roxanne realized it had four legs, a tail—and the sharp curved horns of Liam's ram.

Maxwell reeled. *"Oh,"* he said. *"The power."*

The sphere morphed again. Its snout grew thicker, sprouting fangs. *Pig,* Roxanne thought. Then its hooves widened and its horns grew back, straighter this time: *Ox.* Finally, a sharp beak, a proud plume of metallic feathers rising above piercing eyes—

Rooster.

"Part of the *jiānyù* is very old," Carlos explained, gesturing at the bronze object. "And part of it is new—my own work, in fact."

Roxanne watched in horror as the artifact—the *jiānyù*—ebbed and surged. It drew in on itself, becoming almost spherical again—then expanded back out into the shapes of the power it was absorbing. Ram. Pig. Ox. Rooster.

Roxanne searched deep inside herself. She reached for the Zodiac power, tried to grab on to it and hold it tight. *It's not gone yet,* she told herself. *You can do this. Don't let go of the power!*

But she was too late and too weak. The power drainer, enhanced by Malosi's abilities, was too strong. The Rooster was slipping out of her grasp, possibly forever.

Roxanne looked up and around, desperate. "Celine," she whispered.

Snake just stared at Maxwell's image, shaking her head.

Roxanne knelt on the platform, surrounded by Liam, Duane, and Ox. All four of them writhed in pain, helpless. Malosi took a step toward them, the merciless Tiger reaching out to wrench the last of the Zodiac energy from its victims' bodies.

With each new surge of power, Maxwell twitched and glowed. All the energy flowing into the *jiānyù* seemed to stimulate him, like a series of electric shocks. He muttered and murmured, lost in his own world.

Carlos shifted his gaze back and forth from Maxwell to Malosi, monitoring the power drain. "That's it," he said. "And . . . we're done."

Suddenly, the pain was gone. Roxanne slumped to the ground, exhausted. Duane, Liam, and Ox collapsed beside her.

She forced herself to look up. Malosi was still glowing with power. Carlos ran the analyzer across his body.

"Levels at ninety-six percent," Carlos said. "Maximum qi absorption." He turned to sneer at Roxanne and the others. "No more super people."

"Hey," Monkey said, pointing up at the hologram. "Is he all right?"

Maxwell stared down, through a haze of Zodiac energy, at the *jiānyù* in his hands. It shifted, changing shape faster and faster. Pig. Ox. Rooster. Ram. Pig, Ox, Rooster, Ram. PigOxRoosterRam—

"Sir?" Malosi asked.

Maxwell looked up. He peered through the energy, and his eyes seemed to focus.

"I'm fine." Maxwell nodded. "Son."

Malosi's Tiger roared with pride.

"The power," Maxwell continued. "It's . . . overwhelming. . . ."

On the platform, Snake hissed in a breath.

Malosi raised his arms. He looked like the embodiment of triumph, like a conquering general. Roxanne could picture him striding across the world, laying waste, vanquishing states and countries in the name of his leader—a leader who watched from afar, his electronic visage four times the size of a normal man.

Liam and the others were struggling to rise. Roxanne crawled over and touched Duane's shoulder. He jumped slightly, startled.

"Our powers are gone," Duane said.

"I know." Roxanne kept her voice low. "Which means we've got nothing left to lose."

She looked back at Maxwell's holographic image. It reeled, glowing with power.

"Maxwell's disoriented," Roxanne said. "I don't know if we can take Snake and the others, but this is our only shot. You guys ready for a last, hopeless stand?"

Liam and Duane nodded.

Ox's face was steely. "I'm with you," he said.

"Okay." Roxanne glanced over at Malosi and sucked in a deep breath. "On my signal . . ."

Something flashed over the platform with a sudden, deafening roar. Roxanne barely had time to glimpse a small human figure, a metal harness, and a trail of flame. The smell of rocket fuel filled the air—

—as the figure slammed into Malosi and carried him, soaring, off the platform.

Everyone scrambled to the edge at once. Roxanne ran ahead of Liam and Duane, pushing past Ox and Snake and Monkey. Only Carlos hung back.

Malosi and the figure dwindled rapidly from view, spiraling down toward the center of the Vanguard complex. A flare of rocket fire illuminated them briefly, and then they were lost in the glow of the domes below.

Above the shack, the Maxwell hologram frowned. *"What happened?"* he asked. *"What was that?"*

Roxanne raised an eyebrow. Things still looked bleak; her team was depowered and outnumbered. Maxwell glared down at them from the hologram, bristling with power. Jasmine was missing, and their greatest ally—Carlos—had turned against them.

But even so, Roxanne felt a surge of hope. She found herself starting to smile.

"That," she said, "was Steven Lee."

CHAPTER TWENTY-FOUR

STEVEN HUNG ON tight. Malosi squirmed and twisted in his grip, struggling to break free. Locked together, they lurched and swooped through the air, arcing down toward the glowing domes.

For just a moment, Malosi turned his face to look directly into Steven's. The Tiger energy burned around the Vanguard agent, mirroring the rage in his features.

"YOU!" Malosi screamed.

He pulled away from Steven, tipping them off balance. For a split second, the sky reeled. The floating platform spun in Steven's vision like a coin tossed in the air.

Then the jet pack flared bright, and they found themselves accelerating—straight down.

Steven felt a moment of panic as the ground rushed toward them. He fumbled for the controls on his waist, at the base of the harness. *Stupid thing!* he thought. Rat had given him the jet pack—the "other toy" the rodent-man had promised in Sydney. But Rat hadn't stuck around long enough to show him how to use it.

Steven jabbed at the lateral thrust button. He and Malosi lurched sideways as their descent slowed. But Malosi had freed his arms. He rained down blows on Steven's shoulders and head.

"Let go!" Malosi yelled.

Steven clamped both arms tight around Malosi's waist.

"No way," he said.

The white Tiger flashed on and off around Malosi like a faulty light bulb. *He could break free in an instant,* Steven realized, *if he knew how to wield the power. But he's not used to it. That gives me an advantage.*

Not a big one. But an advantage.

They swooped between two of the small domes, narrowly missing them. The main dome rose up, dead ahead of them. There was no way to avoid it.

Watching the dome grow larger, Steven felt oddly calm. *I've lost my powers,* he thought. *I've probably lost my team. It's just me now.*

All I can do is my best.

The featureless white wall of the dome loomed close. *Wait for the right moment,* he thought. *Just a little longer . . . one more second . . .*

He twisted violently, turning Malosi toward the dome. *Make him take the impact. He's got the power—*

But Malosi's eyes went wide. The Tiger flared around him, its roar filling the air. He reached out and grabbed Steven's shoulders, then whirled in midair.

The jet pack struck the dome first, sending a jolt of pain through Steven's back. The plastic wall cracked and gave way under the impact and the blazing Zodiac power. The jet pack sparked and caught fire.

Then they were falling.

Steven flailed, instinctively trying to summon the Tiger power. Nothing. He barely had time to remember his combat training. He bent his legs and landed awkwardly, stumbling over something hard and rocky.

He looked around and drew in a sharp breath.

The room was crowded, filled to overflowing with artifacts. Paintings, sculptures, steles and columns from ancient temples. A pile of gold bullion spilling out of a very old trunk. A large table with sculpted legs, rows of beautiful carved pots and jeweled necklaces covering its surface.

The jet pack was still smoking. Steven shrugged it off. It clattered to the floor, landing next to the object he'd tripped over: a broken statue of a king with a long stylized beard and haunted eyes. Its lower half was missing.

"The House of Property," Malosi said.

Steven looked up. Across the room, past a row of carved pots, Malosi stood blazing with power. He stared at Steven with pure hatred.

Steven remembered the tunnels, the artifacts crammed haphazardly into Maxwell's subterranean warren. *He piles up the extra inventory down here,* Josie had said. But Ox's intel had also mentioned Maxwell's houses: twelve rooms, each representing a different aspect of a person's life, spread in a ring around Maxwell's garden.

"So this is where he keeps the good stuff," Steven said. "The treasures he steals."

"The treasures he *rescues,*" Malosi corrected.

Steven stared at him for a moment. Then, despite himself, he laughed.

"Dude," Steven said, shaking his head.

Malosi's anger flared brighter. "You mock me," he replied. "You mock *him.* But he's the only hope this world has."

"Yeah?" Steven gestured around the room. "I think the *world* would like its stuff back."

Malosi walked stiffly to the table. He picked up an ornate decanter lined with silver and studded with large jewels.

"This was looted from a Middle Eastern museum," Malosi said. "If Maxwell hadn't taken it, it would have been lost forever."

"That's what he told you, huh?"

"The nations of Earth are destroying themselves," Malosi continued. "There's no order anymore, no rule of law. Maxwell knows that. That's why he wants the Zodiac power. That's why he's preserving the heritage of the human race, right here."

Steven walked toward him. Malosi stood across the table, about three meters away.

Steven picked up a heavy necklace mounted with diamonds. "It looks to me like he just wants a big pile of bling."

Malosi flared with anger. He brought a fist down, splintering the table in half. The decanter crashed to the ground and shattered into a thousand pieces. The other pots and dishes followed, smashing into a pile of multi-colored shards.

"So much for the heritage of the human race," Steven said.

The Tiger was bright around Malosi. Its eyes glowed yellow.

Steven stepped back. He reached into his pocket and felt around. His fingers closed on a cool metal object: the qi amplifier—the gift from his mother.

Malosi leaped over the broken table, roaring with fury. Steven watched him soar through the air and calmly pressed the button on the amplifier.

Nothing happened.

Steven's instincts kicked in just in time. He leaped aside, and Malosi's elbow grazed his face. Malosi flew past and tumbled to the floor, crashing into a pile of gold coins.

Again the Tiger roared.

Steven looked down at the qi amplifier in horror. Then the horror turned to anger.

Thanks, Mom, he thought. *You failed me again. Why did I think this time would be different?*

Malosi was climbing to his feet. *He's still not used to the Zodiac power,* Steven remembered. *But I won't get another chance like that. Next time he'll kill me.*

Steven glared at the heart-shaped gadget in his hand. He pulled his arm back, intending to throw the useless amplifier away—and then his mother's words came back to him:

Try to use it outdoors.

He cast a quick glance upward. The curved roof of the dome loomed above him. But over by the far wall, where Malosi stood, was the hole they'd punched on their way in.

"The Tiger," Malosi said. "It's everything I thought it would be. It wants to eviscerate its enemy—to rip you to shreds."

Steven looked from Malosi back up to the hole in the wall. Outside, through the small opening, he could see the twinkling night sky.

It draws its energy directly from the stars.

"But I'll give you one chance," Malosi continued. "Surrender and you can walk away. I'll *force* the Tiger to be merciful."

Steven swallowed hard, crouched down, and charged.

Malosi reared back, startled. Steven weaved and dodged, propelling himself off the remains of the table. He jumped onto an antique chair and vaulted into the air. When he passed underneath the hole in the wall, he pressed the button again.

The qi amplifier surged to life.

Time seemed to slow down. Steven paused, hanging in midair. Above him, the stars appeared brighter than before. A shaft of light stabbed into the room.

Steven looked down at the startled Malosi. The white Tiger blazed above him, full of fury and uncontrolled power.

But something was happening to Steven. The Tiger, the power of the Zodiac, surged again—within *him*, as well as Malosi.

Steven opened his mouth and roared.

He slammed into Malosi, and time snapped back to normal. Steven reached out and grabbed the Vanguard agent, swinging him around and throwing him into the wall. A huge painting, a medieval battle scene, cracked and hung loose on the wall.

Malosi bounced back, not missing a beat. He whirled around and scooped up a chipped stone bust of a woman. He hurled it at Steven, who dodged easily.

Above them, in the air, the twin Tigers blazed. Steven's was fierce and righteous, with dark stripes and sharp fangs. Malosi's was pure white, a beast of incinerating rage.

Steven jumped up, reaching out for a high kick. Malosi sidestepped, but Steven's foot grazed his neck. Malosi fell back, clutching his throat.

"Now it's an even fight," Steven said, landing easily on his feet.

Malosi glared up at him. "Never," he hissed. "I *am* the Tiger."

"Only till Maxwell doesn't need you anymore. Then he'll steal your power, too."

"You don't know anything."

"He already did it to Horse and Dog," Steven said. "I saw them."

"You're lying."

"He's probably draining Snake and Monkey right now—"

"*Shut up!*"

Malosi charged, surprisingly fast. He punched Steven in the head three times, rapid-fire.

Steven shrank back, dazed. Then he leaped into the air, hands and feet moving in concert. He kicked out multiple times, left-right, left-right: one blow to Malosi's shin, then his knees, then his stomach. Then the shin again.

Malosi reached out, grabbed Steven's legs, and flipped him over his shoulder. By the time Steven recovered, the

wall was rushing toward him. He was headed for the cracked painting, the same spot Malosi had struck before.

When the impact came, not even the Zodiac power was enough to protect him from the pain.

Then Malosi was on him again, charging and butting him in the stomach. Malosi pressed him up against the tattered canvas of the painting, cutting off his breath. Steven's Tiger howled in agony.

The wall splintered and burst open. They tumbled through the hole together, grunting and grappling.

A splintered wooden beam scraped Steven's side, drawing blood. He cried out. He raised both hands, broke Malosi's grip, and scurried away.

He looked around, disoriented. The room he found himself in was completely different from the first one. It was decorated like an English mansion: flowered wallpaper, gilt-edged railings on a spiral staircase, ornate chandeliers hanging at odd angles from the domed ceiling. The floor was a black-and-white checkerboard of marble.

Everything about the place screamed Old World wealth.

"Maxwell's House of Karma," Malosi said, glaring at Steven. "A fitting place for you to face your sins."

"My *sins*?" Steven asked. "What are you talking about?"

"You're a child," Malosi replied, "a careless little brat. You walked out on your friends . . . abandoned them. Do you even *want* the Zodiac power?"

"I didn't abandon them."

But Malosi's words had struck home. Steven had made the wrong decision, he knew, traveling to Berlin alone. He'd left his team leaderless and vulnerable at the worst possible time.

"You should just walk away," Malosi continued. He gestured at the wide balconies, the meticulously wrought railings. "Let *this* be your destiny—to grow old quietly, someplace where you'll never have to hear the word *Zodiac* again."

Steven blinked. He thought of the old man dying alone in his bed in Berlin.

Above Malosi, the white Tiger blazed. Steven tensed, waiting for the attack. But Malosi just shook his head.

"You're no Tiger," he said.

Then he whirled around and pressed a hidden stud next to an ornate doorway. The entire wall swiveled, taking Malosi with it.

In a second, he was gone.

Steven paused, catching his breath. *I could leave him here,* he thought. *He's wrong—I am the Tiger again. And my friends need my help.*

But he had unfinished business. And somehow he knew: *If I'm going to beat Maxwell, Malosi is the key. I have to defeat him.*

I have to tame my other self.

He took a last look around at the House of Karma: its

wide doorways, its beautiful oak furnishings, the gas lamps shining from its walls. It felt like a trap. A guilty indulgence, an escape from his responsibilities. A fantasy.

He reached into his pocket and hefted the qi amplifier again. It was warm, like a parent's embrace. Like a living heart.

He walked to the wall and pressed the stud. The room whirled around him—and suddenly he was in another chamber.

It was dark and musty, filled with ancient weapons—maces, swords. Flaming torches were mounted on the walls. A huge catapult filled one corner, loaded and ready to fire.

Steven looked around, frantic. *Malosi—where is he?*

Then a sharp metallic sound rang out, again and again. Steven whirled around, the Tiger energy blazing above him.

"The House of Elders," Malosi said.

Malosi strode forward with measured, unhurried steps. He clanked a massive rusty chain up and down in his hands, whipping the floor.

"You followed me," Malosi said. "I guess you're a Tiger after all."

Steven nodded. "And the Tiger never hides from a challenge."

For the first time, Malosi smiled.

Steven clenched his fists. He reached deep inside

himself, tensed, and summoned the power that was his birthright.

In the dark room, lit only by torchlight, two Tigers rose up and prepared for their final battle.

CHAPTER TWENTY-FIVE

JASMINE WOKE SLOWLY, as if from a deep sleep. On the hard surface beneath her, a familiar face looked up, meeting her eyes. She blinked, startled, and scrambled to her knees.

All around her, the same expression stared out of a thousand mirrors. The face was her own.

She concentrated, summoning her power. The snake-like Dragon hissed into being above her, its head whipping back and forth. Then a memory of pain bubbled to the surface of her mind and she paused.

Carlos designed this prison specifically with me in mind, she thought. *He knows how powerful the Dragon is, and he knew he couldn't defeat it. So he arranged to use its power against it.*

He knows me, too—*better than anyone else. If he's designed a trap for me, it's unbeatable.*

The Dragon faded from the air.

She paced the circular room for a moment, her boots tapping on the mirrored floor. Her mind was a whirl of emotion. *Carlos,* she thought, *how could you do this? How could you betray me like this?*

She turned toward the wall and stared into a mirror. She looked exhausted, defeated. Not like a hero or a leader. Just a tired woman who'd been fighting too long.

Then an idea struck her. *The Dragon power. It's not just for combat or brute strength. It's much more than that.*

It transcends time and space.

She reached out and touched the mirror. Zodiac energy flared at her fingertips, sparking on contact with the glass. The image in the mirror—her own face—began to shimmer and change. In its place she saw an old painting, a broken pot, an antique table cracked in half . . .

. . . and then she saw Steven, grappling with a muscular man in his twenties. Above their small forms, two Tigers raged and clawed at each other.

She studied the image for a moment. Steven was battling for his life, but he and his opponent seemed evenly matched. What about the others? Liam, Roxanne, and

Duane? Carlos had threatened them by name, vowed to kill them.

Jasmine cast a last glance at Steven. *Hang in there, kid,* she thought. *I'll get back to you.*

She waved her hand in front of the mirror, and the image changed again.

It took her a moment to understand what she was seeing: the elevated platform, hovering in the night above the glowing domes of the Vanguard complex. She concentrated, zooming in on the image. A large hologram of Maxwell rose up from a shack in the center of the platform.

She zoomed in closer . . .

"Oh, no," she said aloud. "No, no, no."

Snake and Monkey were leading a line of helpless captives toward the shack: Duane, Roxanne, Ox, and Liam. They seemed passive, defeated, barely looking up as they marched past the giant Maxwell hologram.

Instantly, Jasmine knew: *They've lost their powers. They're beaten.*

Monkey swung open the door to the shack. Inside, a strange web of crystal circuitry rose up from the floor of the platform. *That's it,* Jasmine realized, *the gizmo that keeps that huge disk in the air.*

Duane, Roxanne, and Ox filed inside. But Liam hesitated. He glanced up at the giant Maxwell hologram, and a devilish look crept into his eye.

Liam reached out and *punched* the holo-transmitter mounted on the side of the shack. Maxwell's face vanished in a flash of static.

Snake and Monkey jumped on Liam.

Jasmine watched, helpless, as their fists pummeled her teammate. Zodiac energy started to build on her hand, rising along with her frustration. Without thinking, she reached out and let loose a bolt of Dragon-fire.

The energy struck a mirror and backfired at her, knocking her off her feet. For several minutes, she lay gasping for breath.

When she looked up again, her heart sank. Liam was being pushed into the shack after his teammates.

Jasmine concentrated on the image, following Snake and Monkey inside. She could see, built into one side of the shack, a cramped prison cell with a transparent door. Monkey snapped open the door, and Snake ushered the prisoners into the cell.

Liam, Roxanne, Duane, and Ox stared helplessly at the crystal antigravity machinery filling the center of the shack. It stood mere inches from them, but the clear plastic cell door kept them away from it.

Especially without their powers, Jasmine thought.

She followed Snake and Monkey back outside—and her heart sank. There was one other person on the platform—a man she was trying very hard not to think about.

Carlos strode across the elevated disk, taking readings

and consulting his analyzer. He didn't look like a brain-washed madman. He might have been working in his lab back at Zodiac headquarters, losing himself in some obscure experiment.

But he wasn't Carlos—not really. Not anymore.

Jasmine felt despair. Willingly or not, Carlos had betrayed her and trapped her in that cage. Now, step-by-step, he was helping Maxwell destroy her friends.

As if on cue, a small figure rose up from the complex below. Jasmine recognized it immediately: Maxwell. He rode a small hover vehicle, much like the one he'd used during the Convergence. He held a small ball glowing with Zodiac power.

Not Dragon power, Jasmine thought. *I've still got that. This is something else.*

Maxwell swooped up gracefully, surveyed the scene for a moment, and then came in for a soft landing on the platform.

Snake and Monkey watched as Maxwell stepped out of the vehicle. Monkey wore his familiar nasty grin, but Snake looked distinctly uneasy at the sight of her employer.

Carlos strode over to greet Maxwell.

Watching Carlos's smug face, Jasmine felt despair rising again. She told herself: *Don't let them beat you. Don't despair. Don't give up. Get angry.*

She waved a hand, dismissing the image in the mirror. It vanished, replaced once again by Jasmine's own face.

All around the mirrored trap, her visage stared back at her from a thousand warped reflections.

She concentrated, and the Zodiac energy began to build.

The Dragon blazed in all directions. It hissed and shrieked, whipped and coiled through the high chamber. No power could defeat it. No trap could hold it.

This is gonna hurt, she thought.

She closed her eyes and screamed.

The blast of energy tore the roof off building five. Shards of plastic flew in all directions, flaming away into the night.

Beneath her feet, the mirrored floor cracked and melted. Machinery hissed and sparked; circuits turned to liquid. Small fires broke out all along the floor.

The pain was incredible. Jasmine nearly passed out. *No,* she told herself. *Keep pouring it on. You have to save them.*

You are the Dragon!

When she opened her eyes, she was hovering above the wreckage. The walls were broken struts with jagged pieces of mirror still clinging to their frames. The ground had burned away, leaving a crater almost a meter deep.

The Dragon was free.

Jasmine clenched her fists and shot into the sky.

As she passed over the central dome, she spotted the hole in its roof. *That's where Steven is,* she realized.

But the Tiger would have to wait a little longer. Jasmine banked right and headed straight for the floating platform.

She glanced back nervously, suddenly worried that Maxwell might have witnessed her explosive escape. But all she could see was a slight wisp of smoke rising from the ruins of building five. The wreckage itself was blocked from view by the main dome.

The platform hung like a giant coin in the sky. As she approached, Jasmine powered down, forcing the Dragon glow to fade. She didn't want to be seen.

The first thing she heard was a high, sad cry of pain.

Is that Roxanne? she wondered. *Or Duane?* But no: they were out of sight, presumably still locked up inside the shack.

The cry rang out again. It sounded like an animal being struck by its master.

Jasmine moved in closer, staying dark and silent. When the scene came into focus, she gasped.

Maxwell was next to the shack, crouched over Monkey. Zodiac energy flowed out of the hairy Vanguard agent through a metallic drainer implanted in his neck. In Maxwell's outstretched hand, the bronze sphere glowed bright, drinking in the power.

Carlos stood nearby, admiring his own dart gun. "Drainers," he murmured. "Amazing tech. I *am* good."

Monkey looked up groggily into Maxwell's eyes. "Why?" he asked.

Maxwell looked down at him, past the flow of energy. It traveled in one direction: from Monkey into Maxwell's sphere. "Because I can," he replied.

Then he paused and frowned. Jasmine had the strange feeling he'd just caught himself speaking the truth—a truth he couldn't face.

"It's . . . it's for the best." Maxwell added.

Jasmine wafted closer to the platform. No one had seen her yet.

The sphere in Maxwell's hands began to morph and shift. It sprouted mottled brown legs, long-fingered hands, and an extended tail. For a moment, it looked just like a monkey.

Then it grew longer, the tail thickening and stretching. Soon it formed the unmistakable shape of a snake.

Jasmine looked across the platform. Celine—the Vanguard Snake—lay off to the side with another of the drainers in her neck. She was staring straight ahead, muttering to herself in a low voice. There was no hope on her face—and no Zodiac glow around her body or in her normally shining eyes.

He's already stolen her power, Jasmine realized. *It's inside that thing, along with Monkey's.*

Jasmine couldn't feel sorry for Maxwell's agents; they'd made their choices. But the more powerful Maxwell became . . .

Carlos leaned over Maxwell's shoulder. He watched in

fascination as Maxwell's sphere absorbed the last of the Zodiac energy from Monkey's body.

"This is risky," Carlos said. "We agreed you'd stay in seclusion."

"You mean you'd rather perform your experiments alone?" Maxwell asked. "The Tiger is occupied elsewhere, so I must perform this task myself."

They don't trust each other, Jasmine realized.

Maxwell tossed Monkey aside. The man rolled on the ground and scuttled over to join Snake. His hands and feet seemed smaller, less hairy than before. His power, too, was gone.

Maxwell rose to his feet, staggering slightly. He stared at the glowing, morphing object in his hands. It ran through a spectrum of shapes, a catalog of the Zodiac powers: snake, monkey, horse, dog, ram, rooster, pig, ox.

"So much power," Maxwell said. "But the Dragon—my birthright—still eludes me."

As she floated closer to the platform, Jasmine realized she was trembling. The memory of Carlos's words, his cruelty—the way he'd described killing her friends—came back in a flood.

Steady, she told herself. *Sneak up on them. Stay quiet!*

Maxwell turned and stumbled into Carlos. As Carlos caught him, Maxwell whispered something into his ear.

Uh-oh, Jasmine thought.

Maxwell stepped aside gracefully. Carlos whipped out his dart gun and turned to smile straight up at Jasmine.

"I have one for you, too, Jaz," he said, and fired.

Her hand blazed with Dragon power. With barely a thought, she melted the dart in midair, along with the drainer attached to it.

"Give it up, Carlos," she said, moving in to hover just before him. "Transfer the Zodiac power back to Roxanne and the others, and let's go home."

Carlos exchanged a glance with Maxwell.

"'Home,'" Carlos echoed, his voice tense. "With you? With a group of powered freaks who see me as . . . ordinary?"

"'Ordinary'?" Jasmine blinked. "I don't—Carlos, you're the smartest, most logical man I've ever met."

"That's why I'm doing this," he said. "It's logical."

This isn't working, she thought. *Try something else!*

"How's this for logic?" she asked. "You're working for the biggest 'powered freak' of all." She pointed at Maxwell.

Maxwell turned and glared at her.

"That's right, Maxwell. I've still got the Dragon power, remember?"

"And I have the *jiānyù*." Maxwell held up the sphere. "It holds . . . let's see . . . eight of the other eleven Zodiac powers. That might be an interesting contest."

Jasmine frowned. She didn't know how the sphere—the *jiānyù*—worked. But if Maxwell could use it as a weapon . . .

Carlos is the weak link, she thought. *I've got to get through to him, and fast.*

"Carlos," she said. "I know there's some good, some of the *real you*, left inside. You didn't kill me back there in the mirror dome."

"Kill the Dragon? I'm good, Jaz, but not that good." Carlos paused, examining her. "Still, you escaped my trap. Perhaps I haven't found the Dragon's weakness, after all."

The Dragon's weakness, she thought. *You found it all right. But it's not some hall of mirrors.*

It's you.

"You're dangerous, Jaz," he continued. "If I knew how, I *definitely* would have killed you. Planted you in that red earth so deep you'd never—"

Her Dragon-bolt struck him in the chest. He gasped, stumbled, and toppled forward on his face.

"Well," Maxwell said, "I guess now it's you and me."

She came in for a soft landing directly across from him.

"What are you gonna do with that thing?" Jasmine asked, gesturing at the *jiānyù*. "Toss it at my head?"

Carlos lay still on the platform's surface. Snake and Monkey just watched from a distance.

"The Dragon's more than a match for the entire Zodiac, Maxwell," she continued. "You know that."

Suddenly, the platform lurched beneath them. Jasmine stumbled, then floated up into the air. When she looked back at Maxwell, he was smiling.

"I don't want to *fight* you, Jasmine," he said. "The epic

good-versus-evil confrontation—it's kind of a cliché at this point, don't you think?"

She looked around, disoriented. Wind whipped her face as the platform continued to move. Below, through the transparent surface, the domes were coming into sharper view.

"Surprise," Carlos said.

She whirled around. Carlos lay on the ground, holding up a small cylindrical remote control. Jasmine looked from him to Maxwell—then down again. The central dome was just sliding into view.

"This is gonna hurt," Carlos said.

As the platform passed over the exact center of the Vanguard complex, a series of mighty generators hummed to life.

Then, all at once, a web of energy beams flashed from the sides of the domes. The beams reached out, connecting the small buildings in a massive network of electromagnetic power.

Two beams, from buildings four and six, flashed harmlessly into the empty air above the ruins of building five, the mirror trap.

"Seven and eight are offline, as expected," Maxwell said. "But five isn't responding, either. Will that short it out?"

"Cutting building five out of the circuit," Carlos replied, twisting a knob on the remote. "Don't worry. We've got power to spare."

On the ground, a group of soldiers scurried out of the way as the beams from buildings four and six swiveled away from the blasted-out crater. Their energy met in a blinding flash, just meters from the edge of the central dome.

Jasmine stared at Carlos. "What—" she began. "What are you *doing?*"

From each of the small buildings, the beams turned to fire at the main dome. Hidden receptors on its outer walls flared and became visible, absorbing and amplifying the energy.

The main dome glowed like a star. A circular hole slid open in the very center of its roof.

Jasmine turned in panic and took off into the air, climbing as fast as she could—

—just as the brightest, most powerful beam of all erupted from the top of the central dome. It stabbed straight toward the platform, passing harmlessly through its transparent surface—

—and grabbed Jasmine like a magnet.

She flailed, Dragon power flaring, and tried to fight it. But it drew her down, face-first, with a steady, inexorable pull. She smashed down onto the platform's surface, coughing and spitting dirt.

She struggled, but it was no use. She was pinned, stuck fast to the transparent plastic. The energy held her like a mounted insect.

She couldn't turn, could barely move. But she knew Carlos and Maxwell stood above her, watching.

"No little power drainer for you, Jaz," Carlos said. "Not for the Dragon. That requires a very special piece of machinery."

"Fueled by all the power of my complex," Maxwell said. "I was hesitant to commit such a resource. It took Carlos weeks to convince me."

Jasmine still couldn't move. With a sinking feeling, she realized something even worse: the Dragon power was beginning to leech out of her, seeping into the dome below.

"Still," Maxwell continued, "for the power of the Dragon, I would risk anything."

"You're—" Jasmine gasped. "You're not *man enough* to fight me personally."

Maxwell's mocking laugh hovered in the air above her.

"I fought you hand to hand once, Jasmine. And I lost. Believe me, I value victory over pride."

She squirmed, but it was useless. Maxwell had finally caught her, finally managed to tame the Dragon's power.

No, she thought. *Not Maxwell—Carlos. I underestimated him again. Because despite everything . . . I can't let him go.*

Her power was fading. She could feel the Dragon being pulled out of her, absorbed through the beam into the unseen machinery within the dome. From there—soon—it would be transferred into Maxwell himself.

Then he'd be unbeatable.

With a tremendous effort, Jasmine wrenched her head to the side. Maxwell hung back, shining bright, staring at the glowing bronze orb in his hands. He seemed almost in a trance, as if he were viewing some prophecy in his mind.

Monkey and Snake watched from a distance, standing near the edge of the platform. They looked defeated, betrayed, like children whose parents had abandoned them.

And Carlos stood nearby, the remote control in his hand. His eyes were glassy; his gaze was cold and utterly mad.

I could take him out, Jasmine realized. *I've got just enough power left. I could zap him head-on, knock him off his feet—and maybe interrupt the power transfer.*

But at this range, I might kill him.

She couldn't do it. It was impossible. Even if it cost her everything, even if the entire world paid the price, she could not kill Carlos.

So she lay pinned like a fly, watching helplessly as her power flowed away. Below, the domes glowed brighter and brighter, the receptors flashed, the soldiers scurried back and forth.

The Dragon screamed.

CHAPTER TWENTY-SIX

STEVEN LEAPED AND RAN, kicked and jumped, swiped and grabbed, and swung his fists at his opponent. Malosi matched him move for move, sprinting and jumping around, swinging maces and nunchakus in the air.

Steven lost track of how long they sparred in the flame-lit House of Elders. He began to feel the ghosts of past Zodiac wielders watching him, long-dead Tigers following his every leap and parry. He thought again of the old man in Berlin, of the mysteries buried in the dead Tiger's words.

Steven cried out in pain as a throwing star grazed his foot. He leaped up onto the wall, grabbed hold of an outcropping, and looked down. The white Tiger blazed up from Malosi, its energy-form shining brighter than the torches lining the walls.

They were both Tigers. Steven had more experience with the Zodiac power, but Malosi was older, more muscular, and better trained.

"Come down, little Tiger," Malosi taunted. "Let your elder teach you a lesson."

Steven thought of his vision. He remembered the old tiger, circling around the baby.

Then he caught sight of a blazing torch, hanging on the wall just a few feet away. *The Tiger,* he remembered. *It's afraid of flame.*

Almost without thinking, he reached out, grabbed the torch, and hurled it through the air. Malosi's eyes went wide; the white Tiger weakened and reared back. Malosi jumped away.

Steven almost laughed. *That's one I owe Maxwell!*

The torch landed in a pile of Roman shields. Its flame puffed out.

Malosi glared up at Steven. Then he turned and strode across the floor to a display of ancient Chinese weapons. He picked up a very old sword with a black blade.

"Iron," Malosi said, not looking at Steven. "Song dynasty, I think."

"Earlier," Steven replied.

Malosi looked at him in surprise. "Maxwell said you didn't care about your heritage."

"He's wrong. As a general rule."

Malosi laughed softly. He threw the sword aside, picked up a stone axe, then tossed that away, as well.

Cautiously, Steven jumped to the ground. "We gonna play with toys all night?"

Ignoring him, Malosi hefted a thick, double-edged straight sword. Steven recognized it from his grandfather's books. In ancient China, it had been an elite weapon—one of the most difficult of all swords to wield effectively.

Malosi gripped it in both hands and turned toward Steven. The look in his eyes was deadly.

Steven snatched up a Roman shield, barely in time, and the sword struck it with a deafening clang. The two Tigers stood locked together for a moment, their Zodiac avatars biting and swiping at each other in the air above.

Then they were in motion again. Steven broke free and danced backward, out of Malosi's way. Malosi roared and charged, tossing small cannonballs. Steven dodged, and the projectiles lodged in the wall behind him. One cannonball grazed his cheek, drawing blood.

Steven charged and head-butted Malosi in the face. Malosi cried out and jumped back, startled. He dropped his sword.

And that, Steven thought, *is one I owe Liam.*

After that, the combat became a blur. One moment, Malosi was dragging Steven across the floor, over fragments of broken shields. Then Steven was slamming Malosi's head into a stone wall over and over. Malosi punched Steven in the face; Steven grabbed his opponent by the hair and yanked him off the floor. Malosi pulled Steven's elbow down and thrust a knee into his stomach. The two Tigers batted and circled, trading blows, absorbing incredible punishment.

Sometime during the battle, another wall came down.

Steven found himself in a small office with modern furniture, including a desk and chair. Fluorescent lights shone from a low ceiling. The whole room looked eerily normal—except for a few chipped Greek columns standing in one corner.

Malosi advanced toward Steven from the hole in the wall. In one hand, he held a crossbow, shooting off rapid-fire bolts. In his other, a particle rifle spat energy blasts.

Steven dodged and leaped onto the chair, then the desk. He caught sight of an ordinary sheet of paper, half-obscured by the desk blotter. The letterhead read CENTRAL BANK OF LYSTRIA.

As Malosi bent down to reload the crossbow, Steven raised a hand. *"Wait!"* he cried.

Malosi looked up. He didn't put down either of his weapons. But he paused.

Crouched on the desk, Steven gestured around the

office. He pointed at the broken Greek columns. "Do you know what this place is?"

"Yes," Malosi replied in a gravelly voice. "It's Maxwell's House of Self."

" 'Self,' " Steven repeated. "Do you know why he calls it that?"

Malosi shook his head, irritated.

"This is *Lystria*," Steven said. "The town Maxwell destroyed when he was making his reputation. This office, this furniture, even those ancient columns . . . they all came from that city." He paused. "Two million people died there."

"That's a myth," Malosi said. "A story Maxwell spreads in order to reinforce his tough-guy image. He told me so."

"He lied," Steven said. "Lystria was real. Ask Carlos. He's seen it."

Malosi just glared at him.

Then a great humming filled the room, vibrating the desk and lamps. A dull glow seemed to rise from everywhere at once. Steven looked around, searching for the source.

Malosi's expression was blank. He took a step toward Steven.

"What is it?" Steven asked. "What's happening?"

Malosi stared at him. Above his head, the white Tiger mirrored his stance, its eyes boring into Steven's own Tiger.

"You want to see?" Malosi asked.

Without waiting for an answer, he turned toward a side wall and fired off the particle rifle. Energy bolts slammed into the paneling, splintering it. In seconds, the wall went down.

"Come on," Malosi said.

Eyes wide, Steven followed him. They stepped into a vast open area covered with a thin layer of gray sand. *Maxwell's Japanese garden,* Steven realized. Ox had told them about it: the place where Maxwell retreated when he wanted peace and serenity.

But there was no peace there. The streams were dry; the trees had been uprooted and removed. Even the hills had been flattened, leaving only low rises.

And in the exact center of the room, a gigantic column of energy coursed up from the ground, pulsing out of some hidden machinery below. The blinding energy beam passed straight up through an opening in the center of the dome.

Steven crept near the beam. When he peered upward, he could see a bit of the night sky around the edges of the opening. Was that the hovering platform, just above?

"What *is* this?" he asked.

"The endgame," Malosi said.

Steven looked sideways at the blinding energy. As with the bars in Maxwell's jail, he could see something in it. Just one image, repeated over and over again, running down the beam into the floor. Winged, spitting fire . . .

"Dragon," he said. "This is the Dragon energy."

Malosi nodded. "Soon it'll belong to Maxwell. Again."

Steven stepped even closer to the beam. Below, the floor parted to reveal a huge cannon-like opening with circuitry all around it. That was the source.

"I know what you're thinking," Malosi said, "but I can't let you do it."

Steven looked at him. Malosi seemed calmer, almost rational. Could he be reasoned with?

"I have to stop him," Steven said.

"No," Malosi replied. "He's the only one who can handle this power."

"He's been lying to you. All along, every step of the way."

"You're just jealous," Malosi said. "He chose *me*."

The beam pulsed even brighter. Steven glanced from it to Malosi and then back to the circuitry embedded in the floor. Could he reach the beam before Malosi stopped him?

And if I do . . . what will the energy do to me?

"He thinks you're stupid," Steven said. "He's playing you."

A flicker of doubt crossed Malosi's face.

"It doesn't matter," he said. "In the end, we'll all be gone. No one will even remember us."

A familiar chill passed through Steven. Again, he thought of the old man's words: *When the power is gone . . . no trace of its hosts remains.*

"Maybe," Steven said. "Maybe not."

He reached into his pocket and pulled out the small heart-shaped qi amplifier.

Malosi frowned. "What's that?"

"It's a gift," Steven said, "from my mother."

Again, Malosi's expression wavered. "I never had a mother."

Steven frowned. He thought of his parents, who had neglected him for most of his childhood. He pictured them plotting and planning, arranging to trick him into receiving the Zodiac power—whether he wanted it or not.

"You haven't answered my question." Malosi pointed at the qi amplifier. "What is that?"

"She said it brought out a person's inner gifts," Steven said. He held the amplifier up to the glowing energy column.

Malosi made his move, as Steven expected. Malosi leaped toward him, angling sideways to stay clear of the energy beam. His hand was outstretched, ready to grab the qi amplifier.

Once again, time seemed to slow down. Steven felt calm, centered. He knew exactly what he was doing—what he *had* to do.

He snatched the amplifier away and, with his other hand, grabbed Malosi around the waist. He twisted the larger man around, forcing Malosi's arms behind his back in a wrestling hold. He wrapped his other arm around Malosi's neck, pulling him close.

"What—" Malosi struggled. "What are you doing?"

"You're a Tiger, like me," Steven said. "And I think you're a good person at heart. But the Tiger isn't just physical power. It's clarity of thought, purity of purpose. It's about seeing through the lies, to the . . . the . . ." Another phrase came to mind, spoken by the old Tiger. "The big picture."

He looked up at the opening in the ceiling. Past the energy beam, around the edge of the hovering platform, a few faint stars were visible.

Without loosening his grip, he juggled the small amplifier on the ends of his fingers. "She gave this to me," he said. "But I think maybe . . ."

Malosi stiffened in panic.

". . . maybe *you* need it more than I do."

The white Tiger raised its head and roared.

Steven pressed the amplifier to Malosi's neck and pushed the button.

CHAPTER TWENTY-SEVEN

IN A REMOTE part of England, an ancient stone monument called the Arbor Low henge began to glow red-hot. Invisible energy pulsed from the stones deep into the earth, charging the mystic ley lines with electromagnetic power. That power surged beneath Europe, down through Africa, and under the ocean floor, all the way to the other side of the world.

Within the Arctic Circle, a team of explorers found their compasses spinning madly. The earth's EM field was shifting, creating ripple effects from the North Pole clear to Antarctica.

In Australia, the Vanguard complex glowed bright. Hidden machines, mounted underneath each of the small domes, sucked energy from every corner of the world. Soldiers stood in neat rows along the pathways, staring at the power beams firing all around them.

That energy fueled the transfer machinery, increasing its strength. Within the central dome, the energy was processed and amplified into the most powerful artificially generated EM field the world had ever seen.

The only field that could absorb the power of the Dragon.

The main beam shot straight up out of the central dome, through the platform hovering directly above. Its blinding glow covered Jasmine's body, pinning her to the platform's surface. She couldn't see; she couldn't move a muscle. She couldn't even scream.

But she could feel the Zodiac energy leaving her body.

At first, Jasmine had found the Dragon difficult to control. The trick had been to keep it contained, to let out just enough of its power when necessary. The Dragon wasn't exactly sentient; it didn't think like a person. But she had the strange feeling it had come to respect her.

Now, lying on the platform, she realized something else. The Dragon had kept her going. She'd become obsessed with the search for Carlos, possessed by the idea of attacking Maxwell and ending his reign of terror. The burning Dragon power had seen her through weeks

ZODIAC

without sleep, through countless dead ends in her quest.

Now, she thought, *it's all over.*

The beam faded slightly. For a moment, she wondered: *Has something gone wrong with the machinery?*

Then Maxwell crouched down and took her chin in his hand. She tried not to flinch.

"You came into my home," he said, his voice deceptively gentle. "And you took what's mine."

"It's not yours." She glared up at him. "It's *mine.*"

He looked down at the beam, then back at her and smiled. "Not anymore."

Jasmine clenched her fists and struggled. But it was no use. The beam held her tight. And as its power ebbed, she realized something even worse:

The Dragon was gone. The machinery hadn't malfunctioned; it had just finished its work.

Carlos walked up, looking calmly at his analyzer. "Just a moment," he said. "The dome machinery is processing the Dragon power now. Every branch must be distributed properly."

Maxwell rose and turned toward Carlos. "You've served me well," he said, placing a hand on Carlos's shoulder. "I knew you would, in time."

Carlos shrugged and turned away, tapping at the analyzer screen.

Maxwell smiled down at Jasmine. "A cold fish sometimes, isn't he?"

Jasmine felt a fist close on her heart.

Carlos looked up from his analyzer. "Ready."

Maxwell's face went hard. With one quick movement, he reached down and threw Jasmine aside. She tumbled across the platform, free of the paralyzing beam, and lay on her back, gasping for breath.

Maxwell stepped very deliberately to the exact spot where Jasmine had been pinned. He raised his arms to the heavens just as a bright flash covered the platform. The beam washed over him, rising past him to stab into the sky.

"Reversing polarity," Carlos said.

All around Maxwell, the Dragon rose up. It was *his* Dragon, not Jasmine's: huge-jawed and sinewy, cruel and fierce. It seemed larger than ever before, its snakelike body coiling and curling all around him.

"Oh, yes," Maxwell said. "I've missed this."

Jasmine watched, helpless.

There's nothing I can do, she thought. *I know the power of the Dragon better than anyone. No ordinary person can challenge it.*

And that's all I am now. An ordinary person.

She gazed at the shack, at the prison that held Liam and the others inside its walls. A wave of guilt washed over her. *They followed me here,* she thought. *I led us to this point. There's no one to blame but myself.*

Then the beam winked off.

Maxwell shook his head in confusion. Carlos stepped forward, frowning at his analyzer.

The power transfer, Jasmine realized. *Something's inter-rupted it!*

She stared at Maxwell. The Dragon still rose up around him—but it seemed weaker than before, less substantial. The Zodiac power hadn't been fully infused into him yet. Maybe—

A rattling noise seemed to descend from the sky, grow-ing louder. Jasmine flinched and rolled aside.

Steven Lee tumbled in for a landing, with Malosi in his arms.

On Steven's back, the jet pack coughed, spat, and caught fire. It was dented, Jasmine saw, and badly damaged. As Malosi leaped away, Steven twisted free of the contraption and tossed it aside.

"Hey, Maxy!" Steven said. "Surprised to see me?"

Maxwell stood, glowing. "I'm more surprised to see *you*," he said, pointing at Malosi.

Malosi moved forward, facing Maxwell. "I've seen the big picture," he said.

Jasmine's eyes darted from Steven to Malosi and back again. The two stood together, facing Maxwell, their fists clenched in a battle-ready stance. What was Malosi talk-ing about? Had he captured Steven, forced him onto the platform?

Above Malosi, the white Tiger began to take form. Steven furrowed his brow, and his own Tiger billowed out-ward to join it. The two Tigers rose up, stared at each other for a moment, and roared in unison.

Then they came together and merged. The giant energy-cat morphed and twisted in midair, shifting from white to orange, from Malosi's Tiger to Steven's and back again.

Maxwell stared into Malosi's eyes. "Son," he began.

"I am *not* your son," Malosi said.

Jasmine smiled.

The two Tigers exchanged a glance, then charged.

Maxwell didn't step aside, didn't move to counter their attack. He just stood there, smiling.

Steven's mind was racing. *There's two of us,* he thought, *and only one of him. But he's the Dragon. Or part Dragon, anyway.*

Before Steven and Malosi had retrieved the jet pack, they'd cut off the power source in the main dome. But there was no way of knowing how much energy Maxwell had already absorbed.

Once again, time seemed to slow to a crawl. Steven's limbs pumped slowly, as if he were running through mud. Malosi had slowed down, too.

Steven looked around frantically. Jasmine was crouched near the shack; Monkey and Snake stood together, watching; and Carlos was near the edge of the platform, staring at his analyzer. All of them were still as statues.

Only Maxwell was moving. The cruel smile was still planted on his face.

"Too late," he said. "You're too late."

Steven tensed for the attack. But instead of turning on them, Maxwell lowered both his arms. He closed his eyes, clenched his fists, and began to glow.

What's he doing? Steven wondered.

Then Maxwell let out a massive burst of Zodiac energy, aimed straight down. The blast passed through the bottom of the platform and stabbed into the main dome.

Power flashed out in all directions from the central dome, even brighter than before. The energy narrowed, coalescing into five distinct beams reaching out to the remaining smaller domes. They began to glow in response.

The main dome exploded.

Time snapped back to normal. The platform lurched, tipping in midair as the shockwave hit it.

Steven and Malosi stumbled backward and tumbled to the platform's surface. Jasmine crawled over to them, struggling to keep her balance.

Malosi climbed to his feet as the platform leveled out. He reached out a hand to help Jasmine up. She hesitated.

"He's with us," Steven said.

Then Steven saw Maxwell, standing at the center of the platform. His hands were rigid at his sides, aimed down at the remains of the central dome.

And the power flow had resumed. Energy surged up from the broken dome, radiating from its exposed core in the floor beneath. Twin beams of power stabbed into Maxwell's hands. The beams were jagged, rough-edged, less sharply focused than before. But they glowed bright.

Above Maxwell, the Dragon writhed and snarled, growing more solid every moment.

Steven swallowed. "He doesn't need the machinery anymore," he said. "He can absorb the Dragon power all by himself."

Down below, the energy feedback continued to spread. Another dome blew open, hurling plastic and metal into the air. A group of soldiers scattered, running to avoid the falling debris.

Jasmine touched Steven's arm. "He's vulnerable," she said, gesturing at Maxwell. "In a moment he'll be too strong. You've got to stop him *now*."

"She's right," Malosi said.

Steven nodded—

—and then something stabbed into his neck. He whirled, stumbled, and saw Carlos holding his dart gun.

Carlos smiled. "My last dart," he said.

Even as Steven reached for his neck, he felt a familiar, cold sensation. *It's another blasted power drainer,* he realized. *Like back in Maxwell's lab.*

No. This can't happen now. It can't!

But it was. And even worse: when he turned back to Carlos, the scientist was holding the bronze sphere—the *jiānyù*. Tiger energy began to flow out of Steven and into the sphere.

Not again, Steven thought. *Not again!*

He glanced over at Maxwell—who glowed like a star, his gravity pulling in every trace of the Dragon power.

With each passing second, he grew stronger. And Steven grew weaker.

Steven reached inside his pocket for the qi amplifier and pressed its button. Nothing. It was exhausted, out of power.

Malosi reached out and slapped the *jiānyù* out of Carlos's hand. Carlos cried out as the sphere clattered to the platform—but Steven's power continued to flow into it.

"I can stop you," Malosi said, turning to face Maxwell.

Maxwell's eyes glowed bright. He cocked his head one way, then the other. He seemed overwhelmed, dazed by the power.

"I am father to the world," Maxwell said. His voice boomed in the air. *"And the world needs discipline."*

On the platform, the *jiānyù* surged bright.

Malosi cried out and fell to his knees.

"No!" Steven yelled. He staggered toward Malosi. But Carlos was standing over the second Tiger, watching as Zodiac energy fled from his body.

"The drainer's already inside him," Carlos said. "We've been planning this for a long time. Did you think we'd build a Tiger without giving him an off switch?"

"Oh," Maxwell said. *"Oh, my."*

Above him, the Dragon blazed bright. It snarled and reached a wing toward the *jiānyù*. The bronze sphere lay on the platform, glowing with the full energy of the Tiger.

Steven watched the *jiānyù* levitate. As the Dragon

beckoned, it swooped up and around, then landed softly in Maxwell's outstretched hand.

Like a single being, Maxwell and the Dragon turned to stare at the *jiānyù*. Again, it began to melt and shift in Maxwell's hand, morphing into the other Zodiac signs, one by one. The ram. The rooster. The slithering snake. The snorting ox.

Zodiac power surged from the bronze artifact—leaping through the air like a bolt of electricity. The Dragon opened its mouth to receive the energy.

Maxwell stiffened. The glow around him doubled in intensity. He stared into the cloud of energy, almost hypnotized by its power.

Yet another dome exploded below. Fires were breaking out all across the complex. Soldiers rushed around, grabbing fire extinguishers and dragging injured comrades to safety.

Jasmine touched Steven's shoulder. He looked over at her in surprise and saw that Malosi was with her. They were both staring at the glowing, reeling Maxwell.

"What's happening?" Steven asked. "It looks like the Dragon is taking control of all the other powers."

"That's not all it's taking control of," Jasmine said. "We're about to have an even bigger problem. No time to explain . . . the point is, he's disoriented."

Malosi grimaced. "We tried attacking him once. And we had the Tiger power then."

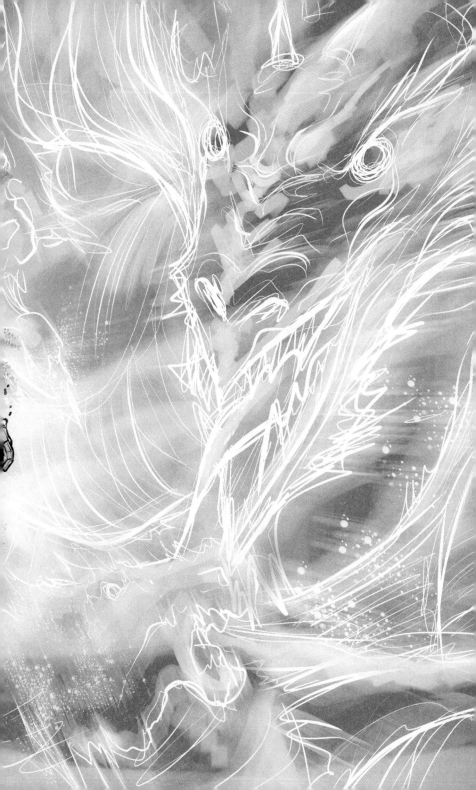

"I'm not saying this is a good option," Jasmine replied. "But the rest of the team is being held captive in that shack."

Steven thought quickly. "If we provide a distraction, can you free them?"

Jasmine smiled. Strangely, Steven felt a wave of relief. She seemed like the old Jasmine, the woman who laughed at danger.

"I'll do more than that," she said.

Steven turned to Malosi. He thought of the blows they'd traded, the vicious battle they'd fought just minutes before, down in the main dome.

Before we were Tigers together, he thought. *Before we were brothers.*

"Together?" Malosi asked.

Again, they charged.

Jasmine ran for the shack—then veered toward Carlos. He turned in surprise as she jabbed a rigid hand into his neck. He made a strangled noise and went down.

When the Tigers collided with Maxwell, Steven felt like he'd slammed into a wall. The energy, the combined Zodiac power, flared through Steven like a high-voltage shock. He heard Malosi gasp in pain.

The energy was blinding; Steven couldn't even see. He felt something hot and metallic brush against his hands. *The* jiānyù*!*

He grabbed it, wrenching it free of Maxwell's grip. Zodiac signs filled Steven's field of vision, flickering in and out, winking and shimmering in the thick ion field. The roaring pig, the charging horse, the laughing monkey.

Maxwell was still on his feet. *Still absorbing the energy,* Steven thought. *Burning out his whole complex, every machine in this base. Whatever it takes to absorb every bit of the Dragon.*

We've got to keep pushing. Knock him down, stop him any way we can. Nothing else matters.

Not even our lives.

"NO!" Maxwell roared.

Energy exploded from him, feeding back into the sphere in Steven's hands. He cried out and threw it in the air. He watched, dazed, as the *jiānyù* continued to change shape in flight: tiger, rooster, ram. It blazed bright, power flowing back and forth from it to Maxwell, building and glowing like a star—

The shack exploded.

Steven blacked out.

When he came to seconds later, Roxanne was helping him up. "Welcome back, boss," she said.

Steven looked around. Roxanne stood with Liam, Duane, Ox, and Jasmine. Malosi stood just past them, over Carlos's unconscious form.

Maxwell was barely recognizable as human. He glowed white-hot, hovering a few inches above the platform's surface. The beam from below had stopped, and the *jiānyù* lay discarded on the platform.

Liam frowned. "I don't trust that soldier boy."

"I think we have a more immediate problem," Duane said.

Beneath their feet, the platform let out a loud creak and tipped violently. Steven stumbled into Liam, knocking him into the others.

Steven followed Duane's gaze. The shack lay splintered and strewn across the platform, a mass of wood and plastic shards. And in the center of it all, the crystal circuitry lay shattered. Tiny fires flared, arcing like electricity across the exposed wiring.

The platform lurched again, in the opposite direction.

Duane pointed at the sparking remains of the crystal circuitry web. "That," he said, "was a null-gravity generator."

Steven looked at him blankly.

"It was keeping us in the air," he explained.

The platform wrenched violently again, to one side and then the other.

"Uh-oh," Steven said.

THE PLATFORM HURTLED across the sky,

tipping slowly downward. From a distance, it looked like a plate that a child had flung through the air—a plate that was, inevitably, falling to earth.

Maxwell stood rigid on the tilted surface, perfectly still, as the glow around him slowly cooled and faded. Above him, the Dragon rose up, proud and sinewy. But it, too, was still in the fierce desert wind.

Steven frowned. *What's Maxy up to?* He looked at Malosi, and the other Tiger made eye contact with him briefly. Then Malosi turned back to study Maxwell.

Steven had a moment of doubt. With a bit of help from the qi amplifier, he'd managed to convince Malosi of the danger Maxwell posed. But as he stood watching, Steven realized he didn't actually know Malosi at all.

Is he watching Maxwell for us? Or has he been playing me all along? Could he still be working for Maxwell? Where are Malosi's loyalties, really?

A crunching sound at Steven's feet made him look down. Duane sat amid the tangled mass of burned circuitry that had been the anti-gravity generator. His hands moved dizzyingly fast, sorting circuits and laying pieces of wire in neat rows.

"I think I can fix it," Duane said.

Steven crouched down next to him. "Without your powers?"

Duane turned and gave Steven his usual shy smile. "I was pretty smart, even before I got them. And I was watching the generator work, from our cell."

The platform lurched again, tilting almost forty-five degrees. Steven stumbled and tripped over a chunk of the broken shack's wall. By the time the platform leveled out, Duane was hard at work, stripping wires and plugging cables into ports.

"HELLLLLP!"

Steven looked around, searching for the source of the cry. Carlos lay on the surface, still unconscious. Malosi and Maxwell hadn't moved, either.

But Liam, Roxanne, and Jasmine were running toward the edge—where Monkey hung by his fingers from the platform, dangling over the ground far below.

"Help!" he called again. "I'm slipping!"

Snake lay flat on her stomach near the edge, stretching an arm toward him. "Quit squirming!" she said.

As Steven approached the platform's edge, he caught a glimpse of the chaos below. The energy beams had halted, leaving destruction in their wake. Four or five domes had exploded completely, and another was in flames. A thick burning smell filled the air.

Even worse, the platform was arcing downward more sharply. The burning wreck of the main dome loomed dead ahead. They were hurtling straight toward it.

Monkey reached up a trembling hand. Snake grabbed it—just as the platform swerved violently.

Steven stumbled into Jasmine, and they both fell to the surface. Liam and Roxanne reached for Jasmine and managed to grab hold of her. Steven grabbed frantically at the plastic surface of the disk, barely slowing his progress.

As he rolled toward Snake, he saw her slip over the edge. "No!" he cried. He grabbed hard at the platform surface, stopping just short of the edge, and reached down.

Snake's hand clasped onto his arm.

Steven looked down. Snake dangled from his grip now. And Monkey hung from *her*, flailing and panicking as the domes whizzed past.

Steven grimaced in pain. He felt himself slipping, sliding closer to the edge. *I can't hold them,* he thought. *I can't hold both their weight. Not without the Tiger!*

On the ground, the soldiers were beginning to back off. An amplified voice filled the air. *"All hands, Condition Seven. Abandon base. This is not a drill. Secure all classified materials and abandon base. Condition Seven. . . ."*

"Grab hold," Steven called to Snake. "Grab on to the edge of the platform!"

"Do it!" Monkey yelled.

"I can't!" Snake replied.

The main dome drew closer. Steven could see inside, past its cracked white walls. A thick column of black smoke rose from the burned-out machinery in the floor.

"Hey, kid!" Snake called up. She sounded oddly calm. "If we both survive this? Look me up in six or seven years."

"What?" he said.

"When you're old enough." She smiled. "We'll have that drink."

Then she let go.

"No!" he cried.

The disk twisted hard, away from the main dome, and almost flipped over. Steven slid toward the center, scrambling and clawing for balance. He braced himself, lying flat on his stomach, and crawled back to the edge.

The big dome passed underneath, its black smoke filling the air with a burned-electronics smell. There was no sign of Snake or Monkey. Steven shivered. *Did they fall into that?*

Roxanne tapped him on the shoulder, hard. "Steven?"

He whirled around and looked up. Maxwell was striding toward them, the Dragon blazing above his head. Energy leaked out of him—his eyes, his mouth, his pores. He held the *jiānyù*; it had subsided to a sphere again, but it still glowed with concentrated Zodiac power.

Liam, Jasmine, and Roxanne had gathered around Steven. They took a step back from Maxwell, toward the platform's edge.

"Between the Dragon and the pavement," Roxanne muttered.

Steven turned to look down at the ground. It was even closer, whizzing past in a near blur.

"This might be the end," he agreed.

"Look," Jasmine said. "Look at him."

Steven followed her outstretched finger. Maxwell had stopped and was staring straight ahead. He seemed rigid, cold, almost in a trance.

And the Dragon . . . the Dragon above him looked different, too. It seemed more solid, more real than ever before—as if it belonged there around Maxwell's body and it would never leave again.

"He's not there anymore," Jasmine explained. "Maxwell, I mean. The Dragon has taken him over completely."

Steven frowned. "Are you sure?"

When she turned to him, her expression made him shudder.

"It's what I spent the past twelve months trying to avoid," she whispered.

A cold feeling washed over Steven. He remembered watching Jasmine disperse the storm back in Dubai and wondering: *Will she* become *the Dragon?*

With a sudden movement, the Dragon spread its wings. Steven and the others flinched. Liam almost toppled over the edge, but Roxanne caught him.

"Is he—is he *leavin'*?" Liam asked.

"He is." Malosi stepped forward, next to his glowing boss. Steven moved to meet him, not knowing what to expect.

"And I'm going with him," Malosi continued.

Steven darted a glance at Maxwell. The Vanguard leader rose off the platform a few inches. His eyes were utterly blank, his body bathed in Zodiac energy.

"So you are still working for him," Steven said.

"No." Malosi gestured at Maxwell. "You're right about him. I know what he is—what he's capable of. But . . ."

"But you owe him."

Malosi nodded. "Like you owe your mother."

Liam turned to Steven. "What is that bloody tin soldier talking about?"

"Maybe I can change things," Malosi said, staring at Maxwell. "Guide him onto a different path. Hey, Steven?"

"Yeah?" Steven said.

"Try not to die."

Malosi grabbed hold of Maxwell and leaped off the edge.

Steven rushed after them, with Liam and Roxanne right behind. They reached the edge—then jumped back as a dome whizzed by, dangerously close. Steven fell to the platform, rolled over—

—and saw the blazing form of the Dragon carrying two figures up and away into the night.

Liam reached out a hand and helped Steven to his feet. "Think it's too late to ask him to leave that dingus behind? The one with our powers in it?"

"Should we go after them?" Roxanne asked.

Steven stared at her. "How?"

"Daddy issues," Liam said, shaking his head. "Seems like I'm the only one without 'em."

"Never mind that," Jasmine said, glancing nervously at the edge. "We need an extraction plan. And we need it fast."

"By the way," Roxanne said, "has anyone noticed that Ox disappeared?"

"Maybe he tumbled off the side," Liam replied.

"Or maybe he's not so trustworthy after all," Steven said, his voice dark.

Liam didn't answer. He crouched down, sweeping away

the remains of some red dirt to peer through the bottom of the transparent platform. It was flying toward the front of the complex, the direction from which they'd first made their assault. The remains of the guard tower that Jasmine had destroyed loomed in the distance.

And just ahead, building two was still standing. When Steven squinted, he could barely make out the tail of the Zodiac stealth plane, protruding at an angle from the dome's still-smoking roof.

Liam stood up. "The plane," he said. "It might be salvageable."

"Great." Steven stared at him in disbelief. "But how are you gonna get down there?"

Liam grinned.

"No," Steven replied. "Oh, no."

Liam sprinted toward the edge. Steven followed, reaching out for him.

"You've got no powers!" Steven cried. "You'll be killed!"

They reached the edge just as building two passed underneath. The plane's tail jutted up out of the dome, not more than a few meters below. They were dropping dangerously fast.

The platform tipped again, and they both stumbled back. When Liam turned, his face was very serious.

"I guess we all gotta grow up sometime," he said. "And Steven, if I don't make it . . ."

Steven swallowed. "Yeah?"

"Tell the British Army I'm sorry."

He turned and dove over the edge.

Before Steven could even cry out, a burst of acceleration sent him tumbling back toward the center of the platform. He whirled, thinking: *Liam. Liam! I've got to see if he's still alive!*

He crawled along the platform, squinting to look down through its surface. As building two flashed past, he thought he saw Liam shimmying down the plane's fuselage into the hole in the dome. But he couldn't be sure.

The ground was passing very fast—and very close. Fires raged all across the complex. A smattering of jeeps and trucks fanned out from the base in all directions as the evacuation order continued.

Another dome erupted in flames—Steven couldn't make out its number. Up ahead, past the complex, red desert sand stretched out, broken only by the access road and a small half-wrecked guard booth at the checkpoint.

"Oh, no," Jasmine said.

Steven turned to look. Toward the middle of the platform, Carlos was marching toward Duane, who still sat in the ruins of the shack.

"Return of the mad scientist," Roxanne said grimly.

Jasmine frowned. "Next time I'll hit him harder."

"Come on," Steven said.

They picked their way across the lurching platform. When they reached the shack, Steven stopped, shocked.

Duane sat on the platform's surface, surrounded by crystals and circuits. As Steven watched, Duane picked up a stripped wire, licked it once, and recoiled from the live current.

But that wasn't the strange part. Carlos stood over Duane, watching him calmly. They were having a discussion.

". . . picked up many of the principles of my work," Carlos said pleasantly. "I'm impressed."

"Thank you," Duane replied, not looking up. "As always, your conceptual leaps were the difficult part. The engineering is simple."

Carlos raised an eyebrow. "It's not *that* simple." He seemed slightly insulted.

Steven watched in confusion. Roxanne and Jasmine stood with him, one on either side.

"What is this?" Roxanne whispered.

"I think . . ." Steven paused. "It looks like a meeting of minds."

"Anyway, you can't recharge that," Carlos said. He didn't seem to have noticed the intrusion. "The battery is fused; you'll never get enough juice to the field generator."

"Not true." Duane smiled and held up a large battery pack. "It's a tricky conversion job, but this is all one system. I should be able to patch in the batteries used for the cell door lock."

Steven glanced at Jasmine. She stood perfectly still, staring at Carlos. She seemed to be in shock.

Carlos was staring, too—at the battery pack.

"That's true," he said. His voice was almost a whisper. "It's possible. Why didn't I see that?"

"Perhaps your logic centers have been compromised," Duane said.

A hint of panic entered Carlos's eyes.

The platform swung wildly again. Carlos stumbled. Several of Duane's components slid across the ground; he snatched them up easily, without hurrying.

"By every objective measure, Maxwell is a danger," Duane said. "To himself, the people around him, and to the world, as well."

He turned and looked up at Carlos for the first time.

"Yet *you* served him," Duane continued. "You helped him to achieve nearly limitless power. Does that not indicate a lapse of rationality?"

"Rationality? No. No, my brain is rational." Carlos shook his head, a wild look in his eyes. "That's what my whole life is built around. It's the essence of who I am."

Duane gestured at the sprawling circuits. "You designed all this, right?"

"Yes." Carlos nodded very fast. "With my mind."

"But you couldn't see how to repair it."

"What is Duane *doing*?" Roxanne whispered.

"I think he's trying to fix a null-gravity generator," Steven replied.

"*And* a man's mind," Jasmine breathed.

Carlos was shaking his head again. He looked down at Duane, almost accusingly. "No," he said. "No, it's not true. You're lying. I *am* rational. Serving him, serving Maxwell, was a rational choice."

Duane worked furiously, connecting wires to circuits. "Maybe I'm not the person you're trying to convince," he said softly.

"You're lying," Carlos repeated. "Lying, lying liar. *LIAR!*"

He whirled and ran off.

Jasmine started after him but stopped as Duane said one word:

"Seventeen."

Steven looked at him. "What?"

"I've managed to steer us out into an open area," Duane said, "but I can't keep the platform from crashing. In about seventeen seconds." He looked up. "Make that fourteen."

Roxanne, Jasmine, and Steven looked at one another.

"I suggest you fasten your seat belts," Duane said.

Roxanne stared at him.

"That's supposed to be funny," he explained.

Surprisingly, Jasmine laughed. Then she reached out and pulled Roxanne and Steven to the floor. She scooted up against a half-standing wall that had been part of the shack, gathering the others to her like a mother hen.

"No seat belts," Jasmine said. "Just us."

Steven felt suddenly overcome with emotion. He closed his eyes, partly to brace for the impact and partly so he wouldn't cry. Despite the danger, the loss of their powers, the fire and destruction, it was *so good* to be back with his friends again.

Roxanne wrapped her arm around his shoulder. She was singing softly to herself, but he couldn't make out the melody.

"Hey, Duane?" Steven called out. Duane was still working furiously, manipulating some sort of makeshift joystick.

"Yes?"

"Still not so good with the funny."

Six seconds now, Steven thought. *Maybe five.*

Duane laughed. "I know."

CHAPTER TWENTY-NINE

THE PLATFORM CRASHED down edge-first, shaking the ground and sending red earth jetting into the air. A squadron of soldiers jumped out of the way, then leaped into their jeeps and sped away.

On the platform, Steven clung to Jasmine and Roxanne. The three of them slid across the surface, smashing into Duane.

Duane grunted and looked up. He sat hunched over his equipment, frantically moving switches and manipulating his patched-together circuitry.

"We've landed," he said.

Roxanne stared at him in disbelief. "You think?"

Jasmine was crouched down, peering through the transparent floor of the platform. "Huh," she said.

"What is it?" Steven asked.

"First thing I did when I got here," Jasmine said, "was attack a guard tower."

"So?"

"So I think we just landed on it."

Steven stood up, and together they walked out to survey the scene. The platform was unsteady, wobbling atop the smashed remains of the guard tower. Dirt had settled across its surface, painting everything a grimy red.

Duane had managed to land the platform at the front of the complex. Behind them, fires raged and small explosions rose up from the remaining domes. Trucks fanned out all around them, heading into the desert.

"They're evacuating," Steven said. "All of 'em."

"Carlos?" Jasmine looked around the platform, almost frantically. "Where's Carlos?"

"Steven? You better get back here." Roxanne said.

He cast a worried glance at Jasmine, then walked back to the wreckage of the shack. Roxanne stood over Duane, who sat surrounded by jury-rigged machinery.

"Curious," he said. "I don't believe I can move."

Steven and Roxanne crouched down together. As Roxanne moved Duane's jacket aside, Steven gasped. A shard of crystal from the circuitry protruded from a blood-crusted wound in his leg.

Duane looked up at them. His eyes were unusually wide.

"Ah," he said, pointing calmly at the crystal. "That explains it."

"He's in shock," Roxanne said. "Should we move him?"

"We can't stay here," Steven said. "We're sitting ducks for any twitchy Vanguard soldiers who haven't left yet."

"*Not* my best landing," Duane continued. There was a little blank smile on his face. "But considering the state of the . . . uhhh . . . equipment . . . I think I did all right."

Roxanne helped him to his feet. "Come on, brainiac," she said. "We gotta bounce."

Steven helped her drag Duane across the tilted platform. Duane seemed pliant, willing to be led. *Like she said: in shock,* Steven thought.

A motion caught his eye. Jasmine was running across the platform, toward the far side—the side that was tipped up a meter or so off the ground. She was heading toward another figure. . . .

Carlos. He sat on the raised edge of the platform, his legs dangling over the side. He was clutching his head.

"Come on," Steven said.

As they approached Carlos, they could hear him speaking. The words were low, almost like a chant.

"Doesn't work," he said. "It doesn't add up."

Jasmine took a half step toward him. "Carlos?" she called. She sounded scared.

She really loves him, Steven realized. *This must be killing her.*

Carlos turned. His eyes were manic, terrified. He cast a quick look at Steven, then stared up at Jasmine. Slowly, he held up a hand and started counting compulsively on his fingers: *One-two-three-four-five,* over and over again.

"Doesn't add up," he said again. "Every move has been rational, every step I've taken. Yet the outcome is wrong. It's all wrong."

Roxanne approached, with Duane limping after. He seemed more alert now.

"His mind is rebelling," Duane said, gesturing at Carlos. "The conditioning—the brainwashing Maxwell gave him. It's destroying him."

Duane stumbled and winced in pain. Roxanne placed an arm around his shoulders to steady him.

Jasmine crouched down and held out a hand. "Carlos," she said. "It's okay. Come with me."

He stared into her eyes for a long moment. His expression flashed from terror to hatred, then back to fear.

He shook his head, turned, and leaped off the platform.

Jasmine started after him, but Steven grabbed her arm.

"We can't," he said. "We have to *go.* We don't have our powers anymore, remember?"

When Jasmine turned toward him, there was a new kind of desperation in her eyes.

"I can't," she said. "After all this . . . I can't abandon him. I just can't do it."

Steven opened his mouth to argue. Then he remembered Horse and Dog. He'd run off on them in the tunnels, left them to be taken by Maxwell's guards. That guilt had been weighing on him ever since.

Can I do that again? he thought. *And with Carlos—a friend? Even if he's been brainwashed, turned violently against us?*

"I don't care about powers," Jasmine continued. "I don't even care what happens to me. I can't leave him."

An energy bolt sizzled over their heads. Steven whirled to see a squadron of soldiers on the ground nearby. They were pointing up at the figures on the platform and aiming their weapons.

Then a flaming piece of debris slammed down right behind the soldiers, knocking them off their feet. Steven couldn't tell what it was—a hunk of one of the domes, maybe? The soldiers dropped, their weapons clattering to the ground.

"Lucky break," Steven said.

Roxanne looked around, her arm still around Duane. "We gotta find shelter," she said.

Jasmine pointed. "There."

Steven followed her gaze. In the gloom, he could just barely see Carlos running toward the access road.

"Come on," Steven said.

He and Jasmine jumped off the platform.

Steven touched down awkwardly, almost twisting his ankle. *The Tiger usually helps me land,* he realized. *I'm not used to being normal!*

He recovered quickly. By the time he caught up with Jasmine, she had a finger to her earpiece.

"Roxanne, you copy?" Jasmine said. "We're in pursuit. I think Carlos is heading toward that smashed-down checkpoint station, at the curve in the access road."

Suddenly, Steven remembered something. "There's a tunnel there!"

"You get that?" Jasmine said into her earpiece. "No?" She turned to Steven, annoyed. "Where's your radio?"

"Maxwell kind of took it. Along with my phone. And the rest of my stuff."

"Great," Jasmine said.

She repeated the information about the tunnel into her radio.

"I have an oracle bone," Steven said weakly.

"That's very nice."

"And, uh, Rat gave me a flip phone."

"Rat?" Jasmine repeated. "We're gonna have a talk about that."

A few scattered soldiers passed in front of them. Steven and Jasmine dodged sideways, staying in the shadows.

Up ahead, Carlos had almost reached the checkpoint. Before the assault, it had been a small booth with windows on all sides, marking the entrance to the Vanguard complex. Now it was a cracked mass of plastic and metal.

A guard's limp body lay draped over the remains of one wall.

"Carlos!" Jasmine called.

Carlos didn't look back. He picked up the guard and tossed him aside. The man landed on the road with a faint moan.

Then Carlos lifted up a hatch and disappeared into the ground.

They reached the tunnel entrance. It was open, leading to a dimly illuminated cavern below. Steven hesitated, remembering his previous experience in the Vanguard tunnels.

"You coming?" Jasmine asked.

He followed her down, past the rusting pipes in the ceiling, along the dripping stone walls. They landed in a wide area leading to a narrow tunnel that curved rapidly out of view.

Jasmine peered down the tunnel. "You've been down here before?" she asked.

"Yeah," he replied. "But I came from the other end. Didn't make it this far."

"Well, there's only one way he could have gone."

She sprinted down the tunnel. Steven followed, stumbling once and glancing off the curved stone wall. Their feet splashed through puddles, the way lit only by old incandescent bulbs spaced at uneven intervals along the walls.

Slowly, the tunnel widened. As before, they passed artifacts, stolen treasures crowded into the tunnel for storage. A carved wine server from ancient China. A full-size Egyptian sarcophagus. A pile of very old coins.

From above, an explosion shook the chamber.

The whole complex is collapsing, Steven thought. *We better find Carlos quick.*

Jasmine pounded forward, staying a few steps ahead of him. She stumbled over something and almost fell. As she stopped, Steven looked down and saw it was a Vanguard soldier, lying unconscious.

"Huh," Steven said.

Jasmine shrugged, turned, and started running again.

They passed two more soldiers, both out cold on the tunnel floor. And then something familiar loomed up ahead. A huge Sherman tank, wedged in so tightly that it almost blocked the passageway.

"I've been here before," Steven began. Then Jasmine stopped dead in front of him, so suddenly that he almost slammed into her.

Carlos stood in front of the tank. His face was dirty, his eyes wide with madness. He raised a Vanguard energy rifle.

"Stay back," he said. "Stay away."

Jasmine took a step forward. "Carlos," she said.

"My brain," Carlos said. "Its components are faulty."

"No," Jasmine said. "Not the components."

"But it doesn't work." He shook his head rapidly, as if trying to knock something loose.

"I know," Jasmine said. "That's because of Maxwell. He did something to you."

Carlos stared at her for a moment.

"Maxwell." He kept the rifle raised. "It was logical to help him. Only he can control the Zodiac power. Only he can be trusted with it."

"Carlos," Steven began, "take it easy."

"Maxwell is—he's the champion of the human race," Carlos continued. "Only he can be trusted with all that power."

"He *can't* be trusted," Jasmine said. "He's not even in control of it anymore."

"He can. He . . . he told me."

"Carlos," Jasmine said. Her voice was cracking. "Maxwell did something to your mind. He made you believe."

"I did everything rationally," Carlos replied, shaking his head violently again. "I followed the proper steps, acted according to consistent guiding principles." He paused and looked around wildly. "Yet it all led to this. The results are all wrong."

"Yes," Jasmine said, taking a tentative step forward. "They are."

Carlos turned and stared at her. "He made me *hurt you*!"

Jasmine just stared at him. Tears were forming in the corners of her eyes.

"My brain," Carlos said. "Oh god, it doesn't work." The rifle quivered in his hands. "I am the Operator. The Operator. My brain my brain *my brain*—"

"It's okay," Jasmine said. "We can help you. Just—"

"No." He shook his head. "The Dragon power . . . it's *his* now. Only the Dragon can fix my brain. Are you the Dragon?"

Jasmine stopped. She shook her head.

He's still thinking, Steven realized. *As damaged as that mind is, it won't stop working.*

Carlos stepped back against the tank. Steven glanced up at the ceiling, then down at Carlos. *If I had my powers, I could take him,* he thought. *Swing off the pipes, knock him away from the tank.*

But Carlos's energy rifle was trained on Jasmine. One twitch of his finger and Jasmine would be dead. Without his Tiger powers, Steven couldn't take the chance.

Carlos studied Jasmine. "Maybe if I kill you," he said, his voice disturbingly calm, "maybe then the pain will go away."

"No," she said.

"Yes." He nodded his head. "It's logical. It's rational. It's the only way."

"Carlos," Jasmine said, her voice breaking. "I came down here to get you. I came back for you."

Steven watched the two of them. There was no way out. If he tackled Carlos, Carlos would shoot Jasmine. If he didn't, Carlos would probably shoot her anyway.

"Don't," Jasmine said. "Don't do this."

But she didn't move. Steven remembered her words, back on the platform: *I don't even care what happens to me.*

Carlos's finger tightened on the trigger.

I have to try, Steven thought. *I have to do something.*

Jasmine closed her eyes.

A flash of light swung down, slashing into Carlos from behind. He cried out and fell forward, dropping to his knees.

The energy rifle went off and struck the ceiling. A pipe burst, spewing steam into the air.

From behind the tank, out of the shadows, a small figure stepped forward. She held up her hand, revealing an electrically charged glove studded with bright claws. It glowed and sparked like a second skeleton over her hand.

It took Steven a minute to recognize her: the blue eyes, the unwashed hair. He shook his head in shock.

"Mince?" he whispered.

She smirked, waving the claw in the air. "Invented this myself," she said. "Pretty tight, huh?"

At her feet, Carlos groaned once and collapsed.

Jasmine blinked in confusion. "Who is this?"

"She works for Maxwell," Steven explained, watching Mince warily. "She's his number two scientist."

"Number one," Mince said, "as soon as you take *him* away."

She kicked Carlos, not too gently.

Jasmine rushed to Carlos and took him in her arms. Carlos's back was gashed and bleeding from Mince's claw weapon, but he was breathing.

"I don't understand," Jasmine said.

"You and the kid trashed this place pretty good," Mince said. "And Maxwell's—well, I'm not sure exactly *what* he is now. But let's just say I'm hoping to advance in the new power structure." She looked around and laughed. "There's always opportunities in the face of disaster."

Steven peered at Mince. She was crazy as ever, but she seemed sure of her plan. Her manner was almost calm.

"You don't want to kill us?" he asked.

"Not if you get rid of my problem." She pointed at Carlos.

Jasmine and Steven exchanged a quick glance. Jasmine rose to her feet, lifting Carlos in her arms. He moaned once but remained limp.

"Thanks," Steven said. He reached out to help Jasmine support Carlos.

Mince laughed—a crazy, nasty laugh.

"Don't thank me," she said. "Once Maxwell learns to tame the Dragon, you'll *wish* I'd killed you."

Yep, Steven thought, *crazy as ever.*

Steven and Jasmine trudged back down the tunnel, with Carlos propped up between them. Mince's laughter followed them. When they rounded a bend and she passed out of sight, Steven felt relieved.

Jasmine raised an eyebrow. "You made some very strange new friends while I was out of action."

Despite himself, Steven smiled. "That's the first joke I've heard you crack in a while."

"Huh," she said. "Felt pretty good."

They retraced their steps, walking past the downed guards. Now Steven noticed the electrical burn marks on the guards' backs and necks.

Mince planned all of this, he realized, *just to get Carlos away from Maxwell. She's dangerous. Very dangerous.*

Somehow, he knew they'd meet again.

When they rounded the last bend, a surprising sight confronted them. Roxanne stood in the tunnel, just below the surface entrance. Duane sat at her feet, his leg wrapped in an improvised bandage made out of his jacket.

"Thought we'd meet you downstairs," Roxanne said. She gestured upward. "It's not too safe up there."

Another explosion sounded overhead. The air smelled like burning plastic.

Duane gestured weakly at Carlos. "You found him."

"Yeah." Steven rested Carlos's heavy form against the tunnel wall. "We found him."

"Now all we need is a way out," Jasmine said. She turned to Roxanne. "Any word from Liam?"

"Good news: he's alive," Roxanne said. "Bad news: he says the plane can't be fixed."

An explosion shook the tunnel.

"Well," Steven said, "we better figure out someth—"

A low rumble filled the air around them. The ground began to shake. At first Steven thought it was another explosion, but the noise grew steadily louder, filling the tunnel.

Roxanne and Jasmine gathered together with Steven against the wall. Jasmine pulled Carlos's limp form closer. Roxanne held out a hand to Duane, and he limped over to join them.

"What *now?*" Roxanne asked.

The wall beneath the tunnel opening began to buckle and collapse. A pair of metal treads appeared, cracking and smashing through the wall. The ceiling crumbled, stone and pipes raining down.

Steven gestured to the others. Together they backed away from the opening, retreating a small way into the tunnel. Jasmine reached out to take Steven's hand in a trembling grip.

As the strange subterranean vehicle rumbled into view, Steven suddenly recognized it.

"That's the Vanguard drill-ship," he said. "The one they used at Dragon's Gate."

The drill-ship ground to a halt, its engines subsiding to a dull rumble. With a rusty clang, the ship's outer hatch swung open.

Roxanne smiled. "Ox!"

Ox hefted himself halfway out of the ship and ran his eyes across the group.

"Couldn't abandon my team," he said. "Come on."

Jasmine's hand slipped from Steven's. When he turned to look at her, she was slumped against the wall, exhausted.

"You heard the man," Steven said.

She smiled weakly.

Ox helped them, one by one, into the cramped ship. Steven and Jasmine picked up Carlos's limp body, passing it to Ox inside. Ox grabbed on to Carlos with strong, thick arms, maneuvering him through the narrow passageway into the main cockpit.

Jasmine followed. When Carlos was safely inside, she reached out and softly ran a hand down the sleeping man's face.

Steven helped Roxanne with Duane. They stepped down and took a spot on the floor of the interior cabin, in the cramped space behind the cockpit.

"Don't forget Liam," Steven said. "We'll have to pick him up at the weapons depot."

"That loser?" Ox said, seating himself in the pilot's chair. "No way."

Steven and Jasmine both turned to stare at him.

Ox grinned. "Just kidding," he said. "You think I'd leave that crazy cannonball behind? He owes me a rematch at chess."

The hatch slammed shut, and the drill-ship rumbled back to life. Steven Lee slumped against the cold metal wall, exhausted.

In less than a minute, the Zodiacs were gone.

EPILOGUE ONE: GREENLAND

THE THIRD-FLOOR LAB was a strange place

for a meeting. A piece of the party banner still hung from the ceiling, and a paper plate covered with congealed icing lay on the counter next to the sink. The previous few days had been so busy, no one had bothered to clean up properly.

But Steven wanted to talk to the whole team as soon as possible. Duane and Dafari were still finishing up their scans for Zodiac energy, and there were only two places they could do that: the lab or the war room.

Steven studied everyone in the group, one at a time. Duane sat at a computer console, his leg in a cast, tapping away at a keyboard. Every now and then Dafari pointed at something over his shoulder and Duane shot him an annoyed look.

Liam and Roxanne sat nearby, chatting in low voices. Liam's arm was in a sling—he'd broken it in the jump from the platform—and he seemed unusually serious.

They're all different now, Steven thought. *They look so . . . normal.*

He walked over to Duane. "Anything?"

"The Australia base is still offline," Duane said. "No energy signature at all."

"Vanguard has suspended all known activities," Dafari added, "including ongoing wars in several countries."

"No sign of Snake and Monkey. Or Horse and Dog, for that matter. If they're alive, they're all laying low."

"Maxwell?" Steven asked.

Duane shook his head. "It's like he's vanished."

"Okay." Steven took a deep breath. "Dafari, would you excuse us?"

The scientist looked at Steven in surprise. Then he nodded quickly, clapped Duane on the shoulder, and left.

Liam and Roxanne approached. They leaned against a counter, waiting. Duane blinked a few times at his screen, then swiveled to face Steven.

Suddenly, Steven couldn't think of a thing to say.

Ox strode in. "Just went over the new security protocols

with Mags," he said. "Without Zodiac protection, we're gonna have to double the patrols and enlist everyone in sentry duty. That should—" He stopped and walked over to join Liam and Roxanne. "I mean, sorry I'm late. I got the e-mail this time."

"Well," Steven began. "Here we are."

They all stared at him.

"Okay, look," he continued. "I'm no good at speeches. We all know that. But here's the thing: none of you asked for the Zodiac power in the first place."

"I did," Ox said.

Everyone glared at him.

"Ox, mate," Liam said. "Let the kid talk, hey?"

"Sorry," Ox said. "And it's Malik."

"Malik," Steven said, "you're new here, but I've had long talks with the others over the past year about the power. Duane, it made things impossible for you back home. Roxanne, it ruined your musical career."

"I never minded," Liam said. "Being the toughest guy in the room, I mean."

"I know." Steven pointed at Liam's cast. "But now you're *not*. And I just want you all to know . . . Jasmine and I appreciate everything you've done here."

"Where is Jasmine, anyway?" Roxanne asked.

"With Carlos," Steven said. "Again."

Everyone looked down for a moment.

"Anyway," Steven continued, "I just want you to know there's no hard feelings. You've all got lives to lead, and now that your powers are gone, there's nothing to keep you from leading them."

Steven felt tears rising to his eyes. He turned away, lifting a hand to his face—unobtrusively, he hoped.

When he turned back, four sets of eyes were staring at him.

"Mate," Liam said, "you think we're *leaving?*"

Steven blinked. "But . . . I . . ." he gestured at Liam. "Didn't you want to go square things with the British Army?"

"Aye, I'll have to do that eventually," Liam said. "But Maxwell's still out there, mate. And I never liked leaving a fight while the other guy could still walk away."

"Roxanne?" Steven asked. "What about your mother?"

"She *told* me to stay." Roxanne gave him a crooked smile. "You need us, dude."

Malik shrugged. "I just got here."

One by one, they all turned to Duane. He looked troubled.

"I don't know," he said. "I'm still not sure if I'm of value to the team."

Liam and Roxanne exchanged astonished looks.

"Mate," Liam said, "you fixed an experimental antigravity dingus in less than a minute."

"*While* performing psychoanalysis on a madman!" Roxanne added.

"Well," Duane said, "I *do* have some new ideas for tracking Maxwell. Dafari and I have been working on refining the analyzers, maybe even converting them into feedback devices. That would allow us to weaponize some tech that we've so far only been able to . . ." He trailed off, then flashed a shy smile. "I guess I'm staying."

"If nothing else," Roxanne said, "we *gotta* make sure Kim's okay."

Steven really felt like he might cry then. "I don't know what to say."

"Look at it this way," Liam said. "Yeah, we lost our powers—but we still managed to destroy Maxwell's base. We prob'ly set him back years and saved a lot of lives around the world."

"Powers or not," Roxanne added, "we're a pretty good team."

"This place existed before the Zodiac Convergence," Malik said. "You've got ordinary people risking their lives here every day. You think I'd quit just because I can't make a big dumb animal appear over my head anymore?"

"One second, please," Duane said. He tapped frantically at the computer for a moment. Then he stood up, balancing unsteadily on his injured leg. He looked from Steven to Roxanne, then to Liam and Malik. A scared look flashed across his face.

Then he held out his arms. "Group hug," he said. "Grug."

Steven frowned. "Is that a thing?"

"It is now." Duane gestured at his computer. "I just added it to Wikipedia."

Then they were all laughing. Roxanne wrapped her arms around Steven and Duane. Malik hung back, hesitant, but Liam motioned to him, and soon they were all gathered together in one big embrace.

"Thank you," Steven whispered. "Thank you so much."

He heard the sound of a throat clearing. He disengaged from the group—from the "grug." Jasmine stood in the doorway, her head cocked, an amused smile on her face.

"Clearly I've missed something," she said.

The others filed out quickly. Steven could tell they all sensed the same thing: he and Jasmine needed to talk.

"See you in the training room," Roxanne said to Steven.

"You're on guard duty tomorrow, 0600," Malik told him.

"I'll have those new scans ready in a few hours," Duane said.

Liam just smiled and clapped Steven on the back, so hard that Steven winced.

Then he was alone with Jasmine. And for the second time that day, he wasn't sure what to say. They both paced around the room for a few minutes, lost in their own thoughts.

" 'He's not there anymore,' " Steven said, finally. "What does that mean?"

"Uh, what?" She didn't look at him.

"Maxwell. That's what you said about him. You also said, 'The Dragon has taken him over completely.'"

She looked away, a haunted expression on her face.

"I'm not sure," she said. "But I know Maxwell. I worked for him. . . . He killed my parents. And that thing, back on the platform at the end—that *wasn't* him." She turned to Steven and smiled sadly. "You're Zodiac—or you were. But the Dragon . . . it's on a whole other level. I can't even explain it in words. It's like comparing a flashlight to the sun. Or a gentle breeze to a sandstorm."

"When he took my power—the *first* time, I mean—he said, 'Only I can control the Dragon.' Wrong again, Maxy." Steven turned to Jasmine. "So he's different now. Is that a good thing or a bad thing?"

"I wish I knew."

They were silent again.

"You, uh," Jasmine said, "you must still be processing all the stuff your mom told you."

Steven nodded.

"Did she and your father really arrange for you to be present at the Convergence?"

"It all makes sense," he replied. "Even *you* were suspicious about that—about why I was there when it happened. Remember?"

"Yes," Jasmine said.

"When my mom told me about it," he continued, "at

first I was really angry. They've never really been there for me, you know? And then they do this. Once the fighting started, things got so crazy I barely had time to think about it."

"Mm."

"But then, on the ride home, I got to thinking. However it all happened—whatever *reason* there was that I wound up in that room—do I wish it never happened? Would I rather I'd never had the Tiger power, never felt it run through me like a bolt of hot lightning? Never helped people all around the world?"

Jasmine smiled. "I'm guessing the answer is no."

"A lot of bad stuff has happened, this past year." He smiled back. "But I wouldn't trade the good stuff for anything."

"I wouldn't, either." A dark look crossed her face. "Though the bad stuff is pretty bad."

Steven sat down in Duane's vacated computer chair. Jasmine paced again, faster this time. Steven had the feeling she was trying to avoid talking about something.

"You met two other Tigers," she said.

"Yeah. Malosi and the old man."

"Malosi went off with Maxwell."

"Yeah, but . . . I think in the end he'll do the right thing." Steven paused. "Mince is the one who scares me."

Jasmine nodded, not looking at him. "There's a lot to be scared of."

"The old guy," Steven said, "he talked about the past Zodiac users, the ones you mentioned before. What *really* happened to them? Do you know?"

She shook her head.

He watched her for a long moment. She seemed very far away, thinking grim thoughts. When she finally spoke, her voice was barely more than a whisper.

"We blew it," she said.

He frowned. "What?"

"You and me. Both of us." She turned and grimaced straight at him. "You went off to Berlin by yourself, to learn the secrets of your power. And I pushed the team into that assault, against everybody's advice. I was so obsessed with . . . with finding *him*. . . ."

He nodded.

"We both thought we were helping the team," she continued, "but we weren't there when they needed us. That's why all this happened."

He tried to smile. "I think the team forgives us."

"We're lucky to have them," she said. "But we need to start running a tighter ship."

She reached up for the party banner and ripped it off the wall.

"The Dragon is out there," she continued. "In hiding, learning how to live in our world. But he'll be back. *It'll* be back."

"At least we got Carlos," Steven said. "How is he, anyway?"

Jasmine looked at him, her lip quivering. Something in her eyes scared the hell out of him.

Then she let out a loud primal cry. She burst into tears, releasing all the emotion she'd been holding in for so long. Steven rose, surprised, and reached out to embrace her. She buried her face in his shoulder and sobbed.

"It's okay," he said. "We'll cure him. We'll make him better."

She kept crying, digging her chin into his shoulder. He patted her on the back. Her tears soaked into his shirt.

"I was . . ." She sobbed, gasping for breath. "I was the Dragon. I thought I could do anything . . . thought I could do it all alone."

He reached down and felt the heart-shaped object in his pocket—the qi amplifier that had helped him get through to Malosi.

The gift from his mother.

"Nobody can," he said. "Nobody can do it alone."

For just a moment, very deep down, he heard the Tiger roaring. Just loud enough to say: *I'm still here. I'm always with you.*

"I didn't think I needed other people," Jasmine continued. "But I do. I need you. I need *all* of you."

Suddenly, Steven flashed back to a year before—to a time when he'd thought about quitting the Zodiac team. Maxwell had attacked Jasmine, trying to draw the Dragon power out of her. And Steven had reached out with the power of the Tiger, lending her his strength.

I'm still lending her strength, he realized, *just in a different way.*

"That's what I'm here for," he said.

She pulled back, smiling in embarrassment. She reached up and brushed at his shoulder, trying to wipe the tear stains away.

"There's only two Zodiacs left, you know," she said. "One is your friend Rat."

"He's not my friend," Steven replied.

"But your parents are working with him. We may need to exploit that connection."

He nodded unhappily.

"And the other one," he said, "isn't showing up on our trackers."

They stood facing each other for a long moment. Jasmine reached out a hand, and he took it. They shook awkwardly, like old friends who hadn't seen each other for a long time.

"Let's get to work," she said.

EPILOGUE TWO: LOCATION UNKNOWN

"HEY, THERE. Just calling you back. First of all, you don't sound lame. You never sound lame. Second, my dad's doing better. . . . They're gonna let him out of the hospital today. I better stay out here for a while, though, because he needs a lot of help. I hope you're okay. . . . Say hi to everybody. I want to hear all your adventures. Oh, this is Kim, by the way! Duh, back at you."

Click.

Maxwell sat at the long table, his eyes glowing bright in the dark room. He didn't speak; he didn't move. The Dragon rose up from him, dark and solid, its bat-like wings folded.

For a moment, Mince wasn't sure whether he'd understood the message. "You want me to play it again?" she asked.

He turned to face her directly. The glow in his eyes faded, and for just a moment Maxwell seemed to return. He looked at Mince, and his mouth formed two silent words:

Help me.

Then the Dragon surged brighter. Fire filled the room, blazing across the top of the conference table. Mince ducked down.

When she looked up, Maxwell's eyes were filled with Dragon-fire again. He stared straight ahead, unmoving.

Mince shrugged. She held up the cell phone that had belonged to Steven Lee and pressed REPLAY.

"Hey, there. Just calling you back. First of all, you don't sound lame. You never sound lame. . . ."

END BOOK TWO

THE ADVENTURE CONTINUES!
HERE'S A SNEAK PEEK AT THE NEXT PART OF:

THE BALANCE OF POWER

STAN LEE
STUART MOORE
ANDIE TONG
DISNEY
THE ZODIAC LEGACY
THE BALANCE OF POWER

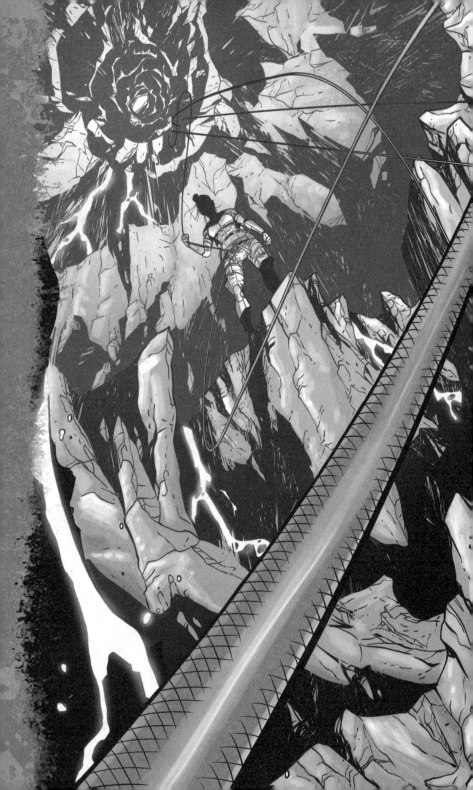

PART ONE
THE MOUNTAIN OF FIRE

CHAPTER ONE

STEVEN LEE inched his way down the rocky wall, grabbing at one handhold after another. *Don't look down,* he told himself. *You're not gonna fall. There's a rope holding you up, a big thick cow-wrangler-type rope strapped to the harness on your back. You're not gonna fall.*

Just don't look down.

He looked down. The chamber was wide and dark, made of yellow-and-brown rock dotted with shiny mica deposits. Little streams of water trickled down the walls. The cavern floor was at least six meters below, with a surface almost as jagged as the walls. If he fell, he could really hurt himself.

Okay, he thought, reaching for an outcropping in the wall. *You looked down. That was a mistake. But it's okay. Just don't fall. Don't fall. Do. Not. Fall.*

He fell.

The rock wall whizzed by at a dizzying speed. His harness pulled tight against his waist, but the rope went slack. *Great,* he thought. *The rope's no good if it's not tied tight enough!*

He scrabbled and grabbed, slowing his fall, but his gloves kept slipping off the slick rocks. He twisted his body, willing the Tiger—his Zodiac avatar—to emerge, to take control of his reflexes. But the Tiger was silent.

Stupid, he thought. *The Zodiac powers are gone, remember? That's why we're here!*

A thick hand grabbed his arm, arresting his fall. Steven cried out; his shoulder felt like it was being pulled out of its socket. Another large hand grabbed his harness.

Steven looked over at his rescuer, a big man in paramilitary gear with a pack on his back. The man, Malik, had anchored himself against the side of the wall by digging a pair of mountain-climbing pitons into the rock and hooking them on to his own harness.

"Welcome to the volcano," Malik said.

Volcano. The word echoed in Steven's mind. He'd been trying not to think about that.

"You're all right," Malik continued. "Just flex that shoulder a few times."

Steven nodded, struggling to catch his breath.

Malik shifted his muscular body, depositing Steven easily onto a small outcropping. Like Steven, Malik had once wielded the Zodiac power; as the Ox, he'd been almost supernaturally strong. Now he was merely *very* strong.

"You two havin' fun up there?"

Steven squinted down, his eyes adjusting to the dim light. About a meter below, another big man was anchored to the wall, grinning up at Steven and Malik. A long scar ran from the man's thick blond hair down his face, through his missing left eye.

"I wouldn't call it fun, Nicky." Malik's voice echoed off the rock walls.

Nicky reached up. "Want a hand down, kid?"

Embarrassed, Steven shook his head. He turned toward the wall and grabbed for a handhold, then stepped off the ledge onto the next small outcropping. Slowly, hand over hand, he descended to the floor of the chamber.

When he reached the bottom, he shrugged off his harness. *With the Tiger's power,* he thought, *I could have made that descent in half the time. Being normal is overrated!*

Nicky and Malik made their way down the wall above him. When Nicky—Dog—had held the Zodiac power, he'd boasted a carpet of yellow fur over his entire body. Dog had been a fierce fighter. He was both heavier and stronger than Steven, but when they'd fought hand to hand, Steven's agility had made them an even match.

Nicky and Malik had both worked for Maxwell, the man the Zodiac team had been formed to stop. After

Maxwell turned against his own agents and stole all their powers, they joined Steven's team. Like Steven, they were just ordinary people now.

"Kid?" Nicky asked, jumping the last meter or so to the floor. "You still breathing?"

"I just fell twenty feet," Steven protested. "Give me a minute."

Nicky turned to Malik, laughing. "I don't think the kid's used to working with this team."

"We're all adjusting." Malik smiled. "I'm not used to taking orders from a fourteen-year-old, either."

"Fifteen," Steven said. "I'm fifteen."

Nicky and Malik were right. Steven was used to operating with his old team, the team he'd worked with so many times in the past. He missed having them by his side: Ram, Rooster, Pig, and especially Rabbit.

But those particular teammates were occupied elsewhere. And if Steven was to pull off this mission, he'd need the help of every ex-Zodiac he could find—even those, like Nicky and Malik, who'd been enemies in the past.

Nicky turned to stare up at the hole they'd entered through, a hundred meters above. It was barely visible in the dim light, a dark spot on the yellow rock ceiling.

"Josie!" Nicky yelled. "You comin', girl?"

A fourth figure dropped into view, descending in a perfectly straight line. She let out her support rope with even, expert movements. Like Malik and Nicky, she was a trained soldier with years of combat experience.

And I'm just a kid, Steven thought. *But I've got to lead them. Somehow.*

Josie touched down and shook off her harness. Her eyes were blank; her movements seemed unenthusiastic, almost robotic. She didn't look at any of them.

"Joze?" Nicky said. "You with us?"

She turned and walked away.

"We shouldn't have brought her," Malik said.

Nicky glared at him. "Maybe we shouldn'ta brought *you*." He turned and followed Josie over to the far wall.

Steven frowned. When he'd worked with her before, Josie—Horse—had been a ball of energy, a determined fighter who never gave up, with or without her powers. She'd guided Nicky in their defection from Maxwell's Vanguard army, leading him and telling him what to do.

But something had changed. Josie seemed almost hollow now, a shell of her former self. And Nicky was taking care of *her*, instead of the other way around.

"We're not very deep yet," Malik said, running his eyes up and down the wall. "This volcano goes hundreds of feet farther down. How 'bout a scan, kid?"

Steven nodded. He reached up to his forehead and flipped down the lenses of a thick headset. A night-vision HUD schematic appeared before his eyes, bright against the black background projected by the virtual-reality device.

Green lines sketched out the uneven cavern floor and the angled walls rising up all around. Three red dots, indicating Steven's teammates, shone within the chamber. Readouts scrolled down the left side of his vision: SEN-SOR RANGE 3.2 KM. BATTERY LEVEL 94%. CHAMBER HEIGHT 24.7 METERS. WIDTH (MAX) 16.7 METERS. FLOOR PITCH 8.4°.

Along the right side, a menu of options presented itself. ZOOM. SEARCH. BRIGHTNESS/CONTRAST. INFRA-RED LEVEL. REFRESH/REBOOT. He selected ZOOM and panned the image down.

"You're right," he said. "There's another chamber below this one. I don't see any life signs down there."

"That doesn't necessarily mean anything," Malik replied. "If Maxwell's got Vanguard soldiers hiding in here, they'll be shielded from our scans."

The image zoomed out, revealing the volcano's entire shape: a mountain bisected by a large open mouth. Below the main caverns, a network of tunnels and corridors snaked through the earth. Steven zoomed in on one of those passageways, four or five levels beneath the ground. Three more red dots winked on, smaller ones this time.

The second team, he thought. Their objective was as important as his—more important, actually. He wanted to contact them, to make sure they were all right. But he had to maintain radio silence for now.

"Any Zodiac power signatures?" Malik asked.

Pain stabbed through Steven's forehead. The HUDset was Vanguard tech, stolen by Malik when he'd made his exit. They'd managed to equip only one unit for the mission, and Steven had barely had any time to practice with it. It gave him a headache.

"What?" he asked.

"The *Zodiac tracker*," Malik said impatiently.

"Right, yeah." Steven reached into his pocket and pulled out a small device, the size of a thumb drive. He pressed it into a port on the HUDset, just above his ear. A large menu item appeared on the HUDset display, flashing blue: ZODIAC TRACKING.

"Is it scanning?" Malik's voice seemed far away. "That's your tech, not ours. I don't know how well the devices sync together."

"I think so." The entire display went black for a moment, then winked back on. "It's kinda buggy."

"Hurry up," Nicky called from the other side of the room. "I wanna get my powers back!"

Once again Steven zoomed the schematic view up through the chamber, to the volcano's mouth high above. He panned back down, past the three red dots indicating the positions of the second team, and plunged deeper into the subterranean labyrinth. The ZODIAC TRACKING text blinked blue the entire time. Steven waited for the device to detect something—anything—infused with Zodiac energy.

"Nothing," he said. "No Dragon, no artifact, no energy traces at all. No nothing."

"Again: not a surprise," Malik said. "Maxwell has wave blockers, same as you, that can shield the Zodiac energy so it doesn't show up on scans. Doesn't mean the artifact's not here—but we're not gonna find it the easy way."

Steven glanced at the readout menus on the side of his display. The power level read 46 percent. That seemed low. "This thing's getting hot," he said, tapping the HUDset.

"Zodiac scanner's probably draining the battery. Better turn it off for now."

Relieved, Steven flipped the lenses up off his eyes.

Malik was already walking away, across the chamber. Steven followed him over to Nicky, who stood above Josie. She was down on one knee, staring at the floor.

"Joze?" Nicky said. "We gotta go. We gotta find the jee—the jin—the juju—"

"*Jiānyù*," Steven said softly.

"The thing," Nicky said, "the artifact, the old brass widget that's got all our powers in it. You wanna get your powers back, don't you?"

Josie turned halfway around. There was hardly any expression in her eyes.

"We don't even know if that 'widget' is here," she said.

"We'll find it!" Nicky turned to Steven and Malik, his eyes pleading for help. "What's this jye-annie thing look like, anyway? Is it a *boring* artifact like a pot or an urn, or a cool one with skulls all over it?"

"The *jiānyù* is a sphere," Malik explained, "a little

bigger than a softball. It's built to absorb and contain the Zodiac powers. When it's holding them, it's been known to morph into the shapes of those powers: an exaggerated ram or tiger. I dunno how it does that . . . something to do with the tech inside it."

"The tech enhances it," Steven said. "But the *jiānyù* was built centuries ago . . . during the Shang dynasty in China."

"And what do we do when we find this medieval basketball trophy?" Nicky asked. "Blast it to pieces? Lay our hands on it and chant like monks?"

Steven and Malik exchanged glances.

"Unclear," Malik said.

Josie snorted. Nicky glanced at her with concern, then ushered Malik and Steven away, out of her earshot.

"What if she's right?" Nicky whispered. "Maybe it's not here. The Jay-Z—the jazz hands—"

"*Please* stop trying to say *jiānyù*," Malik growled.

"I'm just sayin'. Maybe Vanguard ain't stationed here at all. Maybe this is just an *ordinary* deadly volcano."

"No," Steven replied. "We know Kim is here, so this has to be one of Maxwell's bases. I just can't believe the big jarhead left it undefended."

"I *don't* believe it," Malik said.

Maxwell had kept a very low profile in the weeks since he'd stolen the Zodiac powers. He hadn't made any aggressive moves; his private army had pulled out of even its most routine military contracts. He seemed to have diverted his resources toward some secret objective, but every time Steven and Jasmine thought they were closing in on that secret, the trail went cold. The ex-Zodiac teams had explored a half dozen of Maxwell's former lairs, using information supplied by Nicky, Josie, and Malik. They'd come up empty every time.

"We've gotta keep searching," Steven said. "Find a way down to the next chamber. And remember: be ready to create a diversion, in case the second team needs one."

"Search covertly *and* create a diversion?" Malik shook his head. "Those are contradictory objectives. We can't risk this entire mission for one person."

Steven glared at him. Malik was a great fighter, even without Zodiac powers; the team was lucky to have him. But sometimes he could be *too much* of a soldier.

"Kim's a very special person," Steven said.

He turned away, thinking of Kim—the Zodiac's Rabbit. Steven had wanted to lead the other group, the one assigned to find her. But the mission required careful deployment of every team member, especially since none of them had their Zodiac powers anymore. Steven was the most likely person to locate the *jiānyù*, so he had to lead this group.

As team leader, he'd made that decision himself.

Josie was still staring at the ground. Steven crouched next to her, touched the uneven surface—and felt something.

A rush of energy, warm and familiar, ran through him.

Zodiac energy.

A man's face appeared, filling Steven's field of view, wavering and shimmering as if it were made of fog—a very old man's face, with wrinkles all over and eyes sunken into the flesh below the brows.

Steven reached up for his HUDset, but it wasn't covering his eyes. This was a vision—one of the strange by-products of the Zodiac power. When the power had been stolen from him, the visions had gone with it. He hadn't had one for a long time.

He started to tumble forward. He felt Malik's and Nicky's arms steadying him, but their voices seemed very far away. The face filled his mind, focusing on him with an expression of alarm and concern.

Now Steven recognized that face. It belonged to an old man he'd met in Berlin, a man he'd seen die before his eyes—the man who'd been the Tiger before Steven, before Steven had even been born, in fact.

"Do not seek out the power," the old man whispered.

Somehow Steven knew what he meant. "I must," he replied. "I have to find the power."

The old man shook his head.

"I have to," Steven said.

The man grimaced. He nodded, seeming to understand Steven's words, and cocked his head downward. Then, in a flash, he was gone.

Steven shrugged away from Nicky and Malik, shaking his head to clear it. He looked down at the floor, at the spot the old Tiger had indicated. He glanced quickly at Josie.

Almost imperceptibly, she nodded.

Together they scrabbled away at the dirt. Nicky and Malik stared at them as if they were mad.

Josie's hands were rough, calloused from a lifetime of military operations. Steven had no such experience; he winced as his fingers began to bleed. But he kept digging.

Seven or eight centimeters down, they uncovered a round manhole cover. Steven grabbed hold of its edge and tried to pry it loose. It didn't move.

Josie grabbed it with both hands and flung it into the air.

The passageway stretched almost straight down. It was dark, curved, and narrow, no more than half a meter in diameter. Steven shone his flashlight into it, but he couldn't see the other end.

Once again, he heard the old man's voice. *Don't,* it said. A chorus of voices joined it, warning Steven in unison. *Don't,* they said. *Don't. Don't. Don't.*

He knew who the voices were. The other Tigers. The men and women, young and old, who'd wielded Steven's particular Zodiac power in the years and centuries past.

Josie's voice jolted him out of his vision. "If we're gonna do this," she said, "let's do it."

She hoisted herself up and vaulted into the hole feet-first. In less than a second she was gone.

Steven looked up at the others. Nicky spread his arms and shrugged. "You said we should find a way down."

Steven nodded. But in his mind, he could still hear the Tigers, warning him:

Do not seek out the power.

The passageway led down through the rock, its walls jagged and sharp. Malik led the way, with Nicky following and Steven bringing up the rear. The end of the passage remained out of sight, beyond a seemingly endless series of twists and turns.

"Can't see Josie at all," Malik grumbled.

As they made their way down, Steven's sense of discovery grew stronger. *We're close,* he thought. *This is the place. The power is here, somewhere.*

The tunnel began to widen. "Finally!" Nicky said. "I was tired of smellin' you guys' armpits."

Malik gestured for Nicky to be quiet. The passageway veered sideways, almost leveling out. When it grew large enough, Steven climbed down next to Malik and Nicky. He could see light just ahead, where the tunnel ended.

They crept up to the lip, looked down—and froze. The chamber was smaller than the one above: barely three meters high, with fluorescent lights mounted on the ceiling. Luminescent blue stones lined the walls.

Josie stood below, her back to them, hands raised in defeat—facing a virtual wall of Maxwell's Vanguard agents, all in full body armor and protective helmets. Their glowing energy rifles were raised and pointed at the hole in the wall where Steven's team had appeared. Malik hissed in a breath.

"Come on down," the lead soldier said. "Slowly."

Steven felt the soldiers' eyes on him, even through their opaque helmets. He looked around, frantic, at the chamber below. Door-sized entryways were arrayed along the walls, but there was no way Josie—or the rest of them—could reach one before the soldiers picked them off.

I'm the leader, he thought. *I have to figure out what to do—*

"I'm surrenderin'," Nicky said. "Unless you got a better plan."

Steven shook his head.

Nicky slipped down out of the passageway, followed by a reluctant Malik. As he watched them, Steven remembered the Tigers' warning: *Do not seek out the power.*

Looks like we don't need to worry about that anymore, he thought.

He raised his hands and dropped to the floor, the Vanguard energy rifles tracking his every move.